FULL OF FIRE

JENNIFER MILLIKIN

JNM, LLC
Scottsdale, AZ
85255
jennifermillikinwrites@gmail.com

ISBN-10: 0-9967845-2-7
ISBN-13: 978-0-9967845-2-8

To my husband,
the man who inspires and challenges me.

I love you twice as much as yesterday
and half as much as tomorrow.

There, how's that for a compliment?

CHAPTER ONE

I am so above all this. Either that or I totally don't fit in. A quick look around reminds me that I don't have any friends in this room. The cafeteria at UNLV is a microcosm of my life. Groups of people sitting together, laughing and taking selfies. Like me, there are a handful of parties of one, but for the most part everyone here has someone else to talk to. I don't mind being alone. I prefer the company of my camera. I raise my chin a fraction of an inch. These aren't my people anyway. The conversation at the table next to me confirms it.

"Dude, do you remember what happened last night? You were sooo wasted," long-haired guy one says to long-haired guy two. The way he speaks reminds me of Southern California beaches and the quintessential surfer. Sometimes I miss the sand and surf—if not the surfer dudes who go along with it.

I open my book, tuning out Wasted Guy and his friend. As the second of four children, I'm excellent at shutting out noise. Besides, the characters in my books are much more interesting than the assholes around me. I finish my salad in a silence that my talent provides me, lost in a love story that is just beginning to unfold.

"Lila Mitchell!"

My head jerks up at the sound of my name, an uncommon event. A girl I recognize from my days in the dorm waves at me like a maniac. Her lunch tray wobbles unsteadily as she balances it on her non-waving arm. She sets the tray down at a table filled with people who are now all looking my way. *Great.*

I respond with a small wave and mouth "hello." She couldn't hear me unless I shouted anyway. I barely manage to stifle a groan as she motions for me to come talk to her. *What is her name?* I'm up from my small table, picking up my bag and tossing my book inside. I take my time throwing away my empty salad container and returning the tray. *What the crap is her name?* Something really pretty, something that matches her perky personality. Sunny! That's it! Thank you, memory.

"Hi, Sunny." I wave as I approach her. "Long time no see."

She stands up and pulls me in for a hug, completely taking me by surprise. When she lets me go, she's smiling broadly with perfect little teeth, cute white rectangles all in a row. They remind me of the chewing gum I used to buy from the ice cream man.

Sunny clasps her hands in front of herself, a pained look on her face. *Are the rain clouds moving in?*

"I know, too long. How are you? Happy that junior year is over? Have you finished your finals?"

Which question am I supposed to answer first? She's throwing them at me like fireballs.

My answers are succinct. "Everything is great. Finals are over. How about you?"

Sunny picks up a book from the table and holds it in front of her, grimacing. "One more this afternoon, and then junior year is officially over, baby!" The frown quickly changes into a bright smile.

One of the guys at Sunny's table lets out a whoop, startling me. Sunny laughs and rolls her eyes. "Ignore Joey. He's crazy."

I nod my head. *Are we done here?* I shift my weight, more aware of my discomfort than ever.

Sunny's voice chirps in my ear once more. "So, I called you over here because a) I am so happy I ran into you, and b) I'm having a party tonight, and I want you to come. My brother just came back from his last year of grad school at Michigan, so it's a welcome home party for him and a good-bye junior year party for us."

A party. *I'm not good at those.*

"Um, well…" My mind races to invent an excuse. *Any plausible excuse will do!*

Sunny grabs my arm, pulling lightly. "C'mon, say yes. Are you still friends with Jessica Jones? You should bring her, if you are. It'll be fun, I promise."

I nod my head. "Ok. Sure."

I barely hide my groan. What did I just say? *Take it back, take it back!*

Sunny's hand is extended toward me. "Give me your phone, I'll put my number and address in it."

I pull my phone from my bag and hand it over, wishing I'd gone home for lunch. Damn my growling stomach.

"There," Sunny announces after she adds herself as a contact. "I really hope you make it, Lila."

I smile, feigning excitement. "See you tonight."

Quickly I back away from the group of happy, talkative people, my eagerness barely contained. I can't wait to get back to my house and the comfort of its relative solitude.

The whirring noise of Jessica's juicer greets me as I open the front door to the cute little house my parents bought when I moved out of the dorm. Real estate is a good investment, my dad declared after he signed the papers. I didn't care about investments. I was just happy to be away from dorm life and all the incessant talking and barging into people's rooms.

"Hi." I walk toward the kitchen to find my roommate and her daily afternoon cocktail of green juice.

Jessica turns around carefully, a glass of juice in her outstretched hand. "Here."

My nose is wrinkled in disgust, but I take it anyway. It's good for me, at least that's what I'm told. "Thanks. Why are you dressed like that?"

Jessica glances down at her bikini-clad self. "I'm going to lay out back and get a tan. Care to join me?"

I watch in awe as she drains her glass of juice and flounces toward the backyard. For the hundredth time I wonder where she gets her confidence. Jessica still has the twenty pounds she gained after a particularly heinous break up, but it doesn't seem to bother her. She owns that bikini, curves and all.

I finish my juice with a pinched nose and head off to change into a bathing suit I don't feel nearly as comfortable in.

"You know this is terrible for our skin." My tone is admonishing as I join Jessica in our backyard. This is the scorching desert after all. People who live in and around Las Vegas aren't exactly short on Vitamin D.

Jessica snorts delicately. "Terrible schmerrible. A little color will be ok."

Honestly you'd think someone who's from this hot as hell place would be better about staying out of the sun. I grumble to myself about skin cancer as I lie down on the towel Jessica has already spread out for me. The warmth of the suns rays instantly permeate my skin. I have to admit, it feels good.

"Just a few minutes." I warn Jessica of my internal timer. "I don't want to burn."

"You don't burn, you tan," Jessica murmurs. "You always have."

She's right, of course.

We're quiet for a minute before I say, "We were invited to a party tonight."

Jessica looks at me with one eye open. "By whom?"

Her question tells me just what I need to know. There is no way she'll want to attend. Jessica dislikes parties and big groups of people as much as I do. It was how we bonded in the first place.

"Do you remember Sunny Blankenship from our first year in the dorm?"

Jessica groans. "Yep. The personality to match the name."

I shake my head solemnly. "I ran into her at the cafeteria today, and she invited us. It's a goodbye junior year, hello big brother from Michigan soiree. I told her we would go."

Jessica rolls her blue eyes. "Why?"

"I felt cornered. She practically accosted me." With annoyance I recall how Sunny had interrupted my novel just when it was getting juicy.

"Fine." Jessica rolls over onto her front, her attitude telling me it's anything but fine. "I guess it wouldn't hurt to go out. Fulfill my quota for the month."

I sigh with relief. There's no way I could have gone alone.

Jessica prepared her famous jerk chicken caesar salad for dinner, I cleaned the kitchen, and now we're headed upstairs to begin the painstaking process of getting ready for a night out.

Jessica is laughing as I trudge up each stair, dramatizing every step. I catch my foot when I get to the top, pitching forward onto my hands and knees. Jessica's bent over in stitches as I roll around on the ground, and we're both laughing so hard that no sound comes out. The only noise is the sharp smack of Jessica hitting her hand on her thigh.

Jessica finally finds her voice. "You didn't have to literally drag your feet."

"Harty har har." I stick out my tongue playfully. "Guess I'll wear jeans tonight, so nobody sees the bruises on my knees."

I stand up and pretend to brush myself off, making Jessica laugh again.

"Ooooh, you know what this night needs?" Jessica's eyes are wide and excited. She brings her hands in front of herself and clasps them. "Pre-gaming."

And now I'm lost. "What are you talking about?"

Jessica rolls her eyes, exasperated by my lack of knowledge. "You know, where you drink while you're getting ready for the party."

Now it's my turn to roll my eyes. "That sounds so stupid."

"Where did my funny friend go who was putting on a comedy skit only three minutes ago? Is she still in there?" Jessica lifts her hand and pretends to knock on my head.

I explain. "We have to drive to this party. So, no, pre-gaming isn't a good idea. And yes, your funny friend is still here."

"Fine, you're right. Ok, shower time. Make sure you scrub-up good. Never know who you might meet tonight." Jessica wiggles her eyebrows at me suggestively and saunters into her room.

Oh, please. Like I'm going to meet anyone at a college party. It's going to be filled with all the same people I see on campus. And I'm definitely not attracted to anybody at school. Tonight won't be any different.

I'm so sure of it that I'm leaving my legs unshaven, just to prove a point. Smiling to myself as I towel off, I picture my mother and the disapproving look she would give me if she knew. But Mom isn't here, she's at home in Newport Beach.

I hang my towel on the rack and begin the arduous process of combing through my long brown hair. Once that's done, I decide to go an extra step and actually use my blow dryer. Usually I let the dry Las Vegas heat do the honor. I flip my head over and begin the process.

When my hair is dry, I move on to make-up... What little I have, anyway. I prefer the bare face look, but since I'm going to a party, I add mascara and lip gloss.

And now to my closet. I really am going to wear jeans, especially since I chose not to shave my legs. I grab my dark skinnies and my favorite red sleeveless blouse, the one with the racerback. I shove my feet into my black wedges and turn to my full length mirror. I clean up all right, I suppose.

Jessica knocks on my door and comes sailing in without waiting for me to answer. She's wearing a short pink skater dress with a matching belt around her middle. White and silver sandals complete her outfit. She looks beautiful and summery.

"I adore that color on you, Lila!" Jessica touches my mid-section. "Ooh, it's soft too."

"Thanks," I murmur. "You look stunning."

And she really does. Jessica has gorgeous strawberry blonde hair that falls to the middle of her back in a natural wave. The pink color of her dress makes her hair color even prettier.

"Yay for hot chicks who are going to a party!" Jessica waves her hands in the air.

My nose wrinkles. She's way too excited. I can't believe how committed she is to this night out.

"I thought you were as anti-social as I am. Did you get laid?" I eye her suspiciously. Jessica doesn't have a boyfriend, but that hasn't stopped her in the past.

"I would have told you the second it was over. I was listening to Britney Spears while I was getting ready. Suddenly I want to gyrate my hips with a Python around my neck." Jessica demonstrates her ass shaking abilities while I watch. *Ok, ok it's amusing.*

"Perhaps we should skip the party and find a Britney impersonator. This is Vegas, I'm sure it wouldn't be hard." I scoop up my purse off my bed and lead Jessica down the stairs.

"In all seriousness, LL, we need to talk." Jessica's voice is earnest as she calls me by the nickname she gave me our freshman year. Apparently there were times when my four-letter name was too long for her.

I'm bent over, grabbing two water bottles from the fridge. "What?" I ask, straightening and handing one of the bottles to her. Is she going to lecture me yet again on my tendency to be rude without realizing it?

"You have to try to have a good time tonight, ok? I don't like big social gatherings either, but I can at least put on a happy face and pretend. You're not so good at that." Jessica's face is stern.

Putting on a fake smile is just so…un-me. It's not what I'm about. I want to meet people I actually like and have a real conversation. Not pretend to smile as some loser with beer breath yells in my ear. Perhaps I should text Sunny and tell her I'm not going to make it.

When was the last time someone invited you to a party? My internal voice chides me. Ugh. The voice is right.

I hold my hands up in surrender. "You win. I'll fake it through, should I need to. And I probably will."

Jessica nods once, happy. "Good. And no camera tonight."

I make a face. "Of course not. Do you think I want to waste my talents on a house party?"

"Knowing you, probably not. But I bet you could capture some hilarious moments with those photography skills of yours."

"I prefer the moments I capture have meaning or beauty." I lift my nose into the air. I'm very serious about my work. Photography is my passion.

"Well then I hope nothing meaningful or beautiful happens tonight, because you won't have your camera." Jessica loves poking fun at me.

I ignore her as I grab my keys from the counter and walk out the front door.

The evening is relatively cool compared to the heat of the day, and it makes me hopeful. Something my mom likes to say pops into my head, and I smile to myself. *You'll never meet anybody if you don't get out there.* Perhaps tonight won't be so bad after all.

CHAPTER TWO

The drive is short, maybe fifteen minutes. I park down the block because there are already cars lining the street on either side. Sunny's house is large and stucco, essentially a big box with a rock front yard. Typical of Vegas.

Awkwardly I climb out of the car in my wedges, something I'm not at all used to doing. It shows. Flats and sandals are usually my footwear of choice. We climb out and walk toward the house. Well, *I'm* walking. Beside me Jessica is dancing her way down the sidewalk. Right now her hip gyrations could rival a pole dancer's. I assume, anyway. I've never actually seen one in person.

"Jessica, there isn't any music playing. How are you dancing?" My inquiry makes perfect sense to me.

Jessica responds without missing a beat in her movements. "There's music in my head, Lila."

I groan. Tonight she's Fun Jessica. My studious, serious, introvert Jessica has morphed into her alter-ego. Fun Jessica comes out every once in a while, usually after Normal Jessica has been under loads of stress. I suppose this behavior makes sense then. Jessica just finished her finals, she has one semester left to go, and her parents are still in the middle of that ugly divorce. *No more raining on her parade.*

I shimmy my shoulders playfully as we reach Sunny's house. "I hear the music too."

Jessica's laughter tinkles into the night, like little bells. She puts her arm through mine and leads me through the open gate toward the sound of the party in the backyard.

"Remember what we talked about, ok?" Jessica sounds positively parental.

I roll my eyes. "Yeah, yeah, yeah. I got it."

There's a throng of people already in the backyard. A keg sits on the patio and next to it, a cooler full of soda and water. Gratefulness fills me at the sight of the non-alcoholic beverages. I'm the designated driver.

Sunny spots us right away and waves.

I elbow Jessica and nod in Sunny's direction, returning her wave. To my credit, I'm waving with excitement. *See, I can play nice.*

Sunny is wearing a yellow polka dot bikini, and I can't help humming the tune in my head. She makes her way over to us and surprises me with a hug for the second time today.

"Thanks for coming, guys! There's beer and regular drinks on the patio. Please help yourself. Did you bring your suits?" Sunny looks at us expectantly, a bright smile on her face.

I shake my head, and inside I'm totally relieved. "Um, no. I didn't realize this was a pool party."

"It's not really, but you know, it's hot and this is a desert, so if anybody wants to jump in they can! Maybe if you drink enough beer you'll be swimming in your skivvies." Sunny tips her head back and laughs at her own joke.

I poke Jessica lightly on the shoulder, nominating her. "You may have to count on Jessica for such a display. I'm the DD tonight."

"Ohhh booo," Sunny exaggerates her pout. I imagine a black rain cloud over her head, and then I'm giggling to myself.

More people are walking in behind us, and Sunny lifts her hand to wave at them.

"Excuse me, I need to say hi. Have to be a good hostess, right?" Sunny smiles and squeezes my arm, then walks toward the newcomers.

Jessica leans into me and whispers, "Why didn't I like her in the dorm? She's really nice."

My smile is sardonic. "I believe you said she's insipid, banal, and saccharine." My hand is up in front of us as I tick off the unkind words on my fingers.

Jessica reaches over and lightly smacks my hand down. "Geez, that's mean. I was so rude back then."

"I would definitely say you're less rude now." My shoulders are shaking with suppressed mirth.

Jessica narrows her eyes. "Lets get a drink. Won't you have just one?"

"No," I say flatly, but Jessica is already ahead of me and shaking her head, as if my choice not to have a drink is some great loss. I sigh. This is going to be a long night.

I have just escaped the company of three girls I know from a community volunteer program I took part in last year. They are beyond boring, spending all their time discussing what's in fashion for fall. I made the mistake of asking *"Isn't it summer?"* when I had so many other remarks swimming in my head. My question made me the recipient of a collective condescending stare. *Right, I'm the brainless one.*

Jessica has run into a guy she had a crush on our freshman year. She's pulling out all the stops: smiling with a tipped head, laughing at his jokes, brushing her hair back from her shoulders, and looking at him through her lashes. So now I'm on my own, and after the bland companionship of the three airheads, I'm ready to be by myself.

Leaving isn't an option, thanks to Jessica's reconnection with her crush. I wander into Sunny's house, looking for a bathroom. I locate one off the kitchen and spend a few minutes freshening up.

I walk out to the dark living room, enjoying the quiet. I can't bear going back out to the party just yet. Absentmindedly I stare at a painting on the wall, my mind hatching an escape plan that includes coming back for Jessica later. Suddenly a deep voice speaks behind me, making me jump.

"Are you lost?"

I whirl around, feeling like a wayward child and embarrassed to have been caught inside the house.

"Um, no. I'm sorry. I just needed a break." I squint in the darkened room, trying to see the person I'm talking to.

The overhead lights go on, and after my eyes adjust, I'm able to see who has caught me in Sunny's house.

Whoa. Who is this blond Adonis? He's tall with a mop of hair the color of straw. His face is chiseled, like a model. He's wearing a white T-shirt and workout shorts. Clearly not a party-goer.

The Greek God strides toward me with an out-stretched hand. My ingrained manners take over, and I respond.

"I'm Cade Blankenship. Sunny's brother." His grip is firm, and he looks me right in the eye.

His good looks are so disarming, it takes me a few seconds to find my voice. "I'm Lila Mitchell. An old friend of Sunny's."

"Nice to meet you, Lila. Not into the party, huh?" He gazes with annoyance out to the lively din in the backyard.

I shake my head. "Parties aren't really my scene." I shrug, then remember something. "Isn't this party for you? At least partly, anyway?"

Cade responds by rolling his blue eyes. "Hardly. It was just Sunny's excuse. I think she was hoping I would meet someone."

I laugh lightly. "Well, that's kind of hard to do from inside the house."

"Apparently not." Cade has an amused look on his handsome face. "I've discovered a stow-away."

My blush is crimson, I know it. Is Cade flirting with me? Oddly, I don't feel attracted to the intensely good-looking man in front of me. But I know someone who would…

"Parties are an introverts worst nightmare." Hopefully this explains my presence in his living room. "But if you get dressed and come outside, I have someone to introduce you to."

Cade eyes me, unsure. Is he getting the hint that I'm not interested? Do I even need to give him one? I'm hopeless when it comes to this stuff.

"I suppose it wouldn't hurt to make an appearance at my own party. I'll go change."

I sigh in relief. I must have piqued his interest about introducing him to someone. I better get outside and wrangle Jessica away from that dumb old crush, pronto.

"I'll meet you outside, ok?" I yell after Cade's retreating back. I return the way I came and find the door that leads outside.

It dumps me right into the line for the keg, and I have to squirm through. More people have shown up, making it harder to find my best friend. I walk the perimeter of the party, finally locating Jessica. She looks pissed.

"Jess," I call out, walking quickly toward her. "What's wrong?"

"What a loser."

I stare at her, bewildered. "Who? That guy you used to like? I thought you were all about him." Talk about a one-eighty. I'm so confused.

"Apparently I wasn't all about him enough." Jessica shudders. "He asked me to go to his car and have sex with him."

"What the fuck!" I hiss. "Where is this asshole?" I'm looking around, but he's nowhere in sight. All I see are the outlines of partygoers, and none of them resembles the loser.

"It's ok. I told him to fuck off." Jessica shakes her head in disbelief. "I always thought he was so sweet, a good guy. Was he really a gross out, and I just didn't know it? Are they all like that?"

I have no answers. My experience in the guy department consists of one long term boyfriend in high school. And I broke up with him to come here.

I reach over and rub Jessica's back. She offers a small, resolute smile.

"Maybe I'll just become a lesbian." Jessica's lip curls even as she makes the joke.

I laugh and glance around, looking for a certain blonde someone who may keep Jessica's sexual preference firmly in the male category. And there he is now, talking to his sister. Cade has changed into a light blue polo and khaki shorts. Clean cut, blonde, handsome. Perfect for Jessica.

"I think you might want to keep your lesbian plan on the back burner," I murmur.

Jessica looks at me, interested.

"This might not be the best time for this after that jerk, but I met Sunny's older brother. And I want to introduce you two. Can you handle that?"

She looks unsure, tossing her strawberry blonde hair as she considers it. "I kind of hate men at the moment."

I point surreptitiously at Cade. "Do you hate the man who's talking to Sunny?"

Jessica eyes Cade, her mouth agape. *Yeah, I was struck dumb too.*

"Oh my God, he's gorgeous. You talked to him?" Jessica looks at me with envy.

17

I nod enthusiastically. "And he appears to be genuinely nice. I met him when I went in the house to use the bathroom. He came out here to meet you."

Jessica narrows her eyes. "Why don't you want him for yourself?"

This is another question for which I have no answer. "Oh, you know me. I like tall, dark and handsome." I shrug, disinterested. Cade is gorgeous, nice, wasn't inclined to attend his own party, and a college graduate with an advanced degree. From Michigan, of all places, so he's also smart. Truthfully, I have no idea why I don't feel attracted to Cade, but I don't.

I wave at Cade as he looks over to us.

Sunny waves back, a look of confusion on her face. *I'm not waving at you, Sunny.*

Cade starts walking toward us, and my very confident best friend walks forward to greet him on her own. *So much for introductions.*

After a minute I follow Jessica and join the twosome. Their enamored smiles tell me they are already smitten with each other.

Ten minutes of their flirting and Jessica's giggling is all I can take. I excuse myself from the conversation, not that I was really a part of it anyhow. I stop momentarily to text Jessica. She can call me when she's ready to leave. I'm going back to my car, where my book is waiting for me. I participated in a social event, and now I'm ready to retreat and be alone.

I settle into my car, open my book and let the characters sweep me away.

CHAPTER THREE

And just like that, Cade and Jessica became an item. And me? My status as a party of one has never been more solid. But that's ok, I'm a loner. I'm not afraid to admit it.

Cade has been at our house three times in the week since he met Jessica. And they've been out on dates on the nights when they aren't at my house. We've already settled into a routine when Cade comes over. Jessica cooks dinner for the three of us, then I retreat to my bedroom and give them some space. They are so new couple-y that I can hardly stand to be around them. Jessica practically swoons every time Cade speaks. And Cade thinks Jessica walks on water. It's nauseating to watch.

And it's possible I'm envious. Will I ever have that weak-in-the-knees feeling with anybody? I just don't know. I'm easily annoyed, my standards are high, and I have trouble connecting with people. Not a recipe for success. At least I have time on my side. I'm young, though by next Thursday I'll be a year older.

Ugh, my dreaded twenty-first birthday. The night where I'm expected to get hammered and act stupid. Not happening. And since my family lives a state away,

I won't have anybody forcing me to celebrate. And Jessica, my adopted family, may not even remember my big day anyhow, given how starry-eyed she is these days. So I might have a quiet birthday, just like I want.

Today is a rare rainy day in Las Vegas. I'm supposed to be at work in an hour, but I can't get up the motivation to get myself into the shower. Spending the day scheduling clients at Alexa Salon & Spa doesn't sound like what I want to do on this dreary day. Rain and dark clouds call for a good book and a warm blanket, both of which I own. I sigh loudly as I drag myself into my bathroom. Bikini waxes and manicures wait for no one.

I'm grabbing a granola bar from the pantry when Jessica walks in the kitchen, hair messy and a lascivious grin on her face.

"What?" I ask, though I'm positive I know the answer.

"Cade stayed the night." Jessica smirks smugly, the cat who ate the canary.

"What?" I feign surprise. I don't want to embarrass Jessica, but I would have to be deaf to not already know that. I spent a good portion of last night with a pillow over my head.

"When's the wedding?"

Jessica takes my hand, her eyes shining bright. Gone is the smug grin. In its place is a smile so sweet it makes me think of cotton candy.

"Oh, LL, I think he's…" Jessica cranes her neck and looks around to be sure we aren't being listened to. "The One."

Oh my. The One? This is big.

"Wow." I don't have time for details now, but I definitely want them. "I want to hear more later, ok? I need to get to The Pain Shoppe before I'm late."

Jessica nods, looking totally sated and in love. "Ok, sure. Call me if you hear anybody screaming again."

"*Waxing doesn't hurt. It just feels like a tug, and then the hair is gone.*" I make air quotes as I cite the words of a technician at my work.

Jessica laughs throatily. "Who was seriously dumb enough to believe that load of garbage?"

I shrug. "Some poor woman whose lady parts are now only partially bare." I give my best friend a quick hug.

"See ya." Jessica turns to the fridge.

I hurry out of the house, eating my granola bar and trying to ignore the tugging feeling in my heart. Of course I'm happy for Jessica, but I'm sad too. Now I'll have to share my best friend.

I have two minutes to spare when I pull into a spot at Alexa Salon & Spa. I jump out and rush into the house of pain.

"Almost," mouths Jeri, the receptionist, greeter and general fetcher at Alexa. She's tall, at least 5'10, with the best haircut I've ever seen. It's a sleek bob, cut just below her ears, and paired with the fact that her hair is black, it totally makes her look like a badass. She also wears outlandish lipstick colors, from magenta to a fiery orange-red. I so envy her confidence.

"One minute to spare," I hiss back as I pass her desk on the way to my own.

I'm at my desk for no less than six minutes when Granite Alexa himself strolls in.

Jeri shoots me an 'oh shit' look and leaps up from her chair.

"Hi, Mr. Alexa, it's nice to see you again. Can I get you a beverage?" Jeri's tone is attentive without a trace of brown nose.

Granite, as he disturbingly calls himself, gives Jeri his trademark look. First he looks down his nose, but not in her direction, and then flicks his eyes off to the side, even farther from her. I haven't been able to figure out why he does this, because it only makes him look odd. We all make fun of him behind his back, specifically for this compulsion.

This man, owner of the most exclusive salon and spa in Las Vegas, gives us much fodder for our imitating. He's a large, well muscled black man and incredibly good looking. He also happens to be a well-known cross dresser by night. To top it all off, he has a very small boyfriend who comes eye-to-eye with me at 5'5". Granite is cranky, moody, and thinks very highly of himself. Which is why he changed his name to Granite, because obviously his body is even harder than normal rock. According to office gossip, his name used to be Sheldon.

Granite finishes the grand production of giving Jeri his signature dirty look. "No," he answers, his tone clipped. He strides past Jeri and back to me.

"Lila." He stops at my desk momentarily, a haughty look on his face. *Yes, I work here. No, I don't get my eyebrows waxed.* I have yet to take advantage of my employee discount. He probably knows that. His eyebrows look far better groomed than mine.

"Mr. Alexa," I respond, smiling politely. I have promised myself and Jessica that on my last day here I'm going to call him Sheldon. Knowing that little secret makes me want to giggle.

"How long have you worked here, Lila?" Granite cocks his head to the side but doesn't have the face of someone asking a question. He looks cold and bored.

"Three years in October, Mr. Alexa." My answer is immediate. What is he getting at? I've never had this long of a conversation with him.

"Meredith says you do a good job." He pauses, waiting for me to thank him for his kind words.

If he thinks I'm going to simper at his convoluted compliment that doesn't even belong to him, he can forget it.

"Oh," I demure. "That was kind of Mrs. Romaneski. I work very hard and enjoy my job." I smile sweetly, picturing Granite Alexa in all his cross-dressing glory.

"Keep it up." Granite is already turning his large back to me, striding out to the rest of the salon. "This is a highly coveted role."

Granite is being extra nasty today. *Did his small boyfriend choose not to put out last night?* I sigh. Granite is full of shit, and I shouldn't let him get to me.

"Oh my gosh, why does he hate me?" Jeri is suddenly at my desk, leaning down and whispering intensely in my face. I'm having a close-up with her hot pink lipstick. How does she get it on so perfectly?

"You don't have a pen 15?" I joke, answering Jeri's question. "Or do you? This is Vegas, after all."

Jeri narrows her eyes at me. "Haha, very funny. Seriously, what's his deal? He barely acknowledges me."

I reach up to pat the forearm draped over my desk. "Don't worry, you've only been here for six months. That was the most he has ever spoken to me, and I've worked here for almost three years. And he managed to threaten my job." I shrug.

Jeri's blue eyes bulge. "Are you worried?"

I shake my head. "No, not at all. He is the moodiest person I've ever met. As long as you're on good terms with Meredith, it's fine. He trusts her implicitly."

"Ok," Jeri mutters. She has a lost puppy look.

"Go back to your desk. Clients will be here soon. If Granite stays long enough he'll get to see you doing your job, and maybe you'll feel better."

Jeri nods her black bob enthusiastically and pivots, returning to sit at the reception desk.

Honestly, I don't know why she's so worked up. Her family has more money than sense. Jeri's last name is Tyson, as in Tyson Construction. Her family built most of Las Vegas, including a couple of the hotels on the strip. No matter what happens to her job, Jeri will be just fine.

The day is here. Happy birthday to me!

I didn't feel any different when I woke up this morning, not that I expected to. Jessica treated me to my favorite breakfast in bed. Nothing more special than lemon ricotta pancakes with blueberry compote. The girl can cook.

I'm on my way to work now, air conditioning blasting in this insufferable heat. SoCal is hot too, but not like this. At least in Newport Beach there's a breeze coming off the ocean. This place is like an oven, dry and hot.

"Happy birthday!" Jeri exclaims when I walk in. Three clients waiting for their appointments turn to look at me, and one of them echoes Jeri's sentiment.

"Thank you," I smile graciously at her. She's a regular.

I turn to Jeri. "How did you know?"

Her answering smile is secretive. "A little birdie told me."

I'm not amused. "Spit it out."

Jeri bends down and pulls a bouquet of fragrant calla lilies from below her desk.

"These are for you," she announces, handing them to me. "They came for you about twenty minutes ago. The card says happy birthday."

My mom has been giving me calla lilies every birthday for as long as I can remember. My face scrunches up in a smile, and suddenly, I really miss her. I'm still not going home for the summer though, no matter how many times she asks. I have a job and Jessica.

"Thanks." I take the flowers from Jeri, who looks like she's about to die of curiosity.

"They're from my mother," I explain, to put poor Jeri out of her misery. I carry the flowers back to my desk and set them down. Time to work.

The day is nearly done, only a handful of clients still finishing up their treatments. I sigh and rub my eyes. I'm ready to be at home. Maybe I'll buy a bottle of wine, now that I can, and get drunk. *To what end?* I giggle to myself. Getting drunk is totally not in my repertoire.

I sit up straight and smile warmly as the last clients of the day approach my desk. They are all three beautiful, two blondes and one redhead. To me the redhead is the most beautiful, because she's so unique.

"Hello, ladies. How were your services this afternoon?" I wait expectantly for the same answer I usually receive. Most people answer with a "good, thank you" or a "so relaxing."

"Good, thank you," answers one of the blondes, just as I expected. She has a neck tattoo, but it's not obnoxiously large. I think it's a dahlia. "Now we have to go home and get dressed like vixens."

Hmmm…this comment is different, but not completely out of place, given our location.

"Well, you have fantastic haircuts that will make it easy to look the part." I smile again. "Would you like to book your next appointments now?"

The other blonde shakes her head. "No, that's ok. We'll call individually when we're ready."

I nod my head automatically. "Sounds great. Are you paying separately?"

The redhead speaks up. "No, I'm paying for everything. I lost a bet." She steps up and hands her credit card to me.

Bet? I'm curious, but there's no way I am asking. I bet Jeri would.

With a straight face I recite the total. She asks me to add a 25% gratuity, which I calculate quickly before I run her card through the machine. This person is beautiful and generous too. The industry standard for good service is 20%.

"Your flowers are beautiful," the redhead says offhandedly as I wait for her receipt to print.

"Thank you." No need to tell her that today is my birthday. I've been the recipient of enough attention already, thanks to the flowers.

"Are they from your boyfriend?" The question catches me off-guard. I haven't had a boyfriend in three years.

I laugh softly, mostly because I'm uncomfortable. "My mother. It's my birthday."

"Why are you working? Happy birthday!" The redhead, Genevieve Waters, according to her credit card, clasps her hands together. "Please tell me you're twenty-one."

I smile and nod. "As of 12 a.m."

"Perfect. Do you have any plans tonight?" Genevieve looks hopeful.

I contemplate telling her my thoughts about tonight being about me and a bottle of wine, but decide against it. That's more pathetic than not having any plans at all.

"Nope, none."

"Good. I want you to come to the club where we work." Genevieve glances at my name plate. "What's your last name, Lila?"

I swallow. Oh my goodness. A club. A place where a massive amount of people listen to ridiculously loud music and dance up against each other. It's so beyond not my scene, it makes my visit to Sunny's house party look like high tea.

"Mitchell," I hear myself say. I want to smack myself, but what am I supposed to say, *no thank you?*

The two blondes behind Genevieve are smiling.

"Lila Mitchell, I'm Gigi Waters." Genevieve reaches her hand over my desk. I shake it firmly. My response is a mumbled "Nice to meet you." I'm still wrapping my mind around this whole club idea.

Gigi points back to the blondes behind her. "This is Lucy and Becca." They wave in unison, and I'm not sure who is who.

"Nice to meet you." I glance behind them, hoping Granite won't decide now's a good time to check up on me.

"So, you'll be on the list at Townsend. I'm giving you a plus two. That means you can bring two people with you. Tonight you'll be our special guest." Gigi winks at me.

"Wow, thanks," I say, stunned and practically speechless. Why me? I'm dying to ask, but my own mortification saves me.

"See ya around eleven," Gigi says, signing the receipt and pushing it back across to me.

Eleven? That happens to be my bed time. *Who cares? You're off tomorrow.*

"See ya," I echo.

They start walking out, but Gigi stops and turns back. She leans in, and automatically I lean toward her. She smells of the designer shampoo we use.

"No offense, Lila, and please don't be embarrassed, but maybe see if one of the techs can wax your brows?" Gigi squeezes my shoulder lightly and then turns around, rushing after Lucy and Becca.

Holy. Shit. The embarrassment is threatening to consume me, but I swallow it down and wave at Gigi before she walks out the door. Somewhere in the background of my own humiliation I hear Jeri wish the three girls a good night.

Oh my God. Gigi just told me to get my eyebrows waxed. Are they that bad? They must be, if she noticed after only five minutes with me. Crap crap crap.

Am I even going to go to Townsend? I sort of have to. Gigi is putting my name on a list, some arbitrary list that will supposedly make me her special guest. And she knows where I work, so it's not like I can just skip out on her invite. No, it would be very bad manners to not show up. So I'll go for an hour. Hopefully Jessica and Cade are available. How embarrassing would it be to show up alone?

I stand and walk out to the rest of the salon. I don't even know if any of the waxers are still here. I can't believe that I, Lila Mitchell, am willingly subjecting myself to the torture chamber located in the house of pain.

CHAPTER FOUR

I'm on my way home from work, eyebrows stinging. I've been told to put ice and aloe vera on the area to reduce the swelling faster. Thankfully Rosie, my favorite waxer, hadn't left for the evening. Once she heard my plans for the night, she was game to let me squirm in her chair while she ripped my hair out with hot wax. It wasn't as painful as I thought it would be, but it didn't feel good either.

Rosie was so excited for my big night out that she commissioned one of the stylists to trim and curl my hair. So now I'm waxed and my long brown hair is expertly curled and, according to Rosie, I was just invited to one of the hottest new spots in town.

I feigned excitement so my coworkers didn't think I was crazy, but mostly I'm having a mini anxiety attack at the thought of going to a club and being around so many people. At least it will be loud, so hopefully I won't be forced to make conversation.

Jessica stares in awe at me when I walk in the door. "Oh my. The Pain Shoppe finally got you. You're no longer a waxing virgin."

My hand shoots up to my sticky and tender brows. "I have so much to tell you. Starting with, please tell me you're free tonight."

Jessica frowns. "Of course. I told Cade I wasn't going to see him tonight. It's your birthday, after all."

Thank goodness. I should have known Jessica wouldn't leave me to celebrate my birthday alone. "Thanks, bestie. It's just that you and Cade have been so hot and heavy, I wasn't sure if all the sexing would distract you."

Beaming, Jessica plunks herself down on the couch.

"Ah, yes, the sexing. We did it again this morning." She giggles. "You tell me why your eyebrows are waxed and your hair looks magnificent, and I'll fill you in on the sexing."

I hold up one finger. I need to attend to the redness on my face, stat. Rosie said it would fade within the hour, but I'm nervous it won't and I'll show up at Townsend with red and swollen eyebrows. "Let me grab a cold compress and aloe." I scoot off to the kitchen.

"So, is beauty really pain?" Jessica asks when I come back to the living room, her eyes squarely on my eyebrows.

I arrange myself on the couch with my head back so I can lay the compress across my lower forehead. "Not as much as we thought." I answer. "But I'm sure this area is the least painful."

"So, why the wax and curls?" Jessica asks again.

I launch into the whole story, beginning with my mothers flowers and ending with the invite that prompted my visit to the torture chamber.

"Wow, Townsend. That's crazy. I can't believe you're on the list for that place." Jessica shakes her head, sounding and looking in awe.

"You are too." I retort. "And how do you know about Townsend? Have you been there?"

Jessica gives me a derisive look. "What do you think?"

I laugh and shake my head. "Stupid question."

"Ok, we have another hour before we need to start getting ready. Let's go make dinner, and I'll tell you all about last night. And this morning." Jessica has a wicked grin on her face. She jumps up from the couch and starts for the kitchen.

Oh my... Do I really need all the dirty details? I would rather not know *everything*, but Jessica tends to be an over-sharer when it comes to personal matters.

I stand up from the couch and move cautiously toward the kitchen, my head tipped back so I can keep the compress against my face.

"Keep it PG, Jess."

Jessica huffs. "You're such a prude."

No, I'm not. I just don't want to hear about Cade's size, girth, stamina, how he kisses, where he kisses, or anything of that nature. And I already know they both enjoyed themselves. Our rooms aren't soundproof.

"PG-13," I concede. I sit at the kitchen table and watch Jessica from underneath my compress.

"Fine. I'll try." Jessica walks into our pantry and grabs various items to make dinner.

"So, it started last night when you went to your room…"

And Jessica is off, lost in a world where the man she's already in love with is making her feel things she has never felt before.

I'm standing in Jessica's room and she looks annoyed. "For the last time, no, you cannot wear jeans to a club. Not even your darkest wash. They won't let you in, even if you're on the list." Jessica has her fists clenched tight on her hips.

My hands go up in surrender. Nothing is worth battling with Jessica. She fights dirty.

"Fine," I mutter. "How the hell was I supposed to know there was a dress code?"

"Of course there's a dress code. How do you think Townsend became the best club in Vegas? They sure as hell aren't letting in losers with baggy jeans and girls in yoga pants." Jessica is looking at me with exasperation and pity. "Your laid-back SoCal roots are showing."

"Your 'I Grew Up Here So I Know Everything' arrogance is showing." I'm speaking in a sing-song voice so my words don't seem quite so blunt.

Jessica ignores me and marches into her closet. "I have something you can wear. I bought it last year, back when I was twenty pounds lighter, so I know it'll fit you."

Whatever Jessica has, I'll have to wear it. I literally own nothing appropriate for a club.

"This baby will look amazing on you!" Jessica produces a fiery orangish-red strapless mini dress from her closet. The tags still dangle from it.

"I bought this last year before loser face broke up with me." Jessica still won't say his name, not that I blame her. A break up through text. What kind of limp shit is that?

The dress is gorgeous and the color is stunning, almost like the sun just before it peeks over the horizon.

"Try it on," Jessica urges.

I fight to remove my tightest and darkest skinnies. With Jessica's assistance the jeans finally clear my ankles. By then, we're laughing hysterically.

"How the hell did you get those on?" Jessica says between howls.

"Very carefully," I reply with a smile. "Now for the dress."

Jessica unzips it and hands it over.

I step in and Jess zips me up, then I step back for her review.

"Wooowww, LL," Jessica draws out the word. "Keep that dress. It was made for you, birthday girl."

I turn to look at myself in the full length mirror. The bright dress, paired with my olive skin and brown hair, looks, well, spectacular. The curls give my hair way more volume, and my eyes look bigger and rounder, thanks to the excess hairs being removed from my brows and the dark brown eyeliner Jessica has applied.

Am I really that beautiful girl staring back at me? I look just like someone who would go to a club like Townsend should look. Not that I'd know, but maybe…maybe it's time to find out. Suddenly, I'm not dreading this night anymore.

The strip is bright, noisy, and packed. Throngs of pedestrians crowd the sidewalks, and traffic is bumper-to-bumper. I have to remind myself that this is just the beginning of being in a crowd. At least right now, in the relative safety of the cab, I still have my own space.

It was Jessica's idea to take a cab tonight, and I'm secretly grateful to her for suggesting it. That way, if I do decide to celebrate my birthday in the typical fashion, I'm not stuck coming to get my car in the morning. I already made it clear to Jess that I'm not going to get hammered and act like a moron, but this dress and the skyscraper heels she forced me to wear have put me in the mood to celebrate.

Townsend is inside The Martin, a new hotel and casino on the strip. We pull up and I manage to exit the cab without flashing my lady part at anyone while Jessica pays the fare.

The Martin looks incredible. The tall building appears to sparkle, and when I look closer I see that the outside is mirrored, and there are tiny lights in the mirrors. It shimmers and reflects the lights of the other hotels on the strip. It's absolutely beautiful.

"Can I help you ladies get somewhere?" A friendly valet approaches us, offering his assistance.

"Townsend," I say with authority. It must be these killer heels.

"This floor, ma'am. Past the casino." He nods and takes off running, rushing to open the door of a red Ferrari that has just pulled up, engine roaring.

Jessica loops her arm through mine, and we enter The Martin. The floors are a spectacular white marble, while gray leather couches dot the oversized reception area. Large crystal vases filled with the most fragrant arrangements of white flowers sit atop gray metal tables, and enormous rectangular mirrors line the walls. I see myself over and over as we walk past the casino. Bells from the slots ring out loudly, and I watch a handful of celebrating people at a craps table.

"We should play tonight," Jessica suggests.

"This night has enough firsts," I murmur. My excitement is giving way to nervousness now that I'm actually here.

"Gambling will just be another one. And that's ok, you know?" Jessica gives me a one armed squeeze.

"I know firsts are ok. I'm just getting nervous, that's all." I whisper to Jessica.

She shakes her head, her long strawberry blonde hair shimmering. "Don't be. I know you don't like crowds or making conversation with strangers, but you need to get over that for tonight. You were personally invited to the hottest club in town, you're on the list, and you look freaking hot. Please, for once, let's both just let our hair down and act our age." Jessica's look is stern.

I know she's right. Ok, fine, her pep talk worked. "Agreed." I relent. "But nobody our age uses the phrase 'Let our hair down.'"

"Damn,"Jessica says, making a small motion with her hand and snapping her fingers at the same time.

I'm laughing and looking ahead when I see it. The long line, the two large, broad-shouldered men standing guard at the entrance, and the metal sign reading 'Townsend' in small square lights.

I stop short. Jessica stops with me.

"There it is." I nod in front of us. "What the hell am I supposed to do? Just walk up and tell one of the big guys up front that I'm on the list?"

Jessica shrugs. "I guess so."

This was a bad idea. "What if Gigi forgot? What if I go up there and look like the idiot I am for thinking I belong in a place like this? No way." I shake my head.

Jessica sighs and glares at me with exasperation before she marches off toward Townsend, the line, and the two big guys who will laugh me out of The Martin.

I hurry after Jessica to stop her, but she already has the attention of one of the guys. I show up just in time to hear her say my name and tell him I'm on the list, courtesy of Gigi.

He grabs the list and looks it over. His eyes pause momentarily, then he nods and unlocks the velvet rope. "Go on in ladies. Gigi is in the sky tonight, but she has you reserved at table six. Have fun and happy birthday."

I'm stunned into silence, but thankfully my best friend has a working brain.

"Thank you." She smiles sincerely at the man and pulls me into the club.

The music is thumping in my chest the second we walk in. It's dark, but there are blue, yellow, and pink lights coming from all over the place. And there are so many people that we have to squeeze by them as we make our way in.

"Look for table six," Jessica yells. Thankfully I can read her lips, because I sure as hell can't hear her.

We spot a reserved sign on a table and slowly make our way through the writhing bodies. I follow Jess up two stairs and into the reserved area, a u-shaped white leather couch surrounding a glass table.

"It's for us!" Jessica squeals, plucking a handwritten note off the table and handing it to me.

I read it aloud. "Happy Birthday Lila, xoxo Gigi and the Townsend Girls." *Wow, this person is really going above and beyond to make sure I celebrate my birthday.*

"Ladies, hello." A women in a tank top and hot pants takes both steps up and smiles sweetly at us. She leans into me and yells in my ear. "Happy birthday, Lila. I'm Serena. Don't worry about anything tonight. As Gigi's special guests, everything is on the house. She said to start you off with this." Serena sets down an ice bucket and two glasses I didn't even notice she was carrying. With a flourish she pulls the bottle out of the ice and effortlessly pops the cork.

"I hope you enjoy your evening." Serena fills our glasses. "Don't hesitate to ask me for anything." She replaces the bottle back in the ice and retreats with a smile.

Eyes wide, I look at Jessica. Her face mirrors mine. "Holy shit!" we yell in unison.

We both settle onto the couch, and I pick up the glasses and hand one to Jessica.

"Cheers!" We clink glasses. Tentatively I try the champagne.

Oh. My. Gosh. It's delicious. Why have I never had this before? Eagerly I take another sip. The crisp taste and the effervescence are delectable.

A thought occurs to me. I turn to Jessica, who is already dancing from a seated position. I cup my hand and yell into her ear.

"What did the door guy mean when he said Gigi was in the sky?"

We both look up, and I see exactly what he meant. Are those cages?

On the wall opposite our table are three boxes, spaced evenly apart. They have bars on them like jail cells, and inside girls are dancing, one per box. And the one with red hair is none other than Gigi.

I take another sip of the champagne, trying not to gape at the cage dancers. *No big deal. I see this stuff all the time.*

"The middle one is Gigi." I yell to Jessica.

"Wow," mouthes Jessica. "She can dance."

I watch her for a minute as I sip my champagne. The music is hypnotic, and I find myself moving my shoulders, just a little.

"Excuse me, are you the birthday girl?"

The voice is a yell, coming from behind me. I turn around and find myself looking right into the greenest eyes I've ever seen, even greener than my own. His hair is dark, styled perfectly in that crisp and clean way, and his jaw is strong and angled. Suddenly my heart is pounding, my skin pulsing with electricity. Who the hell is this man?

CHAPTER FIVE

Is it the absurdly handsome man or the champagne that causes electric currents to run down my body? Either way, I've never felt more alive.

"I'm Lila," I stammer, then remember I need to raise my voice to be heard, although somewhere in the back of my mind I realize the music isn't pulsing as wildly in my chest anymore.

"I'm Lila," I repeat, this time louder. "The birthday girl." *Get yourself together, you fool.* I pull my shoulders back and smile confidently at the world's most attractive man.

He offers his hand and I take it, shaking it once. More sparks. I knew it wasn't just the champagne.

"And you are?"

He leans in closer to be heard. Automatically I lean in too, my desire to be closer to this man moving me without my consent.

"I'm sorry, I don't know where my manners went." He unleashes a full, mega-watt smile on me. His teeth are perfectly straight and white. Of course.

"I'm Xavier Townsend." His deep voice is clear, strong, assured.

My eyes widen. *Townsend?*

I point a finger in the air and circle it around toward the rest of the club. "As in Townsend the club? Or is it a coincidence?"

He smiles, looking simultaneously proud and arrogant. Geez, he's gorgeous.

Xavier nods his head. "This is my club."

I'm stunned. Is he even over thirty? Where did he get the money to start a club, in The Martin of all places?

"Wow." It's all I can think to say. Suddenly I remember my best friend. I force myself to move away from Xavier and turn to Jessica, placing my hand on her shoulder. I have to yell.

"Xavier, this is my best friend Jessica."

They shake hands, and Jessica's eyes are wide like mine.

"Nice to meet you Jessica." Xavier smiles politely. "Are you enjoying yourself?"

Jessica nods. "Yes, thank you. And nice to meet you too."

Xavier shifts his attention back to me. I look up and lean forward, eager to close some of the distance.

"So, Lila, how old are you today?" His hands grip the back of the couch, and he bends at the waist to talk to me. For the first time I notice what he's wearing. His slacks are charcoal gray, his white shirt is some kind of linen blend with the top button open. His clothes are ironed to crisp perfection, and I wonder if his girlfriend ironed them for him. Or maybe his wife? Surreptitiously I check his left hand. No ring. *Hallelujah.*

"Twenty-one." But I'm not thinking of my age right now. I'm still stuck on his relationship status. Ok, so, no wife. And hopefully no girlfriend either, because this man has me feeling things I've never had the pleasure of experiencing before.

Xavier looks surprised. "That's it?"

I raise one eyebrow at him. "Are you saying I look old?"

He has the decency to look abashed. "Not at all. It's just that you seem older."

We've only just met. How can he make such an assessment?

"Why is that?" I'm intrigued. I've never behaved my age, but to hear it from a stranger? I have to know what kind of vibe I'm putting out.

"Well, for starters, you aren't drunk or dancing." He gestures out to the rest of the club, and I follow his gaze. Everyone is dancing and almost definitely drunk.

I turn back to Xavier. "Ah, but we've only just arrived," I say. "Perhaps drunken dancing is in my plan for the evening."

Jessica sits next to me, silently sipping champagne. I know she's straining to hear every word.

Xavier smiles mischievously. Oh, wow. He looks...playful.

"Well, don't let me keep you from your plans. Gigi should be down soon. I know she's looking forward to spending her break with you. Apparently you made quite an impression on her." Xavier's lip twitches as though he's holding back laughter.

Whatever the joke is, I don't get it. Is there some way I can keep him here, talking to me? I have no idea what to say next. I'm clueless when it comes to men. I can take a photo that will make a person cry with its poignance, but I can't think of a way to prolong my interaction with Xavier? I come up blank.

"It was nice to meet you, Xavier." Why do I feel sad?

"You as well, Lila. Nice meeting you, Jessica."

She smiles at me. How much champagne has she had while I've been talking?

Xavier leans in so his face is tantalizingly close to mine and rests one hand on my bare shoulder. "Happy birthday, Birthday Girl." His voice is seductive, and my breath hitches.

He walks away, and I look down at my shoulder, certain there must be an imprint from his hand. How is it possible I can still feel the heat from his touch?

I'm on my second glass of champagne when Gigi exits the cage. I watch as she makes her way down a ladder that's affixed to the wall. Her body is insane, clad in hot pants and a sequined bra top, and not an ounce of fat on her. Another girl climbs up as soon as Gigi is off the ladder.

I wave at her and she waves back, then motions to the bar and gives me the one minute finger.

"Ask Gigi if she can tell your boyfriend to come back over here." Jessica laughs at her own joke.

"Oh please." If only...

"I'm telling you, Xavier is into you."

Jessica won't let it go. She started in on me the second Xavier walked away, and she hasn't let up, even though I told her he was just being polite. According to Jessica, Xavier was showing classic signs of interest, all of which I missed. I'm pretty sure it's just that she is in love and wants me to be too. It's making her see things.

Gigi walks into our booth, saving me from arguing with Jessica yet again. She's carrying another bottle of champagne and a glass for herself. I stand up to greet her.

"Lila! You came!" She hugs me with one arm, the champagne bottle and glass still in her other hand.

I nod enthusiastically. "Thank you for all this. It's so nice of you." I have to yell extra loud into Gigi's ear to be heard. Is it just me, or has the music gotten louder since I talked to Xavier?

"Everyone deserves to be treated special on their birthday." Gigi turns to Jessica. "Hi, I'm Gigi."

Jessica extends a hand, which Gigi takes. "I'm Jessica," she shouts. "This is awesome. Thanks!"

"No problem." Gigi uncorks the next bottle of champagne and refills our glasses, then pours one for herself.

"To Lila." Gigi lifts her hand in a toast.

I smile as Jessica echoes Gigi's toast. We all sip the bubbly liquid. It fizzes in my mouth, and again I wonder why I've chosen to miss out on something so delicious for so long.

Gigi winks at me from across the booth. "Now, let's party!"

I'm buzzed from the champagne, flushed from all the dancing, and now I can add *famished* to the list. A night of partying can take a lot out of a girl.

We shut down Townsend, dancing and drinking champagne until the last song ended. The bottle of champagne never seemed to empty, so I don't even know how many bottles we went through. But I do know that I had fun. The kind of fun that I judge others for having. Perhaps I'll have to re-evaluate that.

Lucy and Becca were there too, dancing in the cages at different times and visiting our table when they were taking breaks. Somehow Gigi didn't have to go up again for the rest of the night. And I didn't see Xavier again, but the place was jam-packed and, to be honest, my vision got a little fuzzy.

And now we're a group of five very hungry, half-drunk girls headed out to an all night diner. Jessica and Lucy are walking a few feet ahead of us, singing and laughing. I can't pay attention to them right now, because all my concentration is going toward walking straight in these crazy-tall heels.

Blessedly the walk is short, and I'm quickly seated in a booth. I slip my sore feet out of the heels and set them gingerly on top of the shoes.

"The usual, ladies?" Becca glances at Gigi and Lucy. They nod.

"What's the usual?" Jessica asks. She's sitting next to me, and suddenly I feel really grateful for her. She's my dose of normalcy in this whole bizarre night. I reach over and squeeze her hand. Jessica looks at me, the question in her eyes, but she doesn't ask it. I smile gratefully and release her hand.

I look toward the group and see Gigi watching us intently. "The usual is hash browns, sausage, and eggs, and apple pie for dessert. A la mode, of course."

"How the hell do you guys keep those bodies?" I ask, incredulous. I would be a house if that menu was my *usual*.

"We work out. Hard. You can join us sometime." Gigi offers.

Ugh, exercise... not something I enjoy. It's more Jessica's thing.

"Umm, well. I'm not much for exercising." It sounds lame, even to me.

Gigi winks at me. "I'll make it fun, I promise."

After the generous birthday night Gigi has just arranged for me I feel obligated to agree.

"Ok. I'll willingly torture myself."

Gigi beams. "You won't regret it."

After we order, Jessica turns to Gigi. "Thanks for doing all that for Lila tonight. We probably would have been at home drinking wine and eating pizza." Jessica's smile is sincere.

Oddly, Gigi's response is on the cool side. "At home? You live together?"

Jessica's eyebrows furrow, but just barely.

"We've been roommates since freshman year of college," Jessica says.

"I'm guessing you're both juniors? Based upon Lila's age?" Gigi's tone seems to have warmed slightly.

"Actually," I say, "we're both in the middle of our senior year because we've taken summer courses. One more semester to go." I high five Jessica. We're almost there!

Gigi watches us. Is it just me, or does she look relieved? And why? Perhaps she has something else on her mind tonight.

"Well, good for you, ladies." Gigi congratulates us. "I graduated from UNLV too. And I make a fuck ton more money working at Townsend than I ever did as an accountant."

Jessica and I share a surprised look. Isn't that every soon-to-be college graduate's worst fear? Earning a degree and then not making enough money with that degree?

The thought is depressing enough to make me want another drink. I take a long drink of my ice water, and it's refreshing and necessary.

Gigi turns to me. "I saw Xavier talking to you."

I nod. "He came over to tell me happy birthday." I'm trying to sound unaffected, but my insides are rolling. All I can see are emerald eyes and Xavier's flawless face. Not a minute's gone by that I haven't thought of him since I met him.

"Did he try to get in your pants?"

What the hell kind of question is that? Is Gigi joking? One look at her straight face tells me she's not.

I laugh uncomfortably. Gigi might be the oddest person I've ever met.

"Ummm, no." I answer, still bewildered by the question. "Why?"

She shrugs as if her question was totally normal. "You should stay away from Xavier. He doesn't have a great track record."

I sneak a peak at Jessica. Her mouth is open.

No, please don't let this be true. Xavier can't be a bad guy. No way.

"Thanks for the warning, but there wasn't much to our conversation. He spoke to me for a few minutes, and I didn't see him again." I try to look nonplussed. Now I'm the one shrugging with feigned nonchalance. Xavier didn't put butterflies in my stomach. Nope, not at all. Those green eyes, that chiseled face… And there they are, the butterflies, back just because I'm pulling from my memory bank.

"Consider yourself pretty fucking lucky if that's the end of it. Right, girls?" Gigi looks to Lucy and Becca to confirm her words. I smell a story, maybe stories in the plural, but I don't want to ask. I don't want to know.

They shake their blond heads vigorously. Great, the whole Townsend trio agrees about Xavier's bad-boy status.

"He's a heartbreaker, Lila. And you're so sweet and young and innocent." Gigi smiles at me, looking weirdly maternal.

I wave my hand at the Townsend girls and laugh. "Don't worry about me. Nothing is going to happen between me and Xavier." I'm assuring them, and it's not really a lie. When am I ever going to see him again?

Jessica laughs beside me, and I know the sound is forced. We all turn to her. Thank God the attention is off me.

Jessica looks like she is holding a juicy secret.

"Lila may be young, and the sweet part is debatable, but she isn't innocent. So this one time… " And the story begins, leaving me free from further well-meaning and unwanted advice.

Jessica has the Townsend girls full attention, regaling them with the story of me at eighteen, streaking through a frat party because I was dared to. C'mon, everyone knows you can't back down from a dare. Besides, I wore skin colored underwear. And a mask.

"And the best part was, people were placing bets. Most people thought this introvert over here would never do it." Jessica stops to ruffle my hair. "But she agreed to streak as long as the winners of the bets promised to donate their winnings to No Child Hungry. And then she made sure they actually did." Jessica looks at me with affection. She loves that story.

"Wow. I'm *tres* impressed, Lila." Gigi looks pleasantly surprised. "Sweet, pretty and not so innocent after all. Imagine that."

I shrug. "I suppose it was the philanthropist in me. So, does anybody else have any experience in the streaking department?" I'm eager to have the attention removed from me.

Somehow I'm going to have to pay Jessica back for saving me from the anti-Xavier campaign. But first I'm going to let my still fuzzy brain dream up his image one more time. And his deep voice... "Happy birthday, Birthday Girl."

In one short conversation Xavier made me feel more than any man I've ever encountered. How is that possible? It must be hormones. I'm incredibly sexually attracted to him. That's all. And if that's the case... And off I go to daydream about what lies beneath Xavier's white linen shirt.

CHAPTER SIX

The pounding head, the swirling stomach... So this is what a hangover feels like. Good God, I feel like shit. I want to roll over, but I know it will hurt too much.

Thank goodness I remembered to close my curtains last night. Or was it this morning? Either way, the sun would have been an unwelcome guest in my room. My phone buzzes next to me on my bed. I open it and read my text.

Jessica wants to know if I'm ok. I type out my response with one eye open. *No, I'm not ok. I want to puke.*

Less than a minute later my door opens, and Jessica heads straight for my bed. She climbs in and curls up behind me.

"What a night, huh?"

"From beginning to end," I agree.

"And what about Xavier?" Jessica asks the one question I haven't dared to ask myself.

"What about him?" My voice is flat, not betraying even one emotion, but I'm not fooling Jessica.

"Lila, he was...wow." Jessica sounds dreamy.

I finally grow the courage to roll over. I pause for a moment, just to see if I'll puke. When I don't, I say, "What does that even mean?"

"He was so into you. You would have to be blind not to see that."

"I'll probably never see him again. It doesn't matter anyway." Even saying the words makes my heart twist.

"Never say never." Jessica intones. She yawns hugely, and soon I'm yawning too.

"Nighty night." Her eyes are already closed.

"Don't let the bed bugs bite." I close my eyes.

I awaken to Jessica's voice. She's holding that nasty green juice concoction out to me across the length of my bed.

I sit up slowly, groaning. "Is that supposed to be appetizing?"

"It will make you feel better. Besides, aren't you over the hangover by now? It's four in the afternoon."

"Ugh, I slept all day." My voice sounds whiny. I hate sleeping all day. I don't even like sleeping past eight. I always feel like I'm missing something.

"That's what happens when you party all night." Jessica pushes two pills and the juice into my hands. "Take these. Cade is going to be here soon. He's making us something he swears will cure any hangover on the spot."

I roll my eyes. "Then where the hell was he this morning? I barely kept from tossing my cookies."

Jessica suddenly looks lustful. I feel my upper lip curl in disgust. Jessica and that starry-eyed gaze don't even notice.

"If Cade had been here this morning, you wouldn't have had the pleasure of my company." Jessica leans down and taps me lightly on my nose.

I take a sip of the green drink and pretend to gag. Jessica ignores me.

"I suppose your spooning was awfully nice this morning," I admit.

"Not as nice as Xavier's would have been." Jessica eyebrows wiggle salaciously.

I groan and sit up, mumbling. "Drop it."

The doorbell rings, and Jessica jumps up. She speeds out of my bedroom door and thunders down the stairs.

I shake my head at Jessica's eagerness. *Have some dignity, woman.*

I suppose I should head downstairs soon and join the land of the living. But first, a shower.

"All right, fine. This stuff is amazing, Cade. Consider my hangover cured." I lift my hands in defeat.

Cade turns from where he's washing dishes at the sink and winks at me in a knowing way. It's hard to imagine buttoned-up Cade ever needing this magic elixir. He seems so proper.

Who knew chicken noodle soup was exactly what I needed to kick the last of my hangover to the curb? Apparently its healing abilities extend further than the common cold.

Jessica smiles lovingly at Cade and gets up from the table. I watch as she sets her empty bowl in the sink and wraps her arms around his waist.

"My man can cook," Jessica declares, her voice possessive and proud. "I wonder if Xavier can cook?" She asks the question without turning to look at me.

"Since when are you Xavier's biggest fan?" Why does she keep bringing him up?

Jessica nuzzles her face into Cade's back, making her response muffled. "I don't care about Xavier. I'm Cade's biggest fan."

Before I can tell Jessica to drop any fantasies of double dates, Cade asks his own question.

"Lila, I take it you met someone?"

"As you already know, his name is Xavier. Perhaps you can tell your girlfriend to stop bringing him up. We talked for a few minutes, and that was it. No info exchanged. And for some reason, Jessica's already planning our wedding."

Jessica employs her biggest eye roll. "Because he liked you. And you liked him too. Quit denying it." Jessica's voice is stern, my mother all over again. "You spend so much time disliking every guy you meet. Give me a break for getting excited when someone finally piques your interest."

Jessica's right. It has been a long time since I felt attracted to somebody. But last night was about more than just attraction. Xavier struck me on a deeper level. Beneath the handsome face, below the witty and flirtatious conversation, there's something deeper that I'm drawn to. And I'm denying it because I know there isn't a future.

I eye Jessica meaningfully. "You heard what Gigi said."

Jessica shrugs, and I know her well enough to know that she isn't letting this Xavier thing go. She is doing just the opposite, digging her heels in.

Cade looks at me with apprehension. "Did you meet Xavier last night at Townsend?"

"Why?" *Oh no.* Someone with more bad things to say about the one man who has caught my eye since high school. The sinking feeling is heavy in my stomach, even though I've made it clear I'm not going to go after Xavier.

Cade follows up with another question. "Xavier Townsend?"

I narrow my eyes. "Spit it out Cade." My voice is harsher than I meant it to be.

Jessica shoots me a disapproving look.

I watch as Cade takes an annoyingly long time to rinse off the last pot and put it on the towel on the counter next to him. I'm about to ask him if he really graduated from Michigan with an advanced degree. Nobody smart enough to graduate from a school like that could take this freaking long to wash a damn pot.

Finally he turns to face me. I must have a defensive look on my face, because Cade's hands come up in front of him like he's proclaiming his innocence.

"Don't shoot the messenger, ok?" His look is earnest.

Honestly? How does Jessica put up with this guy? "Ok, Cade, I agree not to shoot you. Now talk." My voice is demanding.

"He was a friend of my older brother's. They went to school together, played sports together. Xavier got my brother into trouble. I've always known him to be a trouble maker..."

I hold up my hand. "I'm confused. There's a third Blankenship sibling? I thought it was just you and Sunny."

Behind Cade Jessica shakes her head and closes her eyes.

Cade look downs as he answers me. "Brent died in a drunk driving accident the night of high school graduation."

I soften my voice. "Cade, I'm sorry about your brother. I have a sister and two brothers, and I can't imagine how painful it would be to lose her. We can stop talking about Xavier if you want. Your warning is noted, ok?"

"Thanks." Cade smiles and steps closer to the table. "I didn't know you had such a big family. Tell me about them."

We move to the living room, me with a large glass of ice water, Cade and Jessica with a glass of wine, and I tell Cade about my family. Just like that it's a normal night again. Our new normal, anyway. I'm nestled in the arm chair, telling funny stories about my siblings, and now that my hangover has subsided, it's easy to believe last night and Xavier never happened.

It's Saturday, always a busy day at The Pain Shoppe. I don't mind. It keeps me from thinking too much of Xavier. And of Gigi and Cade's warnings. And of those eyes, those emerald green eyes. And that face. And the wide shoulders. And the smell of his skin when he leaned in closer to me.

Stop! This is pointless. I heard, loud and clear, what Gigi and Cade had to say.

Thankfully the customers are coming in a steady stream. I force myself to focus on them.

Before I know it, it's two o'clock, and my stomach is growling. I pick up my phone and dial Jeri's extension.

"What's up?" Jeri turns toward me from her spot at her desk and smiles.

"Lunch? Can you sit here for five minutes while I scarf down the rest of last nights soup?"

Jeri hangs up and leans over to Camryn, the new front desk girl. She's still in training, but hopefully she'll be ok for five minutes.

"Thank you, thank you, thank you," I say when Jeri arrives at my desk.

"Yeah, yeah, yeah. You're lucky you're such a hot piece. Otherwise I might have said no. Get up."

Hot piece is one of the last phrases I would use to describe myself, but arguing will only keep me from my soup.

"I'll be right back, I promise." I grab my phone and head to the break room.

Once my soup is warming in the microwave, I turn on my phone.

Two texts, one from my mom and the other from Gigi. Mom wants to know what I did for my birthday and why I didn't call her back yesterday. I type out a message telling her that I'll call her when I get off work.

I retrieve my warm soup from the microwave and read Gigi's text. *Ugh.* She wants me to workout with her tomorrow morning. I totally forgot I promised to join her sometime. I really wish I hadn't said that.

Quickly I type another message agreeing to the sweat session, and then I slam down the remainder of my soup. I clean up my mess and head back out to my desk. My five minutes are up.

As promised, I call my mom on my drive home. I turn on speakerphone and dial her number. She answers on the fourth ring.

"Hi, Mom." My voice is cheerful.

"Honey, I'm so glad you called." Her voice sounds relieved. "I was worried about you."

My mother is a world-renowned worrier. It's an art she developed when she had my sister Hannah, and she perfected it through the years. My dad wants her to take anxiety medicine to chill her out, but she refuses. Her worrying annoyed me when I was a teenager, but now I find it endearing.

Despite what I know of my mother, I'm not sure why she was concerned about me this time. I'm the tamest of all four of her children. "Why were you worried?"

She doesn't answer right away. I hear yells and cheers in the background, and then my mom's voice screams right into the phone. "Go Jackson! Come on, come on, come on! Get it in the goal!"

Obviously she's at my little brother's soccer game. I wait patiently.

"Yeah! Good job Jackson!" My mother is still screaming like a banshee.

"Mom?" I ask, when her screaming dies down and she still isn't speaking.

"I was high-fiving other parents. Sorry, that was exciting. OK, where were we?"

I smile. She is such a good mom. "I asked you why you were worried about me."

"Oh. Well, because you had your birthday, and then you didn't answer my calls yesterday. It's not like you. What did you do on your birthday?" Her voice is reluctant, almost like she doesn't really want to know.

"Mom, I did something totally normal." I explain carefully. How much of my night does she want to know about?

"You went out drinking? That's not like you at all. That's not something you're into now, is it?" Her voice sounds horrified.

I'm glad my mom can't see my eye roll. "It was just a really weird situation. I met someone at the salon who invited me out to the club where she works."

"You made a new friend!" My mom exclaims, abandoning the whole partying aspect of my story.

I've been hearing for years about how I should make more friends. And now I have. Of course, my new friend dances nearly naked in a cage suspended on a wall. I won't bother my mom with that detail.

"Her name is Gigi. Short for Genevieve. She's very nice. She made Jessica and me her VIP guests at the club where she works. We had a really fun night."

"It must've been quite a night, if you couldn't answer the phone yesterday." Her voice is dry.

My mom is trying to sound flippant, but I know better. There's disapproval hiding behind the words.

"I'm not turning into Hannah." My older sister was wild at college. She had more than one underage drinking citation, not to mention a trip to the hospital for a broken arm after drunkenly climbing a tree. My big sister and I are opposites in every way. She has a thousand friends and hates books. She's never without a boyfriend and loves being the center of attention. In no way will I ever be like Hannah.

My mom sighs. "I know honey. I just worry."

"I'm fine. Pinky promise, ok?"

My mom chuckles. "Pinky promise."

I pull into my driveway and turn off my car. "I'm home. Pay attention to Jackson's game and give him a hug from me. And Colin too, if he's with you."

"He is and I will. Are you taking care of the house?" She always asks this question at the end of our conversations.

"No parties. No other roommates, just Jessica." I would never break the rules, and she knows it, yet she still asks. Honestly, who would jeopardize the opportunity to live in a real house while in college instead of a small apartment or the dorms again? I will be eternally grateful to my parents for buying a house in Las Vegas.

"Love you honey."

"Love you mom." I reply and hang up.

I walk into the house and right into Jessica and Cade in the middle of a hot make-out session on the couch.

"Good Lord, you two." I pretend to shield my eyes. "I guess I should just be happy you're clothed."

Jessica giggles and sits up, adjusting her shirt. Cade has the grace to blush.

"I'll leave you two alone in a second, but first..." I turn to Jessica. "Interested in joining me at the gym in the morning?"

Laughter bubbles up until she sees I'm not kidding. "You're serious?"

I nod. "Gigi text me."

"As much as I would love to see you attempt to exercise, I just want to be lazy tomorrow. Monday is the first day of my internship, so I want my Sunday to be filled with a whole lot of nothing. We're going upstairs now. Nighty night." Jessica stands and pulls Cade up with her.

"You suck. Fine. Goodnight." I turn and head into the kitchen. I slice up a green apple and put a spoonful of peanut butter on my plate. I'm headed up the stairs when I hear the dreaded sounds of Cade and Jessica getting it on.

Headphones or a shower? Headphones in the shower? I hurry into my bathroom and turn the shower on. I need to eat, get clean and get to bed. I've signed on for a torture session, and tomorrow morning is coming quick.

CHAPTER SEVEN

Nooo... I roll over and throw an arm across my face. How is it already morning? The alarm on my phone is playing loudly on my dresser across the room, a location I chose on purpose. Now I'm forced to get up to quell the annoying noise.

I rise from the warm comfort of my bed and go to my phone and switch off the alarm. My feet are lead as I trudge into my closet and start pulling on the clothes I set out last night. I happen to have some exercise-appropriate clothing from last year when Jessica guilted me into working out with her.

I'm dressed in my black capri's, tank top, and running shoes. After my hair is pulled back into a high ponytail, I stand back to look at myself. I certainly look the part. A quick toothbrushing, deodorant application, and I'm set.

Quietly I pass Jessica's door, where she and Cade are surely sleeping soundly after what I can only assume was a performance of acrobatics last night. How else can I explain the sounds of walls being knocked into? Naked cartwheels? I don't even want to know.

The streets are quiet as I make my way to the gym where Gigi told me to meet her. Idly I wonder if she will have more clothes on than she had the last time I saw her.

I pull up to the gym, and before I get out of my car, I take a deep breath. I'm so not excited about this. *Get in there, Mitchell. Quit being a pansy.* I grab my water bottle and head inside.

Gigi is standing at the front desk, all long legs and gorgeous red hair. This morning it's twisted into a perfect ballerina bun on top of her head. She's wearing pretty much exactly what she wears to work, but these teeny shorts have an emblem from a popular sportswear store. And the top is a sports bra, not a glittery bra top. I try not to gape. It's insane how toned she is.

Gigi smiles and claps her hands together when I walk in. "You made it!"

Why does she like me so much?

I ignore the voice in my head and return Gigi's wide smile. "I'm here, but I can't promise you I'll be a very good workout partner. It's been a while since this body has seen any significant physical exertion." I motion from my head to my feet.

Gigi shakes her head. "That's crazy. You have such a nice figure for someone who doesn't exercise."

"I eat well." I explain. "When I'm not chowing down at diners at four a.m., anyway."

Gigi giggles, but not in an annoying, overly girly way. "I know, right? You ready to work off that pie?" Gigi grabs my hand and leads me past the front desk. It's so damned early that no one is even there to check us in.

"Do I need to sign in or anything?" I ask with worry. I don't want to get in trouble. Or get Gigi in trouble.

Gigi flippantly waves her manicured hand. "I talked to Maria before you came in and told her you would be here with me this morning. She doesn't care."

I look around at the gym as Gigi leads the way. Intimidating machinery surrounds me, making me want to turn and run. We arrive at the row of treadmills, and Gigi hops on one. I step up on the one next to her and put my water bottle in the cup holder.

Next to me Gigi is stretching. I mimic her, feeling totally foolish. Standing there, next to this tall, toned goddess, I feel completely inadequate.

Gigi stands up and starts playing music on her phone. "Nobody's here so I'll just play it out loud for both of us. This is my favorite warm-up playlist."

The thumping music starts and immediately I'm taken back to Townsend. And of course, its owner. Why can't I stop thinking about him? Our exchange was hardly special, and according to Gigi and the other girls, something to be ignored.

Gigi interrupts my thoughts. "Choose level seven on your machine." She presses a button on the screen below her.

I do the same and the machine turns on. At first it's just a walking pace, which I don't mind. After a few minutes the treadmill speeds up, and I'm jogging. I hate jogging.

Before long my throat is burning, and I'm starting to feel cramps in my stomach. As much as I hate to quit, I have to. I reach over and hit the end button.

I walk slowly with the machine as it comes to a stop. Gigi gives me a questioning look and jumps out, feet on either side of the stable part of the treadmill while the tread continues to roll on its own.

"What's wrong?"

"It has just become painfully clear to me that I'm out of shape. Maybe I should go so you can work out without me slowing you down."

Gigi hits the end button on her own machine. "Please stay. We can move on to the next part of my work out. You do as much as you can and then you can stop, ok?"

She looks so hopeful that I nod my head. Since when do I like to be tormented?

"All right, I officially quit." My breath is ragged and my legs are shaking.

Gigi gives me a sweaty side hug. "You did good. Promise."

We replace our weights and kettle balls on the rack. I can't wait to go home and take a shower.

I groan as we head toward the exit. "I probably won't be able to walk tomorrow. I'll have to crawl into The Pain Shoppe."

Gigi looks shocked. "You'll have to crawl into where?"

I realize what I said. "Oh, um, it's just a name I have for Alexa. One time someone freaked out while getting a brazilian. Ever since then, I call my work The Pain Shoppe. Probably not the best thing to tell one of Alexa's customers. Whoopsies."

To my relief, Gigi is laughing hysterically. "Lila, for a second there I thought you were referring to some kind of S&M place."

Now I'm the one who's shocked. "Are you serious? No way!" I shudder at the thought of a place like that.

"Hey, don't knock it until you've tried it." Gigi gives me an impish grin.

Holy shit... I'm going to pretend she didn't just imply that she enjoys S&M. Gigi may be a bit on the wild side. And I'm decidedly not. She isn't someone I would've ever imagined as my friend.

"Anyway..." I say, drawing out the word. Gigi laughs at my discomfort. "Maybe I can join you for your next work out?"

I ask the question as we walk out of the gym and stop on the sidewalk. We both grab sunglasses from our purses and put them on. The sun in Vegas is unrelenting.

"I only use the kettle ball or weights every other day. On the off days I just run. Do you want to join me tomorrow for a run?" Gigi has an amused look on her face. She knows I won't be able to walk tomorrow, let alone run.

I laugh out loud. "Maybe the day after that. Or the day after that. I'll text you when I regain function of my limbs."

"Oh, speaking of text. I almost forgot." Gigi pauses, biting her lip. "Maybe it would be better for you if I'd forgotten." She looks conflicted.

"What?" I ask, bewildered.

Gigi sighs and shakes her head. She digs in her purse for a moment and hands me a piece of folded paper. "Xavier asked me to give you this."

My intake of breath is loud. With a shaking hand I take the note from Gigi. I can't help the smile that has spread across my face. *Xavier wrote a note to me... to me!*

Gigi groans loudly, dissolving my silent exultation. "Don't look so lovesick. Please. Xavier is trouble. He will only hurt you. He hurts every person he gets involved with."

I pull on a straight face and set my jaw. "I don't believe in *lovesick*."

Gigi rolls her eyes. "Umm-hmm. Tell that to the girl who didn't have control of her emotions twenty seconds ago."

I stuff the note into my purse. "Thanks. So, I'll text you when I can walk again. Deal?" I'm in a hurry to get to my car and tear into Xavier's note.

Gigi looks like she wants to continue warning me. A moment passes before she says, "Later, Lila. Have a good day tomorrow at The Pain Shoppe."

My stomach is all butterflies as I climb into my car and close the door. Guiltily I glance around, making certain Gigi is definitely gone. I told her I'm not lovesick, and it couldn't be further from the truth.

I pull Xavier's note out and unfold it. It's so third grade to pass a note. And I have to admit, I love it.

His handwriting is neat, and the note is written in all caps. It's not like normal boy handwriting at all. A smile springs onto my face as I read his words.

HELLO BIRTHDAY GIRL,
I CAN'T STOP THINKING ABOUT YOU.
CAN I TAKE YOU OUT ON A DATE?
CHOOSE:
A) YES
B) NO — PLEASE DO NOT CHOOSE
THIS ONE
IF YOUR ANSWER IS A (AND IT SHOULD
BE), TELL GIGI TO GIVE ME YOUR
NUMBER.
XAVIER

I read the note three times to be sure I'm not crazy. Xavier Townsend, most beautiful man and owner of the hottest nightclub in Vegas, wants to take me out on a date. *Holy shit.* And he's asking in the cutest way.

Is this how he asks all the girls out? Gigi's warning is ringing loud and clear in my head. He hurts every person he gets involved with.

I don't want to believe that Xavier is trouble. My attraction to him was instantaneous. I've never felt like that. About anybody. It's been three years since I dated someone. I'm beyond picky, and most guys fall way short of the mark. All Xavier had to do was talk to me, and I'm smitten. That has to mean something, right? I have a spot-on radar for assholes and losers. And my radar was silent the night I met Xavier.

My first instinct is to text Gigi and tell her to give Xavier my number. Instead, I turn on my car and head toward home. I need to think about this rationally. Right now my heart is too excited to have any real reasonable thought. Why does the one man who has finally piqued my interest also come with baggage?

Jessica has managed to talk me into getting Chinese for dinner. She knows I detest her favorite Chinese hole in the wall, and yet here we are. Where have my juevos gone? First Sunny's party, then Townsend, and now this restaurant.

We've just placed an order for an ungodly amount of food, and Jessica is pouring hot tea into both of our tiny only-in-a-Chinese-restaurant china cups.

"Thanks," I say as she places one blue intricately patterned cup and saucer in front of me.

Jessica crosses her arms and stares at me expectantly.

"What?" My voice is a little on the harsh side. I'm tense and irritated, and I've been that way all day. Xavier's note is to blame. And the warnings that keep sailing through my head. Stupid warnings.

Jessica sighs. "What's going on with you? You've been in a weird mood all day, you haven't told me why, and you didn't make any of your usual snotty remarks about coming here to eat."

"Jess, please... It's just..." I turn my head away so I don't have to meet her expectant gaze. I'm not sure what to say. I haven't told Jessica about Xavier's note because I don't want her to agree with Gigi and Cade.

"It's just what, Lila?" Jessica's tone is challenging.

Fine, she wins. At least I won't be the only person overthinking this.

"Are you sure you don't want to become a journalist?" My voice is petulant. "You have that whole intrusive question thing down."

Jessica takes a sip of her tea and gently sets the cup on the saucer, then looks up at me. Her blue eyes are stern.

"Spill." She commands.

I release everything I've been holding in, starting with Gigi giving me the note that was accompanied by her second warning and ending with the mental hell I've been in all day.

"What should I do?" My voice is small and my heart is pained.

"It has taken you three years to like a guy again. And your last guy, your only guy, was your high school sweetheart. I say it's about time you went for it, heartbreaker tendencies be damned."

Finally, something I want to hear. My insides are doing a happy dance as I picture Xavier's face. I'm definitely going to see him again.

I lift my cup in the air for a toast. "Screw you, warnings."

"Take a hike." Jessica declares playfully, clinking her cup against mine.

For the first time all day I feel calm. The storm within me has subsided, and I can let my excitement over Xavier's note overtake me. Before I lose my nerve, I send a quick text to Gigi. I want Xavier's number. I'm going to call him myself. I'm ending this elementary school means of communicating, even though it was an endearing way to get my attention.

Our food arrives then, plate after steaming plate of Chinese. I put my phone back in my purse and dig in. Perhaps it's the fact that I've finally made a decision about Xavier, but suddenly, I'm ravenous.

CHAPTER EIGHT

Well, this is it. The phone is in my hand, and all I have to do is hit the send button. My stomach is a ball of nerves. I need to calm down before I call Xavier. But how?

Jessica's already in bed. Her summer internship starts tomorrow, and she said she wanted a good night of sleep to send her into a successful first day. For the first time in what feels like forever, Cade isn't spending the night.

So I can't talk to Jessica, and Gigi is definitely out. I had to endure another warning from her just to get Xavier's number in the first place. Hannah? No. My sister is a high school math teacher now. No books, just numbers. Even though it's June, she's teaching summer school for extra money. And Hannah doesn't know that Xavier even exists. I don't want to get into the whole story right now. She's probably in bed already anyway.

Wait, is it too late to call to Xavier? It's ten o'clock. Is that too late for a guy who owns a nightclub? I frown. Surely not.

It's perfectly clear that what I'm really doing is looking for excuses to put off calling him. Because, as much as I want to hear his voice again, I'm completely terrified. I've been out of the game for quite some time. And Xavier? Well, it sounds like he has been very much in the game. What the hell am I supposed to say to him? I was so brave at dinner tonight, texting Gigi to ask for his number.

And now I'm a scared, nervous, inexperienced girl. And with nobody around to give me a pep talk, I have to do it myself.

I square my shoulders and raise my chin, finger poised over the send button on my phone.

"Do it, Lila," I say out loud. "He liked you enough to introduce himself to you at his club, and he went all third grade on you with his note. Fucking call him." And then I hit the send button.

Holy shit! My insides are screaming. I am calling Xavier Townsend.

The phone rings twice. Then he answers.

"This is Xavier." His voice is smooth, detached. Very work-ish and not at all the friendly, seductive voice that is burned into my memory.

"Um, hi." I murmur stupidly. The way he answered his phone has thrown me off a bit. Quickly I remember my confidence. "Hello, Xavier. This is Lila. Or Birthday Girl, as you seem to like to call me." My voice is sanguine with a touch of flirtatious. Perfect. Exactly what I was going for.

"Lila? Seriously?" Xavier sounds genuinely shocked.

"Why are you so surprised?" I feel as though I have the upper hand, and I'm loving it.

"Um... Well..." He says.

His bumbling makes me brazen. "Are you surprised because I was supposed to tell Gigi whether I chose a or b? And then based on my answer, you would have either called or not called?"

Xavier chuckles lightly in response. "Yes, I suppose so."

His sexy, flirtatious voice is back. And, oh, does it do things to me.

"Well, I suppose *I* changed the rules and didn't tell you." Now I'm teasing him. I'm surprising even myself with my confident banter. I have never, ever spoken to a guy like this.

"Birthday Girl, you might be more of a rule breaker than I thought." Xavier sounds intrigued.

Oh, believe me, I'm breaking all my own rules by even giving you the time of day.

I backtrack a little, fearful I've given Xavier the wrong impression. "Not quite. I like rules. Rules are good."

"How about I create a rule?" Xavier is playful again.

"And what would that rule be?" I'm curious to know. I feel my upper hand slipping away. Dammit.

"My rule is, you have to let me take you somewhere tomorrow."

The words hang between us. There's really nothing to think about. Of course I will go. But it won't hurt for him to hang on for a few seconds.

"Yes, I suppose so." It's his response from a few minutes ago, turned back on him.

"Great!" Xavier sounds excited. It's so cute. And totally not what I expected from a guy with his reputation. Could Gigi be wrong about him?

I give Xavier my address, and we agree that he will pick me up at three. He won't tell me where we're going.

"It's a surprise." He sounds patronizing when I ask.

"Surprises are great, but what am I supposed to tell my roommate? She's going to want to know where I'm going with a man I barely know. In his car. Safety first. I'm a rule follower, remember?" The cat's out of the bag now. Xavier is going to know what a rule-following introvert I really am. The dancing and drinking at his club was an anomaly.

"Is Jessica your roommate?" Xavier asks.

Whoa, he remembered her name from one quick introduction? That says a lot.

"Yes." Where is he going with this?

"I'll text her my plans. Just so that you feel safe going somewhere with me, a guy you barely know. Sound good?"

I breathe a quiet sigh of relief. I don't want to be the subject of a Have You Seen Me ad.

"Yes, that works." I rattle off Jessica's number. My mind is already wandering, devising ways to sneak into Jess's room and read Xavier's text on her phone.

"Thanks, I'll text her. Just so you know, my middle name is Michael, I'm 28, a Sagittarius, and my favorite color is blue. There, now you know me a little more." Xavier sounds smug.

Oh calm down boss man. It's not like he has shared anything particularly earth-shattering about himself.

"I feel like I know you so well now," I say dryly.

Xavier laughs at my tone. "Has anyone ever told you how funny you are?"

I consider his question. "My mother says I'm too sarcastic for my own good."

"I like it."

"I'll report to my mother that she was wrong."

"Good luck with that. I'll see you tomorrow at three." Xavier's voice turns husky. Ohhhhh my.

"Yes," I murmur. I'm so pleased with our conversation, I'm practically purring. Geez, before long I'll be as lovesick as Jessica is for Cade.

He hangs up, and so do I.

I grab a pillow from my bed and scream in to it. *Oh my God. Oh my God.* I'm going on a date with Xavier. The gorgeous, successful owner of Townsend. A man who, according to Gigi, is guaranteed to break my heart.

But I can't think about that now. All I can do is lay on my bed, glowing and happy.

My eyes open and the first feeling I register is pain. My legs and my butt are screaming. I squeeze my abs just to see if they are sore too. Yep. That hurts.

I look toward my clock and see it's past nine, later than I like to sleep. Must have been my sore muscles that needed the extra rest. I know Jessica is already gone for the day, so I reach for my phone and send her a good luck message. She has been nervous for her first day, but I know she will do great. Graphic design is her passion like photography is mine.

I toss my phone on the bed next to me and stretch my arms up above my head. My toes are pointed, and I ignore my yelling muscles as I enjoy this long stretch. I'm trying to clear my mind, to keep out the thoughts that excite me. Resistance is futile, and I suppose I should've known that. Xavier fills my head, and I lay there in my soft bed, remembering our conversation last night.

Was it just me, or did he sound excited about our date? For a guy that supposedly gets around, he didn't play it very cool when I agreed to go out with him. What does that mean? Maybe he's not the man Gigi thinks he is. I know it's wishful thinking on my part. My fear is that Xavier really is the man Gigi claims he is, and he will only break my heart.

What is most confusing to me is my own willingness to see Xavier, despite the repeated warnings from Gigi and Cade's story. I'm a strong person, I don't give assholes the time of day. I know who I am and what I'm about. I choose my friends wisely and have no problem shutting most other people out. Loser guys and high-maintenance girls have never received a moment of my attention. I drove Hannah crazy as we were growing up, mostly because I wasn't the little sister who coveted her older sister's friends. Generally I considered Hannah's friends to be brainless.

That attitude didn't win me many popularity contests in high school, but that was ok by me, because I didn't like those people anyway. It was that attitude that caught the attention of Jake, my first boyfriend. He had a bad break-up with a particularly high-maintenance girl and I was exactly what he needed after that experience. We dated for two years until I left for UNLV.

So now I'm here, in my bed, trying to figure out why Xavier is even getting a second glance from me. Physically, I get it. Who wouldn't be attracted to him? With his green eyes and gorgeous face, he should be in some sexy cologne ads, not living in Vegas like a regular person. But from a practical standpoint, I can't figure out why I'm still moving forward. He comes wrapped in caution tape, and therein lies the real question for me. What is it about Xavier that makes me willing to ignore the warnings?

I have no answer. He is a flame and I'm the help-less moth, drawn inexplicably. He's a big shot playboy club owner, and I'm an inexperienced college student. Something tells me this won't end well.

I look good. I feel good. As far as my appearance goes, everything has fallen into place. My long brown hair is loose, falling perfectly into soft curls. Working at Alexa has apparently taught me a thing or two.

Dressing was not so easy, thanks to Xavier keeping our destination a secret. It was only after the onset of a mild panic attack that I remembered Jessica knew where I was going tonight. I sent a message to her inquiring about how I should dress and was rewarded with a quick response. Panic attack eliminated.

Now it's almost three o'clock, and I'm ready. So very ready. Being home alone all day nearly drove me crazy. Normally I'm perfectly content being in my own company, but not today. I felt like a string pulled taut. If I weren't so damn sore from yesterday, I would have gone for a run, just to clear my mind. Well, maybe a brisk walk. Instead I binge watched bad daytime television.

My nerves are making me feel nauseated, but I'm ignoring that. I sit down on the couch and flip through one of Jessica's magazines. An article titled *How To Blow His Mind In The Bedroom* reminds me how long it's been since I've had sex. Perhaps I should read up. Some things may have changed since I was with Jake. And my knowledge is severely limited, since Jake is the only person I've ever slept with, and we were so young. It would probably be completely different with Xavier... *Of course it would. He has enough experience in that department.*

Holy crap! Where did that nasty thought come from? It's like I can't turn off my brain, even though my heart has chosen to see where this thing with Xavier can go.

There's a loud knock on the door, and I jump. I shut the magazine with a loud smack and toss it on the coffee table. I pause and check the mirror in the entryway.

When I'm satisfied that I still look good, I grab my purse from the console table and open the door.

Xavier Townsend is standing at my door, looking as amazing as the night I met him, only four days ago. His dark green v-neck shirt takes his eye color to a whole new level. His jeans are just tight enough without being too modern. *Oh my.* My stomach is starting to pull in an unfamiliar way, down deep in a dark, unexplored place. Words from the magazine article are starting to play back through my head. *Geez, Mitchell, get yourself together.*

"Hello." I greet Xavier with a smile, sounding perfectly proper. Not a hint of annoying breathiness, even though my instant desire is front and center.

Xavier returns my smile. His eyes are lit up. Dare I say he looks eager?

"Birthday Girl." Xavier looks me over appreciatively. "You look stunning."

I look down at my tank top and jeans. I'm glad he likes my outfit because it's basically my uniform.

I walk through the front door and close it behind me. Xavier extends his hand, and I take it. The electricity is still there. It wasn't just the atmosphere, the thumping music, or the champagne. *This is real.*

"You sure know how to compliment a girl. Stunning really is way better than beautiful." I'm joking, but not really. Stunning *is* better than beautiful, in my book. We walk around the side of my house to Xavier's car, parked in my driveway. And what a car it is. The two-door BMW M6 is black with deeply tinted windows. *So fancy, bordering on flashy.* Xavier releases my hand and opens the door for me.

I slide right onto the black leather bucket seat. It's so soft and comfy. The instrument panel looks very hi-tech, with a screen coming up from the dash.

Xavier gets in and smiles at me dubiously. "I can't believe you're in my car, Birthday Girl."

"You can call me Lila, you know. My birthday is over."

Xavier drums his fingers on the steering wheel. "Hmmm. Lila…" His deep voice caresses my name as he tries it out. I've never liked the sound of my name so much.

"Ok." Xavier concedes. "Lila it is." He starts the car and reverses out of my drive way. It hums so quietly, I can barely tell it's on until he puts it into drive. Wow, this car can speed up quickly.

"Now can you tell me where we are going?" I make my best pouty face and bat my eyelashes.

For a second Xavier's face mirrors the way I felt when I first opened my front door. I see this, and my insides are pulling again. *Calm it down, Lila.*

Xavier clears his throat and takes a deep breath. "It's still a surprise, Lila." He enunciates my name, separating the two syllables.

"Fine, Xavier," I say, enunciating his name too, but he has more syllables, so it doesn't sound as good.

Xavier looks like he is trying not to laugh. "Are you feisty, Li-la?"

"Quite." My tone is clipped.

Xavier's responding grin is so arrogant. He must see me as a challenge and he likes that. "I like you, Lila. You're stunning, smart, and feisty."

"Thank you. I'd like you more if you told me where we're going."

Sometimes my smart ass mouth just doesn't quit. Then again, it's better than telling him how I really feel. *Xavier, my mind has recently become obsessed with thoughts of you and that amazing face and hot body and, more important than my desire, I'm really afraid you'll hurt me.* No, I've chosen correctly. Better to be a smart ass than a loose lips.

Xavier laughs at my smart mouth. "Patience." He touches a button on the steering wheel, and the car fills with music. It's an old song, one I've heard my parents listen to. Not a song I would have expected from Xavier.

He grabs my hand, the electricity still pulsing in our touch. We drive on, the music switching to another song I recognize from my parents' collection. There is such comfort settling between the two of us. We barely know each other, so how can that be?

I relax into my seat and turn my gaze out the window. My house and the strip are far behind us. Xavier gives my hand a light squeeze and I reciprocate. I can't believe how good this feels.

CHAPTER NINE

It's like something out of a storybook. The old but beautiful, expansive house is surrounded by green grass. The acres of gardens, so lush and colorful. I've been transported to a place that feels very far from Las Vegas. Part of me expects a pink unicorn and an armored knight to appear. The other part of me is lamenting the fact that I don't have my camera. This place is overflowing with photographic opportunity.

Xavier parks the car in a fluid, expert motion, and we climb out. The air is heavy with fragrance and I pause, closing my eyes and inhaling the sweet scent.

Xavier comes to stand beside me. "Lovely, isn't it?"

He's standing so close to me, I only have to lean an inch to make contact with him, but I refrain.

"Divine." I agree. I glance up and right into his eyes, their green color mirroring my own. His eyes look full, as though his head is swimming with thought and emotion. Whatever he's thinking and feeling, I know it can't be faked. No matter what Gigi has told me, this moment is real.

Xavier breaks our gaze first. He pops the trunk and removes a basket. A perfectly quaint, wicker picnic basket. *Ok, that's adorable.*

Xavier sweeps his hand to the wooden sign hanging from a post. It moves in the light breeze, but I can still make out the words painted in elegant script. *Welcome to Fulton Gardens.* I've never heard of this place, but I already love it.

"So you know where we are, thanks to the sign. And you know that we're having a picnic, thanks to the basket. But there's something you don't know, and I'll tell you after we eat." Xavier's grin in playful. He likes having a surprise. *Either that or he likes keeping a secret.*

I ignore my snide thought and smile back. "I don't usually enjoy surprises, but today they aren't so bad."

Xavier grabs my hand again and pulls me toward the house. "I like surprises. So you're going to have to learn to live with it."

He opens the front door of the house and waits for me to walk through. When I do, I feel like I've stepped back in time.

There's a little wooden desk immediately to my left, the top nearly bare except for a small vase of flowers and a metal electric fan. I wonder if it works or it's just decoration. A sitting area is to my right, the couches a pale yellow with a small floral pattern. The curtains are white lace, and on the wall hangs pictures of individual flowers, each with its scientific name and family. A large stone fireplace sits unlit against the back wall. I wander over to a row of pictures and read through them. Xavier stays standing near the desk, waiting patiently for whomever works here.

Then the sweetest voice chimes from behind me, and for the briefest of seconds, I think it's my grandma Mitchell. Which is quite impossible, considering grandma passed away two years ago.

"Hello, you two. You must be Xavier and Lila."

I turn and join Xavier, who is gently shaking the old woman's hand.

"Hello, Mrs. Fulton. I'm Xavier Townsend. And this is my lovely date, Lila Mitchell." Xavier places his hand on the small of my back, and I offer my own handshake.

Mrs. Fulton smiles sweetly at us, her gray hair bundled atop her head in a bun. Her eyes are bright, and they dance as she talks.

"What do you want to do here at Fulton Gardens today? We're more than happy to give you a tour, or you may explore the grounds yourself."

Xavier answers for us. "I think we'll go out on our own, if that's ok with you."

Mrs. Fulton looks relieved. "My hip thanks you, dear boy. My son isn't here today, and he usually leads the tours." She walks slowly to the wooden desk and pulls a sheet of paper from an open shelf.

"Here's a map. There's a gazebo here"—she points out the spot—"for you to enjoy whatever is in that basket you're carrying."

Xavier steps forward to retrieve the map. I can't help but admire the way his broad shoulders move.

Xavier steps back and offers a warm smile. "Thank you for everything. We'll be back through here in a little while."

She waves at us, and I notice that her fingernails are painted a lovely shade of pink.

"Have fun, you two. Oh, and Xavier, if you don't mind me asking, are you related to Grant Townsend?"

Xavier nods. "Yes, ma'am. He's my father."

Mrs. Fulton claps her hands together and smiles. "Oh, what a small world. My daughter and your father were high school sweethearts."

Xavier smiles fondly at Mrs. Fulton. "I'll have to tell him I was here today. Would you like me to give him a message?" Xavier's tone is polite and respectful. I love it. He is scoring major points right now.

Mrs. Fulton shakes her head. "No, no, that's all right. Obviously he has done well for himself. Good for him." Mrs. Fulton flicks her hands toward the rear exit, as though shooing us out. "You two get on with your date. I'll see you in a while."

"Thank you." Xavier and I both respond in unison.

We walk through the back door and step out into the fragrant air. Again I inhale deeply. I don't usually care for overwhelming flowery scents, but this smell is mixed with enough fresh air and grass to keep it from being too sweet.

Xavier and I stand close, examining the map. Well, *I* am only pretending to see the map. I can't concentrate because of Xavier's close proximity. He smells woodsy and clean and just so…delicious.

Good thing Xavier is actually paying attention. He gestures to the gazebo on the paper and points out the path to my right.

"Lets go that way." His voice is certain. He's in charge of this date, and I sense that he likes it that way.

Xavier grabs my hand for the third time since I got in his car and leads me onto the little stone path. There is just enough room for me, Xavier and the picnic basket. Rosebushes line the pathway on either side, their colorful blooms massive and fragrant. It's obvious how much attention these flowers receive, they are impeccably groomed. Reds, lavenders, yellows, clean whites, and both pale and bright pinks. The kaleidoscope of color is dazzling.

Even more dazzling is the man holding my hand. My mind wanders as we walk, and I find myself thinking of what I've learned on my own about Xavier. He is handsome, charming, successful, acts like a gentleman, thoughtful enough to plan this date, and nice to old ladies. Right now I'm choosing not to think about the negative things I learned from Gigi and Cade.

We continue to walk in companionable silence along the path. This suits me just fine. I'm busy soaking up the beauty surrounding us.

Eventually the path delivers us onto a large, sparkling green lawn with a white wooden structure in the center of it. I should have known the gazebo would be so charming.

Intricate swirls are carved into the wood, and a bench sits in the center, just waiting for a couple of romantics to occupy it. I feel like I'm in a storybook. Could Xavier be my Prince Charming? Right now it certainly feels like it.

"Wow," I breathe.

Xavier lets out a quiet whistle. "Seriously. This place is like a painting."

"How did you know about it?" I ask as we walk across the grass. It's the fluffy kind, not cut too short like a football field.

Xavier plays coy. "I heard about it from someone."

Hmmm... why does it sound like there's more to it than that?

I mentally berate myself. *Chill out with the incessant paranoia, Mitchell.* I seriously need to rein it in.

We climb the two steps up to the gazebo, and Xavier walks straight to the bench, setting the picnic basket down and motioning for me to join him.

I obey, sitting down prettily and crossing my ankles. I smile brightly up at him. I knew he was watching me.

Xavier has a smile on his lips too. He busies himself with opening the basket and removing half a dozen boxes.

"I don't know what you like, so I brought a bunch of stuff. I hope I got at least one right." His eyes look shy and fearful. Where is the confident night club owner? I like this side of Xavier.

"You could have asked Jessica."

Xavier shakes his head. "Where's the fun in that?"

I shrug and smile. "Nowhere, I suppose."

Actually, this whole 'guess what Lila likes to eat' game sounds kind of entertaining.

"Well, lets see what you went with." I reach for the first box and open it. And then I'm immediately tasked with trying to hide my disgust. I hate potato salad.

"How did I do on box number one?" Xavier's voice is hopeful.

"Great, I love potato salad." The lie is through my teeth before I even have time to consider telling it.

Xavier narrows his green eyes at me.

'What else have you got in those boxes? This is fun!" I giggle like a school girl. How annoying. But I'm seriously enjoying this. It's like unwrapping presents.

We go through the next five boxes and, thankfully I like everything else he brought. I especially like the split of champagne. *Nice touch, Xavier.*

Conversation comes so naturally, and I find myself at ease as we go through one another's backgrounds. Xavier is an only child, and he has a degree in business administration from UNLV. His parents are still married and moved from Vegas to Lake Tahoe a few years ago. He seems much more interested in hearing about me than telling me about himself.

Xavier is astonished when I tell him I have two brothers and a wild, crazy sister.

His lips twist, the look on his face forlorn. "I think my parents wanted another child, but it never worked out for them."

I hate seeing Xavier's sad face. Something inside me is moved by it.

"So, do you suffer from classic only child tendencies?" I raise my eyebrows and cock my head to the side.

A smile comes onto Xavier's face, and my insides rejoice.

"And what do classic only child tendencies consist of?" He looks amused. He's testing me.

"Selfish, spoiled, self-centered..." I tick the stereotypes off on my fingers.

Xavier nods knowingly. "Ah, yes, the three S's. Everyone knows about those." He reaches for some grapes and pops one in his mouth. "I suppose I can exhibit at least one of those traits at any given time. I'm certainly not perfect. How about you?"

My look is quizzical. "How about me?"

"It's only fair. We just discussed my faults, or at least the stereotypical faults of an only child. Usually it takes actually having a relationship to learn each others faults. So, lets hear it. What are your issues?"

His green eyes are watching me expectantly. I pause to think, taking a wedge of brie and a cracker and slowly placing them in my mouth. I make a big deal of chewing thoroughly. This makes Xavier laugh. *I love that sound.*

I swallow and brush the crumbs from my lips with the linen napkin Xavier has thoughtfully provided.

"Some might say I'm stand-offish and judgmental. According to Jessica, I have a resting bitch face."

Xavier coughs on his sip of champagne. "Resting what face?"

"Bitch," I repeat calmly.

"What the hell does that mean?" Xavier looks bewildered.

"Just what it sounds like. My resting face looks bitchy."

Xavier shakes his dark brown hair. "Not true. At least, not the first time I met you. You looked wide-eyed and intimidated."

I laugh. Actually, that night I was busy judging everyone for rubbing up against people they don't know. Intimidated? Was I? I suppose it's possible, though not on a conscious level. *Leave the psycho-analysis for professionals.*

"Is that why you came over to me? Was I giving off a *damsel in distress* vibe?" I bat my eyes and tip my head to the side.

"A little. And because I own the club, and you were a VIP that night. And you looked so beautiful in that bright red dress. How could I resist introducing myself?" Xavier takes a lock of my long hair and tucks it behind my ear.

Oh my. Breathe.

I try to be casual, as though incredible guys say things like that to me all the time. "I hate to break it to you, but I'm more of a jeans girl."

Xavier shifts closer while I speak, and the last part of my sentence comes out in my newly acquired breathy voice. I know what's coming, and I can't believe how badly I want it.

Xavier's response is a whisper against my cheek. "Something tells me I would like you in anything."

And then his mouth is on mine, and he tastes of champagne.

CHAPTER TEN

Jessica is on the attack the second I walk in the front door. She is all hot pink pajamas and limbs, in my face, and asking for details.

"Don't hold back, Mitchell. I've spent my entire first day and introductory happy hour distracted, thanks to your big date tonight. Spill." Jessica's hands are on her hips, her face is expectant.

From my place two steps inside the foyer I can see into the living room, where Cade is sitting on our couch. Am I supposed to host a tell-all with Jessica's boyfriend in the audience?

I slide past Jessica and set my purse on the table. One glance in the mirror above the table tells me that I look happy. My skin is glowing, and I'm smiling stupidly, despite having been recently accosted. Apparently Xavier's kisses have a lasting effect. Mmmm… Xavier's kisses… Xavier's lips… On mine. *Ohhhhh my.*

Jessica snaps her fingers two inches from my face. "Earth to Lila. Anyone home in there?"

I blush and Jessica smirks. She is loving this way too much.

I sigh. "Yes, Jess, I'm home in here."

"Soooo... How did it go?"

The beauty of Fulton Gardens comes back to me, the picnic basket filled with goodies, and the final act, picking out a rose bush of my very own to plant. I left it outside next to the front door, just waiting for beautiful dark red blooms to emerge.

I glance at Cade, then back at Jessica. "It went well."

Jessica narrows her eyes. She isn't pleased with my answer.

I point to the kitchen and walk toward it. Jessica follows.

Once in the relative privacy of the kitchen, Jessica grabs my arm and pleads, "Tell me, tell me, tell me!"

"It was amazing," I breathe the last word. "Everything about him is just...so... Wow." I can't even describe Xavier in a way that does him justice.

Jessica bounces up and down in her excitement. "Oooooh, like what?"

"For starters, he took me to Fulton Gardens, which you already know."

Jessica brings a hand to her forehead and pretends to swoon. "That place is so romantic! I took my senior pictures there. It's quite a hike to get out there."

I nod my head. "We met the owner, and she was so sweet. She even knows Xavier's dad. And then we went for a walk, and he had this cute picnic basket and a split of champagne. And he arranged for me to pick out a rose bush that we can plant here."

Jessica's mouth hangs open. "A rose bush, that you plant together? That's like getting a dog together."

"It is not."

"It's something that will be alive as long as your black thumb doesn't kill it. It'll symbolize your first date." Jessica raises her eyebrows, daring me to argue.

I hold up my hands. "I highly doubt Xavier put that much thought into the gesture, but ok."

Jessica shakes her head. "Most first dates consist of dinner, maybe a movie. Not a romantic garden, picnic, champagne, and roses bushes."

"I'm aware." My smile is wide. Xavier likes me. Whoever this guy is that Gigi and Cade have warned me against, he wasn't the same person who took me on a date today.

"What does this mean?" Jessica's face looks intrigued, as though my date has presented a mystery to be solved. *Hot playboy club owner behaves in a sweet, thoughtful manner... But why?*

I shrug. "I don't know, but he wants to go out again on Thursday night."

Jessica nods enthusiastically. "That's good. Very good. He already secured a second date before the first was over."

I'm starting to feel sleepy and ready for the conversation to be over. Cade would probably like his girlfriend back.

I yawn. "Well, it's my bed time. I have to work in the morning. Enjoy your night." I point in Cade's direction and take a step toward the stairs.

Jessica holds up one finger. "Wait a minute, missy. Did he kiss you?"

My annoyed groan is just barely contained. Unlike Jessica, I don't want to kiss and tell. Sometimes it's actually ok for things to be kept private.

I stare at Jessica, and she stares back, not backing down. She doesn't even blink. *Fine.*

"Yes," I allow with a blush.

"Holy crap!" Her voice is loud. "Xavier Townsend kissed you!"

"Calm down, calm down." Knowing Cade, he will pop his head in any second to see why his damsel has raised her voice.

Jessica glances toward the living room. "Tell me how it was, and I'll leave you alone."

"Why are you making me do this?" I pause to rub my eyes. "It was fantastic, ok? Perfect amount of pressure. Soft lips. Good hand placement. Not too much tongue. And we kissed for a long time. It's safe to call it a make-out session."

Jessica dances with glee. She might be more excited about my kiss with Xavier than I am. At least outwardly.

She stops dancing. "Ok, now you can go to bed."

"Thank you. Goodnight." I smile and turn around.

"Goodnight, Xavier-kisser."

Jessica delivers one quick tap on my butt and flounces out of the kitchen.

I shake my head and walk up the stairs. I freaking love that girl, even when she is testing my boundaries.

Work is a good place for me to be right now. If I weren't here, thoughts of Xavier would bombard my head. And I don't need that. Not after only one date.

My day is filled with questions. *How was your treatment? Do you love your new cut? Did Dan-*

iel/Eva/Marco/Skylar take good care of you today? Would you like to book your next appointment? On a normal day these questions make me feel as though a few brain cells are slowly sliding out of my head. But not today.

Today I need the mundane, the humdrum, the monotony. Going through the paces, smiling at the clients as they leave The Pain Shoppe with less hair than they came in with, whether by scissor or wax.

Of course, I haven't been able to eliminate all thoughts of a certain dark haired, emerald-eyed man. Jeri was like a replay of Jessica last night when I walked in the front door. Different front door, same attack.

"Oh my God, tell me everything." Jeri's eyes shine bright with excitement. Her lips, a bright cherry red today, pull back against her teeth in a wide smile.

I'm genuinely perplexed by Jeri's question. I haven't told her, or anyone else at work, about my date with Xavier. I haven't even been at work from the time we planned the date to when we actually went on it. She must be talking about something else.

"Tell you everything about what?" I start back toward my desk, Jeri walking right next to me. We pass her desk, and she keeps walking.

"Your date with Mr. Townsend." Jeri looks at me matter-of-factly. She is quite proud that she knows something about me. I'm way more private than anyone else who works here. There are some things I fervently wish I didn't know about my coworkers.

"Who told you?"

"One of the dancers who works at his club. She came in yesterday for a wax and asked if you were here. I told her you didn't work Mondays. She must have called Xavier or something, because when she left, she told me you had a date with him." Jeri shrugged. "Now tell me how it went."

I put up my hand. "Wait. What color was her hair?"

Jeri sighs. "Red. Like a super dark red. Not just mahogany."

Gigi was here. Asking about me and then reaching out to Xavier?

Jeri cocks her head and taps a finger on her lip. "You know, it was odd. She seemed annoyed when she left. Like, not annoyed with Alexa or anything. She said, "I guess Lila decided not to listen." What was that about?"

I groan. Why does Gigi care whether I take her advice or walk off a cliff?

"Gigi doesn't think Xavier is a good match for me." My accompanying eye roll lets Jeri know how annoying I find this to be.

Jeri makes a face, somewhere between disbelief and confusion. "That's it?"

Clearly she can sense there are more details, but I'm not giving them up. I like my privacy, and I have no interest in explaining why my potential boyfriend could actually be a bad guy.

"But she's wrong. My date was fabulous. We had a great time." The memory brings a smile to my face.

Jeri lets out a low whistle, the kind I can't do. My attempt at whistling is pathetic and laughable.

"I never thought I'd say this about you, but here goes. Girl, you got it bad."

"Calm down. It was one date."

Ready to be rid of Jeri, I sit at my desk and switch on the computer. It awakens, and I type in my password to log on to the Alexa booking website.

Jeri grows bored. And, hopefully, she picks up on my non-verbal clues.

"Fine, don't share any juicy details of your date with Mr. Bigshot Townsend." Her voice is petulant, like a pouting child.

I've seen Jeri employ this tactic before, but having three siblings has taught me a great deal on how to fend off these types of attacks.

Jeri's back is to the front door, so she doesn't see Granite Alexa walk in, but I do.

"Go!" I hiss, surreptitiously pointing toward the front of the store.

Jeri jumps and turns, hurrying to her desk. I have to hand it to the girl, she can make a mad dash in heels look coordinated. Jeri makes it to her seat just two seconds before Granite stalks past her. His icy glare confirms he noticed her absence.

I turn my attention to the computer screen and pick up the phone. By the time Granite is stomping past my desk, I'm already leaving a reminder message for tomorrow's first client.

My work day is over, and now I have to find another way to keep my mind on the right track. Weirdly, I'm leaning toward physical activity. I can't fathom why, but it sounds like something that would effectively banish all Xavier thoughts. And so, with laces tied tight, I'm headed out into the evening heat for a run. I can read Jessica's mind when I pass her on my way out of our house, and I ignore her. She's not the only one who thinks I won't last long. Maybe I should walk instead.

I settle for a fast paced walk, forcing green eyes and a chiseled face from my mind. Instead I'm recalling answers from my last final. Between the physical activity and the brain game, I'm doing just fine.

Jessica's in the kitchen when I return, hot and sweaty from my walk in the oppressive June evening heat. She watches me as I grab a glass of water and gulp it down.

"What was that about?" Jessica throws a thumb behind her, gesturing to the world outside our house.

"What?"

She does her trademark eye roll. "Your run. Or jog. Or walk. Whatever it was that you were doing. What would possess you to do that?"

The truth is that I really don't know. When I think of Xavier, I feel overwhelmed. And when I feel overwhelmed, I want to stop feeling that way. So if I can stop thinking of Xavier… It just seems best for my anxiety level if I distract myself. How can I be so affected by him? It's something I can hardly admit to myself, let alone anyone else. Even my best friend.

"Honestly, Jess, I don't know." It's the best explanation I can give right now.

Jessica looks triumphant. "Ohhhh, I know why."

I give her my best *I'm waiting* look.

"Girl, you got it bad."

My nose wrinkles in disgust. Two times in one day I have to hear that imbecilic line? Good Lord, it's like Jeri and Jessica are conspiring.

I choose to ignore her. "Get this. Gigi goes into The Pain Shoppe yesterday…" I regale Jess with the story of Gigi and her irritation at my date with Xavier.

Jess looks as baffled as I feel. "Why does she care so much?"

"That was my first thought too. It doesn't make sense. She barely knows me. Warning me about Xavier, fine, I get it. But to actually have an emotional reaction? I can't figure it out." I chew on my lip, picturing Gigi's fiery red hair.

Jessica shrugs and rummages through the fridge. "Let's talk about it over dinner. I'll make my chicken piccata. Please go clean your sweaty ass. Your face looks gorgeous with that flush, but you don't smell so pretty. Cade will be here soon."

Jessica pulls away from the fridge, arms filled with ingredients, and I bound up the stairs.

I feel good. Endorphins are pumping after my power walk, and I'm ready to face Jessica and Cade's canoodling.

The smell of the lemony piccata sauce takes me downstairs to the kitchen, but the kissing couple isn't in there. Halfway to the living room, I hear Jessica's voice.

"Thank you. I'll give these to her." She sounds pleasant but detached.

Her? Meaning me? Must be. Quickly I walk to the front door, where Jessica is holding a glass vase filled with giant pink peonies. She shuts the door with her foot and turns around.

"For you," she announces, holding them out to me.

Astounded, I reach for them. Surely they're from Xavier. Such a grand gesture could only come from him.

My arms drop down an inch when I take the vase from Jessica's outstretched arms. Damn, they are heavy. And beautiful. And fragrant.

Jessica reaches out with a now free hand and snatches the card from the center of the bouquet.

"Do you mind?" she asks.

I shake my head. "Go ahead."

Jessica opens the cream card. It's high quality paper, thick card stock. Fancy stuff.

"Birthday Girl, You were an incredible date. Thank you for agreeing to see me again. Please be in the front lobby of The Martin at seven p.m. on Thursday night. Xavier." Jessica finishes reading and mouths a *Wow*.

"I know." I nod my head.

Jessica buries her nose in the peonies, inhaling deeply."This guy knows what he's doing."

Her remark hits a nerve. She didn't mean it in a bad way, but I can't help the thoughts that comes to mind.

This guy knows what he's doing... And therein lies the problem. Xavier *does* seem to know what he's doing. Every one of his moves is so romantic and perfect. The kind of moves that would make any girl swoon. And they probably have. How many girls have swooned over a giant bouquet like this? Are peonies his go-to?

Maybe the florist has a name for it. The Townsend Special. *Oh God… He just gave me the Townsend Special.*

Jessica's stern voice breaks through the parade of negative thoughts.

"Stop." By the look on her face, she knows exactly what I was thinking.

I breathe audibly, forcing the thoughts out with the stream of my breath. "Thank you. My mind was having a field day."

Jessica gazes at me with worry. "I can guess why. Lila, I want to ask you something, and whatever your answer is will be ok with me."

The massive arrangement is growing heavier in my arms. "Shoot," I mutter, switching the vase into my other arm and partially supporting it with my hip.

"This Xavier thing… Are you certain it's a good idea?" Jessica bites her lip.

I sigh. The answer is that I most certainly am not certain.

"Why do you ask? By the way, your opinion is the one that matters most to me. Not Gigi's or Cade's."

A deep voice speaks from the front door, surprising Jess and me. We hadn't even heard the door open. Perhaps the alarm system my mom wants to install wouldn't be a bad idea after all.

"Should my ears be burning?" Cade asks as he strides toward Jess. His blond hair and blue eyes are still striking, even though I've seen him practically every night since I introduced him to Jessica. Clearly Jessica think so too. She goes all moony and lovestruck as soon as she sees him.

"Hi babe," Cade greets Jessica. He puts one finger on her chin and tips her head up for a kiss. Jessica happily obliges.

I wait quietly. When their kiss deepens, I clear my throat. Nothing. Not even the slightest hint they heard me. *Good God, get me out of here.*

I turn away from the two people attached at the mouth and walk toward the stairs.

"The answer to your question, Jessica Noelle Jones, is yes." I yell out my response and let it drift behind me as I climb the stairs to my bedroom.

The flowers look lovely on my dresser. Full and pink, they turn my room from average to feminine. I love them.

Should I text Xavier and say thank you? Miss Manners would probably say yes. But I've made a vow to myself not to talk to Xavier until I see him on Thursday at The Martin. I definitely don't want to seem too eager. I want to convey the appropriate amount of enthusiasm. Not that I have any idea how to do that.

Thank goodness I'm working again tomorrow, because obviously I'm overthinking this. Another day of being busy is exactly what I need. And busy I will be, thanks to the summer heat and legendary Vegas pool parties. Plenty of body hair removal appointments.

Tonight I'll be busy with my latest book. It's sci-fi, not usually my chosen genre, but it got great reviews. I curl up in my bed and let the story take me away.

CHAPTER ELEVEN

Holy shit. How is it already Thursday?

Monday... Date with Xavier.

Tuesday... Busy day at work.

Wednesday... Busy day at work.

Boom, Thursday.

The extra time I took this morning to dry my hair was well worth it. My brown locks are full of volume. And they feel like silk, thanks to the new shampoo and conditioner I bought at Alexa yesterday. Thank you, employee discount.

I don't get off work until six, so I brought my date clothes to change into. And I'll curl my hair on my break. I'll certainly have my pick of curling irons.

I glance at the appointments for the day, a majority for highlights and waxes.

The thought of waxing my body makes me shudder. I grew up near a beach, so I should be more comfortable with the practice. It's just the idea of sticky wax being spread on my skin and adhering to the hairs, and then having the hair yanked out in one fell swoop. The eyebrows seem tame in comparison to the other body parts. It kind of makes me nauseated.

And yet, they come in droves to have their bodies freed of hair. Men do it too. Do they all know something I don't?

My hair isn't highlighted either, but that's fine with me. I love my hair color. The deep brown has a reddish tint in the summer sunlight.

Jeri steers clear of asking me any more questions about Xavier. She even stays tight-lipped when she sees Marco curling my hair in between his appointments. I've wrangled his expert hands. He is far better at it than I.

So now I'm finishing the workday with perfect curls, and I'm starting to feel pumped for my date. The hour leading up to closing time drags, and I find myself glancing too frequently at the clock. Finally at five to six, with no one left in the salon, I shut down my computer and pack up my stuff.

"Going somewhere?" Jeri asks as I sail past her desk. She's getting ready to leave too.

"Yes." I don't offer any details. My stride is quick as I leave Alexa and walk to my car. Every step I take away from work puts me closer to Xavier. And it's safe to say I'm very, very excited.

I pull up to The Martin, and a young man rushes to open my door. I hand him my key, and he gives me a ticket, which I tuck into my white clutch.

The first time I was here, I was wide eyed at the sight of the large, sparkly building, but this is my second visit, and I feel more at ease. I glide through the open door and into the sparkling clean lobby. How this place stays so white and clean is a mystery to me.

I'm unsure where to go or what to do with myself. Xavier has told me to meet him in the lobby at seven, and here I am. I'm nothing if not punctual.

I wander to the carved iron half wall that separates the hotel lobby from the casino and watch the gambling. It doesn't interest me, but there are games I wouldn't mind learning, like roulette and craps. The house can have the slots.

Quickly I grow bored watching people waste their money. I glance back over my shoulder toward the lobby, looking for my date.

Xavier is standing only a few feet from me, watching me as I watch the casino. His gaze is strong, unwavering. My insides squish like jelly, my breath hitches. How can this man do this to me?

"Hello." I greet him with a smile.

Xavier stands beside me, grabs my hand, and squeezes it. "Hello yourself."

His touch is electric and immediately I remember kissing him. Hopefully I won't have to wait too long to experience that again.

As though he can read my mind, Xavier dips his face down to meet mine. Our lips touch briefly, sweetly.

He ends the kiss and backs away just enough for me to see his face. "Ready?"

I'm feeling tingly. "For?" I breathe. *Get it together. One short kiss and I'm a mass of seeping hormones.*

A small smile pulls up one side of his face. He looks amused. Does he know how much I want him?

"Dinner." He explains. "Isn't that what you came here for?" He's teasing me now.

I thought I was coming here to have dinner, but the way my body reacts to him… I'm finding myself hoping for dessert first.

I look away from Xavier's intense green eyes, attempting to break the spell. It works. After a moment I look back to him, having regained control of myself. "Lead the way."

He takes my hand, and I follow just a step behind him. As we walk, I examine his attire. Dark gray suit, lavender and white tiny checked shirt underneath. The shirt looks woven, not just a plain dyed cotton. Very expensive. The suit is cut slim, modern. He looks delectable.

I make a fine sight too, if I do say so myself. I went shopping after work yesterday and fell in love with this dress. Bright white, perfect for summer, and it looks good next to my olive skin. It's a one shoulder dress, leaving my other shoulder bare. It's sexy, but understated.

The ground level of the hotel is like a shopping mall. We pass fine candy shops, gourmet coffee, and luxury clothing retailers. Xavier is quiet as we make the trek, and I don't offer up conversation. I find myself wondering what he's thinking about.

Finally we arrive at the entrance, and I'm grateful Xavier didn't suggest I meet him here. I never would have found it. The entrance is an ornate wooden door with a heavy knocker in the center. No sign.

Xavier grabs the knocker and slams it down twice against the wood. The door opens toward us, and Xavier leads the way.

It's dark inside, but my eyes adjust quickly. Two girls stand in front of us at what I assume is the hostess desk.

"Hello Mr. Townsend. Right this way." Girl One smiles encouragingly and walks away.

We follow her to a table near the back, set off the main area in an intimate nook. Xavier pulls out my chair and I sit, trying not to open my mouth in awe. The walls are stone, the tables and chairs a deep, dark wood, and candles flicker away on every table. The lighting is so subtle and low, I can't tell where it's coming from.

Xavier's watching me as I examine the restaurant. He looks hopeful. I realize he wants me to like it. And I do.

"It's incredible in here, Xavier." I look around again. "Like an upscale cave, if that's possible."

Xavier tips his head back and laughs. "The owner was going for a secret grotto look. But upscale cave works too."

I laugh with him. "Do you know the owner?"

"He's a friend of mine."

Our server arrives then, carrying two bottles on his tray. He introduces himself and offers still or sparkling water.

"Still, please." Xavier and I respond in unison. We exchange a smile at our shared response.

Xavier orders a bottle of wine as I peruse the menu.

Our server leaves, and Xavier sits back, not opening his menu. I close mine and set it on the table.

"Do you know the menu well?" I ask.

Xavier nods. "I helped Dante plan it."

"Dante is the owner?" I guess.

Xavier nods again. "I always get the same thing."

"Then why don't you order for me? Since you're so knowledgable." I smile sweetly. Don't men love to be in the position of power? What could be more powerful than choosing someone else's food?

"Sure," Xavier rubs his palms together, eyes dancing.

Our server returns and presents the bottle of wine to Xavier with a flourish. Xavier nods after the briefest of glances and looks away, a cue to the server that he may open the bottle.

"Serve the lady first," Xavier says.

Once the wine is poured, the server turns expectantly toward Xavier.

"Start with my usual. Then we will both have the steak frites. Medium rare." Xavier rattles off the order.

The server nods. "Very well." He retreats, leaving Xavier and me to create conversation.

Xavier has no trouble starting. He lifts his giant red wine glass into the air. "*A inicios.*"

I cock my head to the side, a small grin pulling up one side of my lips. "Should I know what that means?"

"To beginnings," Xavier translates.

I echo his toast, holding up my glass. The wine is smooth and spicy.

"Am I supposed to be impressed that you can toast in Spanish?" My mind still can't let go of all I know about his womanizing ways. I hate that I'm wondering if every move he makes is practiced, calculated.

Xavier blushes. It disarms me. This is the first time I've seen this shade of red warm his cheeks.

"I was hoping so." He looks embarrassed.

I reach across the table and squeeze his hand. "I'm quite impressed with you, no matter the language in which you choose to toast. Don't worry."

Why does this all-powerful, womanizing Vegas big shot want to impress me? I take another sip of my wine, enjoying the flavor as it slides down my throat.

Xavier sets his wine glass on the table. "Tell me, Lila, how did it come to be that you were Gigi's special guest at Townsend for your birthday?" He raises an eyebrow, that impish smile back on his face. Why does he always wear that smile when we discuss Gigi?

I shrug. "Purely coincidental. She was visiting the salon where I work with Becca and Lucy. She found out it was my birthday and was adamant that I celebrate at Townsend. *Your club.*" I emphasize the words.

"Ahhh, I see." Xavier is still wearing that smug smile, the one that says he's in on a private joke. It's the same smile from the night I met him.

I feel my own smile vanishing. "What's so funny?"

Our appetizer arrives just then. *Perfect timing.* The person who is not our server places two martini glasses full of ceviche in front of us.

Holy crap, I love ceviche... The tart lime, the spice of the jalapeno, the lemony, fresh cilantro. Has this man read a book about me? Steak frites and ceviche describe a perfect meal for me. Let's just see if he nails dessert.

Like a pit bull, I'm relentless. I'm ready to know what he finds so freaking amusing about Gigi.

"I'm waiting," I sing-song.

Xavier sighs. Hesitation clouds his face. "Fine, you asked."

"Lay it on me," I say between bites of the acceptable but not amazing ceviche. I've had better at a little road side shack on the PCH near my Newport Beach house. This is as good as it can be, given that it's so far inland. Maybe one day I'll take him to my hometown and show him how good ceviche can be.

"Ok. Here goes." Xavier takes an ungentlemanly glug of his wine and sets it down. "So, Gigi comes to me last Thursday before the club opens and tells me someone has been added to the guest list. She tells me this person is non-paying, strictly a friend of hers."

I blush automatically. How embarrassing that I visited Xavier's club and didn't pay. My brain starts calculating the cost of all that champagne. No way I can pay that back. It's not like I make much. Booking clients doesn't exactly pay well.

Xavier waves his hand between us, seeing my pained expression.

"Stop, stop, it's fine. Pay attention. Something tells me you'll want to hear this next part."

I wait, silent. I have no idea what to expect. I finish my wine. Xavier refills my glass. *Mmmm... The wine is so good.*

The story continues. "So you arrive and sit at the table. I see you right away. Honestly, I'm intrigued by this person who Gigi has as her personal guest. She doesn't have many personal guests. And then I see you and… " Xavier halts.

I hang on his words, waiting. *You see me and what? Finish the damn sentence!*

He takes a sip, sets the glass down, and sighs. "You were sitting there looking so sweet and innocent. Even in that tiny red dress. I knew right away there was no chance in hell you were into Gigi. You aren't Gigi's type."

My latest sip of wine sputters in my mouth. I'm coughing, and it's all I can do to keep the wine from spewing out.

My brain is still trying to process the news of Gigi's sexual orientation when our dinner arrives. The steak looks mouthwatering, the fries hot and crispy. Frankly, anything would taste good right now. The wine has gone straight to my head, and I'm sure it's not helping me absorb the shock of learning that Gigi is bisexual.

That's right, my new friend exercises like a maniac, has a sailor's mouth, dances in cages and is bi-sexual. And she was interested in me. Until I became interested in her boss. Who is a man. Because I'm not attracted to women.

"I guess this helps explain something," I say off-handedly as I slice into the steak. My knife sinks in like it's going through butter. The taste is incredible. This place may not do ceviche well, but steak they have perfected.

"What's that?" Xavier asks, between bites.

I blush. Perhaps I shouldn't be telling Xavier of Gigi's warnings. I don't want to get her in trouble.

"What is it?"

I hold up a finger signaling one moment. I need to chew and swallow my mouthful of frites.

I gulp them down and then tell Xavier about Gigi's admonishments, but I leave out Cade's cautionary tale. I'd like to preserve the possibility of a double date in the future.

I finish recounting Gigi's repeated warnings. Xavier is sitting back in his chair absorbing it all. He looks annoyed and...resigned? What am I to say to his reaction? There's only one thing I desperately need to know. Where in Gigi's words is the truth?

I don't speak, hoping fervently that Xavier will discount everything he has just heard. The silence stretches on, telling me everything I need to know.

"Gigi's right, isn't she?" My voice is just above a whisper. Who knew the confirmation would hurt so bad?

Xavier sighs. "I suppose." He says slowly. "But I'm not that person anymore. Lila, I swear." Xavier's green eyes are intense, imploring me to believe him. His hand reaches across the table towards mine. I recoil without thinking.

My emotions are swirling. Somewhere in the mass of disappointment and upset, I identify relief. At least it's settled. Now I know. Xavier is the womanizer Gigi claims he is, and I have learned this by his own admission.

Holding my hand away from him, I speak. My voice is much stronger than I feel.

"Gigi says you will break my heart. That you leave a string of broken hearts in your wake."

Xavier shakes his head adamantly. "Gigi doesn't know what she's talking about."

"But you just said Gigi was right. Her warnings are valid." I'm persistent. Right here, right now, I'm making my choice. And Xavier knows it.

"It's complicated, but yes, essentially." Xavier looks pained.

The realization hits me. He doesn't want me to know any of this... *Too bad.*

I stare at him, processing. I'm disappointed he couldn't argue with Gigi's warnings and impressed by his honesty.

Where does this leave us? Xavier admits to being a womanizer yet disputes the notion he's a heart breaker. I don't know what to think.

My thoughts distract me as Xavier reaches over the table again. He grabs my hand and holds it tightly.

"Lila, I'm not letting you go." Xavier's voice is thick with emotion.

"I don't want to go." The words are out before I can stop them. *Damn!* Why can't I play the game better? Why do I have to tell him exactly how I feel?

Relief floods Xavier's face. He lets go of my hand, but only to cup my face in both of his. His kiss is deep, hopeful, and somewhere in there, he is requesting forgiveness for his past.

I respond with vigor, disappointed when Xavier pulls back. His emerald eyes pour into my own.

"Spend the night with me." His voice is a whisper.

Quickly my mind flips through a catalog of my short time with Xavier. Our first meeting at his club, the garden, the rose bush, the flowers he sent to me, our easy conversations. Tonight's admission should stop me, but I'm not compelled to let it. His kiss has told me everything I need to know.

"Yes." I whisper back.

Xavier leans into me again, and I feel his smile against my lips.

CHAPTER TWELVE

Dinner is over, and I'm happy for it. My stomach is a ball of nerves. Xavier takes my hand and leads me back through the gigantic hotel, past the shops and toward the lobby. Are we getting a room? Or Xavier's car? Xavier takes me by surprise with a sharp right turn, heading straight to the elevator bank.

"Was I a foregone conclusion?" I asked, slightly miffed. If Xavier already got a room for us before I agreed to sleep with him, then I have officially changed my mind.

Xavier laughs deeply. "No, Lila. I live here."

"You live in a hotel?" My voice is incredulous. As far as I know, only movie stars live in hotels.

We step onto the elevator, and it shoots us up into the inner sanctum of The Martin.

"It's easier."

I don't ask how it's easier, other than the lack of commute. I don't really care. I'm too nervous to make chit-chat.

The elevator opens up on the twenty-eighth floor, and we step out. I follow Xavier down the hall to a door, my clicking heels on the tile floor counting every step. Xavier removes his room key from his pocket and slides it down the slot. The soft click of the lock sliding away sounds so loud to me right now.

"Ladies first." Xavier pushes open the ornately carved white door and gestures inside.

My steps are timid, and I hate it. *Be confident*, I tell myself. *This is what you want. You're a grown woman. A grown woman who hasn't had sex in a very long time.*

Xavier's place is not a hotel room like the kind I've stayed in before. It's more like a condo that happens to be located in a hotel. There's a full kitchen, all stainless steel and white marble counters, and a sitting area with two big tan couches. I'm guessing the bedroom is through one of the doors on the wall across from the kitchen. I set my purse down on a dark wood console table next to a large vase filled with a colorful floral arrangement. I press a finger to the petal of a rose, expecting to feel silk. They are real. How much does it cost to keep real flowers around all the time? The hotel really pulls out the stops. Or maybe it's just for the owner of Townsend. He probably brings them a lot of business.

Xavier's lips are suddenly in my ear, sending thoughts of the flowers right out of my head.

"Do you want a drink?" His voice is low, seductive. As though I need to be seduced. I'm a sure thing, and he knows it.

I nod my head. "Please."

Xavier moves into the kitchen, and I follow, watching him as he grabs a bottle of champagne from the fridge. He moves with confidence and ease. I like it. It makes me feel safe.

"Is champagne ok?"

"Yes." My mind is working overtime to calm my nerves. I can't manage more than a one word response.

Xavier pops the cork and pulls two flutes from a cabinet. He fills each and hands one to me.

I take a deep, quiet breath and reach for the bubbly. My hand is steady, thank God. I want this, and I refuse to be scared of it. I need to be a part of this instead of letting Xavier have all the control. I'll use what he told me at dinner.

I shake out my hair subtly, knowing how he likes it. Xavier smiles at me, his grin sexy. Does he know what I'm doing?

"You have quite a view." I wander over to the floor-to-ceiling window and stand, peering out to the strip far below us. The sparkling lights from all the other hotels are bouncing off me. I know I look good standing here, the moonlight shining in and the lights of Vegas twinkling outside. Slowly I raise my glass, and our green eyes meet.

"Cheers." My voice is thick with lust.

Xavier watches me silently as I take a sip. He looks like he wants me as much as I want him, but he stands back. Slowly he takes a sip from his glass.

"Yes, the view is quite nice." His eyes are running appreciatively down my body. I stare back boldly, letting him drink me in.

My lack of shyness surprises me, all things considered. It's been so long, and this man can be intimidating. But it's true, I'm not feeling shy at all. I am feeling some other things, however.

I take a nice, long drink of the delicious champagne and smile at Xavier. "Come here."

He comes toward me with measured movements.

My fingers curl around my glass in anticipation. Yes, I want this, despite the warnings.

Xavier arrives at my side and peers down at me, his expression hungry. He tips his head back and drains the rest of his champagne.

"Finish your drink," he instructs with an even voice, eyes on mine.

I gulp down the bubbles. Mmmm. So good.

Xavier takes my glass and turns to set both empty flutes on the table next to me. He straightens and reaches for me. My heart races. Silently I take another deep breath.

Xavier reaches for my hair first, weaving his hands into my long brown tresses. He tips my head back, prompting a short gasp from me.

Xavier starts at my ear, where he takes a little nibble before placing feathery kisses along my jaw.

His mouth is coming closer to mine, and I'm nearly writhing in anticipation. He stops just short of my lips and whispers.

"Birthday Girl, you are so fucking sexy. Please stay the night with me."

"I already said yes."

It's all Xavier needs to hear. Suddenly his mouth is on mine, and his body is pressed up against me. I'm crushed between the glass wall and Xavier's body. The lights of the Vegas strip pound against my white dress.

Xavier's kiss is deep, exploring my mouth. I'm responding with vigor, enjoying the feel of his hands on me.

Without breaking our kiss, Xavier hoists me onto his hips to make the trip to his bedroom. *Such talent,* I muse. I won't allow my mind to think of where he honed his talent.

Xavier sets me down, reaching behind me and unzipping my dress in a single motion. The air whooshes up my bare legs as the dress falls down and pools at my feet. One look at Xavier's lustful face tells me my pale pink lace bra and panties were a good choice.

"Lila." He moans my name against my lips. It makes my heart pound.

How is it possible that I feel this way? I have never been so...wanting. Never felt this much electricity on my skin. And it's all because of him.

Gently Xavier pushes me, and we stumble as a unit, stopping when the back of my legs come up against something. *His bed...*

I climb on the soft duvet and pull Xavier down on top of me. His weight presses me into the bed, and the feeling of safety comes over me again.

Oh, Xavier... Please don't hurt me. Please don't hurt my heart. Please don't prove them right.

My mind knows where I am the instant I'm lucid.

Without opening my eyes, I stretch out, pointing my toes and reaching my hands above my head.

My muscles certainly know what I did last night. A twinge of pain cuts across my backside and thighs, making me wince. *Hurts so good.*

I smile, remembering last night and all of its deliciousness. Xavier has taken my memory of sex and turned it upside down. Speaking of... Where's Xavier?

He's not in bed, and a swift glance around tells me that he isn't in his room either. But I do see my dress on the floor, still in the same pile from where I stepped out of it last night. And Xavier's lilac shirt is lying off to the side, near his shoes and socks.

Naked, I climb from bed. I need to use the bathroom, and I'm betting it's through one of the doors across the room. I grab my dress as I walk by.

The large bathroom mirror only lets me see the top half of my body, but from what I can tell, I still look the same. Should I look any different? *I feel different.*

I splash cold water on my face and finger comb my hair. Xavier's toothpaste is sitting on the counter, so I squirt a little on my finger and place it in my mouth with another handful of cold water. Given my lack of toothbrush, this will have to suffice.

With a fresh, minty mouth, I turn to my dress. If only I had a pair of jeans to change into. I have my clothes from Alexa, but they're in my car. I have no choice but to don the little white number.

The embarrassment at wearing last nights clothes turns my face red. I might as well wear a neon sign around my neck. I chuckle as I picture hot pink letters flashing. Last nights clothes... Last nights clothes.

Suddenly I feel nervous to see Xavier. Dumb, I know. I shouldn't feel daunted by this morning-after situation. We're both adults, and this should not be making me red-faced.

I square my shoulders and lift my chin an inch. Then I march out to find Xavier.

He's standing in the kitchen wearing a pair of shorts and nothing else when I come striding out of his room. His back is so muscled, his torso sliding down right onto his hips without any rolls or bumps. Xavier turns at the sound of my approach and smiles.

His grin is provocative, his green eyes knowing. I feel my face heating up.

I continue my walk into the kitchen, stopping once I've reached Xavier. Standing on tiptoe, I place a light kiss on his cheek.

"I know what you did last night," I whisper into his ear.

Xavier lifts his mouth to my ear and whispers. "Don't you mean *who* I did last night?"

I gasp in surprise and smack his arm. Technically it's true, but saying it like that makes it sound so meaningless. Like I'm just another notch on his bedpost, someone he has *done*.

"What?" Xavier actually looks perplexed. Perhaps morning-after conversation isn't his forte.

"I like to think that I'm more than someone you 'did.' Please tell me you were joking." My hands are on my hips, and I wait for Xavier to speak.

"Are you serious?" Xavier runs his hands through his hair, his frustration evident. "I told you last night how special you are to me. And I told you I'm not the same person I used to be."

Xavier turns this attention to the french press, pouring coffee grounds into the carafe.

Aww, crap. Now I feel bad for overreacting. But the truth is that I'm not sure I believe him. Hormones were pumping through me last night, quite possibly clouding my judgment. He admitted to being the guy that Gigi painted him to be. And then he insisted that he's not that person anymore. But can anyone really change so dramatically? And what happened to inspire his change?

I open my mouth to speak just as someone knocks on the door.

I look at Xavier, who rolls his eyes and stops filling up a pan with water.

Was his eye roll to me or the knock at the door? He passes me on his way, grumbling.

"This should go well." It's a quiet mutter, probably not meant to be heard at all.

I stay rooted in my spot in the kitchen, barely out of view of the person at the door.

"Xavier." The woman's voice is flat and annoyed.

I know this voice, but I've never heard its owner use that tone before.

I'm still standing in the same spot when she walks in. She freezes when she sees me. Her red hair is piled on top of her head, not in the free falling tresses I'm used to.

"Lila!" She's shocked. *The feeling is mutual, Gigi.*

I would love to know what the hell Gigi's doing, showing up to Xavier's room at nine o'clock in the morning.

Still, I'm the one wearing last nights dress. I'm in no position to demand answers from Gigi or Xavier. There's no part of me that wants to look like the jealous girl who stayed the night with Xavier and thinks she has staked a claim on him.

"Hello, Gigi." My voice is pleasant, despite her intrusion. I'm even smiling.

But Gigi isn't interested in niceties. "You're not very good at taking advice, are you?" She crosses her arms, annoyance and exasperation plain on her face.

My eyes fly open in surprise. "I'm a grown woman Gigi and you—"

"We need to have a little chat about all the advice you've been giving Lila." Xavier's voice is menacingly quiet. His green eyes look weary, as though he has had it with her. Would he fire her? Right in front of me?

Oddly, Xavier doesn't look angry, just tired. What is the history here? It appears there's more to their relationship than boss and cage dancer.

I open my mouth to say something that will save Gigi's job. But Gigi speaks first.

"Someone needs to give the poor girl some advice. Who knows what the fuck you'll do to her." Gigi stands her ground with Xavier, her boss, the person who holds her job in his hands. Why? Surely this can't just be about protecting me.

Then Xavier's revelation from last night at dinner comes back to me.

Gigi was interested in me from the very beginning. She warned me off Xavier, and now she shows up at Xavier's hotel room and finds me here. In what is clearly a morning after scenario. I can see how that would upset her. *But how did she know to come here to find me? And why does she know which room is Xavier's?* I know that all of this somehow goes deeper than what I'm being told.

"Get out of my business, Gigi."

"Lila is my friend. When she makes the worst decision of her life, it's my business."

"So now Lila is just your friend? You don't hope she plays for your team anymore?"

Gigi pauses to shoot me a fearful look. At least she realizes I'm in the room. They're talking about me like I'm not standing two feet away.

"I told her last night. She had no idea, by the way."

"You asshole," Gigi hisses. "Was that your way of getting me back after I told her what a cheating jerk you are?"

Now Xavier is full out shouting at Gigi, who responds by turning up the volume of her voice. I don't think I've ever been this uncomfortable in my whole life. Here I am, standing in an immaculate kitchen at a swanky hotel after I have just spent the night with the most insanely gorgeous person I've ever met. And instead of having a replay of last night, I'm watching Xavier compete in a verbal sparring match.

"I want you out Gigi. Out of my room and out of my club."

"Your club?" Gigi's perfectly groomed eyebrows shoot up.

I turn away from them. They keep going like I'm invisible.

"It's mine, Gigi. You're nothing more than a pretty face in a cage. I do all the work for it."

"Do you call bedding various brunettes work?"

Furtively I walk the short distance to my shoes and purse. My presence here is no longer necessary. Honestly, I can't wait to be away from whatever the hell is happening between Gigi and Xavier.

I slip my feet in my heels and walk toward the door. The clicking sound on the shiny tile floor ruins my attempt at a quiet escape.

"Lila, wait." Xavier hurries after me.

Gigi stands silent, rooted to her spot.

But I'm not waiting for anyone. I feel supremely stupid. It's beyond clear that something more is happening behind the scenes between Gigi and Xavier. I won't hang around and watch the scene unfold. I have more pride than that.

I'm out the door and down the hall by the time Xavier rushes out. By some miracle the elevator doors are already open but closing fast.

"Hold the elevator," I call out.

A kind person inside actually holds the door for me, and I skip on, breathing a deep sigh of relief.

Xavier comes into my view just before the doors close. He looks beyond pissed. *Well, so am I.*

Goodbye, I mouth at him.

The doors shut and I'm whooshed down to ground level, away from the opulent room.

Tears prick my eyes but I hold back. I will not cry over that man.

After all, I was warned.

CHAPTER THIRTEEN

Jessica isn't home, and I'm so thankful. I can't handle her right now. She is too eager for me to be in love. She would probably tell me to go back to Xavier, hear him out. Screw that.

I overlooked the warnings. People who knew him had tried to protect me. I heard their words, and I made my choice. I gave Xavier so much more than a chance. I gave him me, my heart, my body, and he hurt me. Just like Gigi said he would.

And Gigi... What am I supposed to think about her? First, I learn she's bisexual and was interested in me. How did I not know that? Was there some massive hint I missed? Second, she shows up at Xavier's place this morning, post amazing sexual encounter, and walks in like she owns the place. She talks to Xavier like she isn't afraid of losing her job. Who talks to her boss like that? Granite Alexa would have me for lunch if I talked to him the way Gigi spoke to Xavier.

I can't figure all this out. And I don't even want to. I'm tired and I want to go to sleep. I was kept up late last night, and thinking of the reason for my late hours just hurts my heart. I lay my head on my pillow and fall asleep quickly, my last thought being the walk out of

The Martin. My very first walk of shame. And how shameful it was.

An incessant pounding on my door wakes me. Did Jessica forget her key? I groggily make my way down the stairs and to the front of the house, pulling open the door without checking to see who it is.

Xavier stands before me, clad in jeans and a white t-shirt, holding the sad potted rosebush in front of him. The wilted flowers and puckered leaves cover him from the waist up. *Oh, I was supposed to water and plant it. Oops.*

"You should have told me you have a black thumb. This rosebush is going to require surgery." Xavier's voice weaves around the bush and reaches me.

I begin to smile and then remember how upset I am. My smile turns to a grim line. I stare at him, not speaking.

Xavier sighs and sets the plant down in front of him on the ground between us.

I cross my arms. "What do you want?"

"Lila, please give me a chance to explain." Xavier extends his hands out between us, pleading.

Just then I notice a bag lying near his feet.

"What's that?"

Xavier shuffles his feet, nervous. Since when is the almighty Vegas nightclub owner nervous?

"What is it?" I ask when Xavier takes too long to answer.

He sighs like he doesn't want to tell me. "Some gardening tools. I came to your door earlier and saw the rose bush looking pretty pathetic out here. I thought maybe you didn't have the things you needed to plant it."

"Humph." It's the best response I can come up with. It's true, I don't have what I need to plant the bush, but after this morning, I have no intention of planting it. I certainly don't need a reminder of my poor decision. And yet, here's the poor decision, standing at my front door.

I can't do this anymore. It hurts too much. "Xavier, is there something you need?"

"You." His response is simple and cuts through me like an arrow piercing my heart.

I can't let the pain from this morning go. And yet, I feel unable to tell him how much Gigi's words hurt me. My instinct for self-preservation is too strong. "You had me. Last night, if my memory serves me right. It was just one night. Let's be over it, ok?"

Xavier looks stunned. "Is that how you think of it?"

No, you fool! We were interrupted this morning, and I don't understand what happened. But I can't say any of that. Instead of communicating, I shrug.

Xavier rolls his perfect emerald eyes at me. "Lila, you're something else. Let's plant this bush, ok? Because I would hate for it to die."

"Fine," I mutter, standing aside and granting him access to my house. I point to the backyard. "Back there."

Xavier eyes rake up and down the length of my body, eyebrows raised. In spite of what we did last night, I feel self conscious.

"Don't you want to change? I mean, I'm all for you gardening in that. But you might feel uncomfortable."

I realize I'm still in my dress from last night. Crap, I fell asleep in it.

I ignore his appreciative glance. Is he remembering when he took it off me last night?

"Go through the house. I'll meet you out back."

A few minutes later I join Xavier in my backyard. My khaki shorts and navy tank top are much better suited to gardening. Xavier stands under the shade of the patio, surveying the backyard. His white shirt is just tight enough to accentuate the muscles in his back. Memories of last night flood my mind.

I shake my head, pushing the sexy thoughts aside. I can't afford to think that way. This man has hurt me, and I still don't understand what happened. For that matter, I don't even know why he's here. Or why I let him in.

Xavier senses that I've joined him and speaks to me without turning around.

"Where do you want it?"

I shrug. I want to remind him that apparently I have a black thumb, so how the hell should I know where the bush should go? But I hold my tongue. I want answers about whatever went down between him and Gigi. I'll play nice for now.

I look around and point to a corner of the back-yard. "There."

Xavier shakes his head.

"You need a place that won't have direct sunlight all day. At least some afternoon shade."

As I watch Xavier strides to the center of the yard and looks around. Is it possible he's competent at gardening?

"Your house faces west. So you should plant closer to your house so that when the sun passes over, the plant will get afternoon shade." He walks over to a spot next to a pillar at the end of the patio. "Like here."

"How do you know all this?" I can't help but feel incredulous. It's stunning to hear Mr. Smooth Club Owner school me in gardening. *He lives in a flipping hotel!*

Xavier's grin is wide. "My mom is an avid gardener. I helped her a lot when I was growing up." Xavier pauses and looks down at the rosebush, frowning. "Never with roses though. But I'm sure I can figure it out."

This is the first time Xavier has mentioned something he did as a child. It's...sweet. *No, no, no!* This morning Xavier made me feel like another notch in his bedpost, not to mention that bizarre clash with Gigi.

I must not forget that. It's just so hard to remember my anger when he comes to my door looking apologetic and handsome and wants to plant the rosebush he gave me.

"That must have been special for you to do together," I murmur.

"And now I need your help. And I get to be the boss since my mom isn't here to direct the proceedings." Xavier smiles brightly at me.

My emotions are warring, but I allow a small, tight smile. I just can't muster up a mega-watt grin to match his.

"Aren't you always the boss?" I ask, my voice light. Duh, of course he is. Which takes my mind back to Gigi and her verbal sparring this morning.

Xavier laughs quietly. "I'm not the boss of you."

"Not by a long shot." At least we can agree on that point.

Xavier empties his bag of gardening tools. They are shiny, brand new. *He went to the hardware store?* It makes more sense than Xavier keeping gardening tools in his hotel room.

Without looking at me, Xavier speaks. "If I were your boss, I would've made you stay this morning. Instead you ran to the elevator. Care to explain why?"

We've been skating around it since I answered my door.

I clear my throat. "Actually, I think you're the one with some explaining to do."

Xavier looks warily at me from where he is bent over the bag. I eye him meaningfully.

"Do you happen to have a shovel? I forgot to buy one."

I hate being ignored.

"I'll be right back." I walk toward the garage.

I'm back in less than a minute, handing the shovel to Xavier. "I keep that shovel handy for when I need to dig shallow graves."

Xavier laughs and quickly grabs the shovel.

I roll my eyes. "I'm kidding."

He keeps the tool in his hand. "I'll be in charge of the shovel, just in case."

A little well of laughter bubbles up. I squelch it, but it's too late.

"So she finally has a crack in the facade."

This back and forth banter is really starting to irritate me. I want answers.

"I want to know what the hell is really going on with you and Gigi. And you better be honest. If you're not, I'll find out." My voice is tough, but my insides are quivering.

Xavier lifts the shovel and drives it into the earth for the first time. Despite my frustration, I can't help but gawk. He looks so sexy.

"Like I told you last night, Gigi isn't completely right or completely wrong. Yes, I've dated a lot of women. I don't think I've left behind a string of broken hearts. And no, I have no intention of breaking yours."

Xavier lifts the shovel and brings it back down. My desire for this man is really distracting me from my anger.

I cross my arms. Any kind of barrier is welcome right now. I'm seriously trying not to jump him. How can I want him so much and be so upset with him at the same time?

"Cut to the chase. What aren't you telling me about Gigi? If she were just your employee, she wouldn't talk to you like that and get away with it."

Xavier leans on the shovel as it sticks in the ground.

"Gigi was my wife."

What the…? How the…? Wife? Gigi and Xavier were married?

At the very least, that explains her antagonism toward him.

When? For how long? Why aren't they married anymore? I finally have one answer, but now I have fifty more questions.

Xavier watches me ingest this bombshell. If my face is reflecting my insides at all, then he's seeing myriad emotions ripple through. Shock, disbelief, comprehension, curiosity.

"Lila, say something. Anything. Please."

I shuffle my feet, trying to arrange my questions.

"Well, um, I have more questions now."

Xavier raises his eyebrows. "Go ahead." He gets back to work digging the hole for the rosebush.

I pick the least important one first. "Did you seriously think it was a good idea to give your ex-wife a note to give to me?"

His eyes flick to me before going back down to the ground. "No. But it was my only way of getting to you. I risked her wrath."

My lips twist into a grin as I choose my next question. A much more important one.

"How long were you married?"

"Three years." He answers without looking at me, continuing his work.

"How long were you together?"

"Four years."

So they married quickly. Ok.

"How old were you when you married her?"

"Too young to know what a mistake I was making. I was 22."

"Why did you marry her?"

Xavier shrugs. "Because I loved her, or at least I thought I did." Guilt rides across his face.

I feel the need to soothe him when I see his guilt. I reach out and touch his arm. His skin is slick with a sheen of sweat.

Xavier pauses momentarily at my touch, but he resumes lowering the rosebush into the ground. He nods at the ground to the right of him.

"Grab the bag of soil and open it. I need you to backfill the hole while I keep the rosebush steady."

I'm eager to have something to do with my hands. After all, this is my rosebush.

After the bag is open and dumped, I use my gloveless hands to push the soil into the hole. My hands are covered in smelly black soil, but I find it oddly comforting. The act of planting something is so organic, so simple, and the smell is earthy.

I have more questions about his marriage, but for now they can wait. I'm just grateful to finally understand his relationship with Gigi.

The rosebush is securely in the ground, and we're both hot and sweaty. I run inside for iced tea.

"Here." I hand Xavier a glass when I return.

He lifts it in the air. "To the rosebush. May she put forth many blooms just for the pure visual enjoyment of my Birthday Girl."

Swoon... Man, that Xavier can be quite the romantic.

"Cheers." Our glasses make a light tinkling sound as we tap them. We both drain our cups.

"What do you want to do now, Lila?" Xavier looks mischievous. It's a relief, considering how upset he looked just a few minutes ago.

I cross my arms. "I'm still mad at you Xavier."

"Please don't be. I should've told you about Gigi before she came barging in on us this morning. I'm sorry."

"Why does Gigi act like that if you're divorced?"

"We didn't end well. And Gigi is used to getting her own way at all times."

"So why don't you fire her? This morning you told her you wanted her out of the club. Make it official."

"I can't. She owns 30% of Townsend."

Shit. This is even messier than I thought.

Xavier squeezes his eyes tight and when he opens them again he looks amused. "Why can't you have baggage, Lila?"

"Give me seven years. Maybe by the time I'm twenty eight I'll have some." *You will probably be my baggage Xavier. And that's terrifying.*

"Are you calling me an old man?"

"Geezer."

Xavier laughs. "This old man has to work tonight. Do you want to come by?" He looks hopeful. It's cute.

I can't help my laugh.

"What's funny?"

"Just the idea of dropping by a nightclub. Like it's no big deal."

"Think of it like coming to see me at work. You know, dropping by the office. Only my office is a club and the hours are at night."

I nod my head. "Precisely what I was thinking."

"So you'll come?"

"Ridiculously loud music, people bumping into me, strangers rubbing up against each other for no reason... No thanks. One club experience in a month is enough to tide me over for a very long time."

Xavier's playful smile vanishes. I'm not trying to hurt him, but I'm not interested in that scene. But Xavier loves the club atmosphere, or he wouldn't have opened up a club. *Oops. Open mouth, insert foot.*

I step forward and put my hands on his shoulders. "How about dinner before? I'll cook. Well, no I won't, because I'm an awful cook. But I can order take-out like a pro." I'm hoping my proposition will stem his hurt feelings.

Xavier exaggerates his thinking face, pretending to consider my offer. "I could be persuaded to stay for dinner. Have you been persuaded to give us another chance?"

My mind has been filled with this same question since he told me of his past with Gigi. And I can't think of a reason to stay angry. Xavier did nothing wrong, other than withholding information, and really, who wants to tell someone they've only been on a couple dates with about an ex-wife?

"We both know you already know my answer. I would've kicked your ass out of my house two hours ago if I were going to refuse to see you again." It's the truth. "However, in the future, full disclosure would be nice. Gigi is someone you have to see at work, and she was becoming a friend to me, so in this situation, you probably should have shared the whole ex-wife tidbit."

"You know, it's too bad you don't need more persuading." His tone changes from solemn to provocative in an instant.

My eyes widen at his innuendo. Like a switch I'm turned on with a flip, my breath hitching, the now familiar feeling in my stomach. My tongue slides out of my mouth to lick my dry lips.

Xavier smiles cockily and looks down at his dirty shirt, then turns his intense gaze to my dirty clothes. He steps forward and runs his thumb across my cheek.

When he speaks his voice is thick with desire. "You have dirt on your face."

I blush. "You aren't exactly clean either." My voice is a breathy murmur.

Xavier raises my hand up to his lips and kisses it chastely. "How about we remedy that?" His voice is deep, full of meaning.

Oh. Yes, let's. My body is standing at attention. A continuation of last night? Don't mind if I do.

CHAPTER FOURTEEN

Five weeks. It has been five weeks since Xavier came to my house and planted the rosebush. And in that short period of time, I've fallen in love. And not just any kind of love. This is capital letter LOVE.

Weak knees, heartbeats in triple time, lose focus love.

Xavier is kind, sweet, and funny. And he's spontaneous, something I've never been. Until I met him, that is.

I've also never been so uninhibited, so free with my emotions. I don't recognize myself when I'm with him.

My summer break has been more fun than I ever imagined it would be. I thought this summer was going to be part time at Alexa and lounging pool side in my backyard, reading book after book. But that was before I met Xavier. I'm still at Alexa three days a week, but when I'm not there, I'm either with Xavier, sleeping, or at hot yoga.

Yes, that's right. Hot yoga. The girl who was allergic to exercise is hooked on seventy-five minute sweat sessions. Look out world. And it's all thanks to my new boyfriend.

Xavier works out five days a week. With a body that muscled, he has to. But hot yoga? I would've never guessed that was his secret weapon. Xavier swears it sculpts the smaller muscles he can't get to by lifting weights.

Xavier has been relaxed since he opened up to me about his marriage to Gigi. He doesn't like to discuss her though. I can see the guilt on his face when she comes up, and I don't understand why. One giant unanswered question looms large in my head, and I'm too afraid to ask it. Everything is perfect between us now, I don't want to rock the boat. But someday I want to know why Xavier and Gigi divorced. As much as I like Xavier, the question looms in the back of my head, making me afraid that whatever ended Xavier and Gigi could one day end us, too.

Speaking of Gigi… She's not happy about my relationship with her ex-husband. At all. I haven't spoken to her since the epic morning at Xavier's hotel room. So much for making a new friend. Xavier has to work with her and says she has been nastier than ever.

For the most part I try not to think about Gigi. My life is a wonderful routine of working, spending time with Xavier, hot yoga, and hanging out with Jessica and Cade. I'm not interested in rocking the boat, even if I want more information.

Cade and Xavier have become best buddies. That was a friendship I didn't see coming. Cade's issues with Xavier dissipated after a heart-to-heart one night. The guys went into our backyard with a six pack and came back in as friends.

Now we are one big, happy family. Aside from my nagging question. The one I'm ignoring for now.

It's breakfast time at the Mitchell/Jones house. I'm in the kitchen making scrambled eggs with cheese for Jessica before she leaves for her internship. I don't have to leave for work as early as Jess, so on the days when we both work, I make breakfast. I love the domesticity of it. Also, scrambled eggs with cheese is one of the few dishes I can't screw up.

I sigh as I fish a piece of eggshell from the bowl. I miss Xavier. He worked last night, which means he won't be awake until at least midday. Having opposite schedules sucks. I'll just have to settle for seeing him after I'm done at work and before he goes in for another night of whatever it is he does while he's at Townsend.

I locate the eggshell and toss it in the trash. My text notification goes off on my phone as I'm pouring the egg mixture into the warm pan. I glance over, hoping to see Xavier's name. My eyes widen in surprise as I see *Gigi Waters* plastered across the screen.

What the hell does she want? As far as I'm concerned, she has been placed in the class of *frenemy*. She never had my best interests at heart when she was issuing her warnings about Xavier. She either wanted to date me herself or she wanted to keep Xavier from being happy. I don't wish her any ill will, but we won't be swapping recipes any time soon.

Wiping my hands, I take my phone and open it to Gigi's message.

Meet me for coffee? I think we should talk.

My initial reaction is to say, *no thank you*, but my curiosity is piqued. Maybe if I talk to Gigi, I will get the answer to my question. Hmmm… ok. I'll bite.

I'm free tomorrow morning. Roasters at 9?

"Good morning, LL."

Jessica's voice makes me jump. I was staring so intently at my phone, imagining what Gigi might have to say.

"Sorry, I didn't hear you walk in." I murmur, setting my phone down on the counter. "Eggs coming right up."

With a final stir, they are ready. I grab two plates from the cabinet and portion out the eggs. They smell downright delicious. Jessica and I settle in with our coffee and eggs.

Another text from Gigi comes through as we're eating. She has agreed to the place and time. *Oh boy.*

"I'm guessing from your frown that isn't a text from Xavier?" Jessica nods at my phone.

I snort. "I wish. Gigi wants to talk."

Jessica's eyes go wide. "Did she say what about?"

My hair falls in my face as I shake my head. I put my fork down and tuck the long brown strands behind my ears.

Jessica points out the obvious. "Surely it's about Xavier."

My sigh is deep. "I'm sure it is."

"Do you need me to tell her to pound sand?" Jessica looks irritated.

I smile. She is all tousled strawberry blonde hair and pinched eyebrows, ready to defend me. I love her.

"No, but thanks, Jess."

She waves her hands in front of her chest. "I know, I know, you can take care of yourself." She adds an eye roll to show her exasperation.

I can't help my laugh. She's right, I can take care of myself. In fact, I prefer to. And the truth is, I want to hear what Gigi has to say.

"I'm hoping Gigi can shed some light on something Xavier hasn't exactly been forthcoming about." I shift uncomfortably in my seat. Jessica knows about Xavier's marriage to Gigi, but I didn't tell her that he left out a certain important detail.

Jessica's blue eyes narrow. "What?"

"The reason they divorced." I bite my lip, thinking of the most logical explanation, the only one that would make Gigi act the way she does. Deep down I know it was not just irreconcilable differences.

"Lila Jocelyn Mitchell, you should wait for Xavier to tell you. Don't go to his ex for information." Jessica's face is stern, her finger pointing at me while she speaks.

The desire to roll my eyes is strong, and I have to work hard to control it. I should have known she would react this way. Jessica is practically the president of the Xavier Townsend fan club. She absolutely adores him, and even more than that, she loves that I'm dating him.

"It's ok. Don't get worked up about this."

Jessica stares at me like I've suddenly grown another arm. "Lila, Xavier is the best thing that has happened to you in a very long time. Don't fuck it up."

Jessica stands up quickly and stomps away from the kitchen as I watch with my jaw dropped. Her footfalls are loud as she takes the stairs two at a time, then her door slams. Slowly I stand, stunned at my best friends reaction, and begin clearing the table. What the hell just happened?

First Jessica's outburst this morning and now this? I want to find a hole and crawl into it.

Granite Alexa has decided today was a great day for an all-employee meeting. Lucky for me, I was already due in. Others were not. Looking around at the group, I notice that even with a last minute phone call, the hair stylists who were off today look amazing. I suppose that's why they can charge so much for a style. Oh, and there's Brandee. I raise my hand and wave to the girl who shares my desk on the days I'm not working.

A few minutes after nine Granite Alexa comes striding through the front door. He's a sight to behold, donning embarrassingly tight jeans and skinny alligator loafers with a white tank top. And a fedora. With a lemon yellow scarf draped around his neck. I can't help but admire his fashion sense.

Despite his casual appearance, Granite is here on business. We've all convened in the back of the salon to hear whatever it is our esteemed owner has come to tell us. *This should be interesting.*

Granite starts his speech dramatically, arms thrown up in the air. "Thank you, employees of Alexa Salon & Spa, for meeting me here this morning. I will only take a few minutes of your time, as our first clients of the day should be arriving soon." Granite scans the employees gathered before him. *We're all here stupid.*

"I've been asked to be part of a reality show." Granite pauses for dramatic effect. The corners of his mouth turn up, even though he's trying to maintain his indifferent expression. Quickly he eliminates any semblance of a smile and continues talking. "They will be filming my ownership of this salon and then my activities outside this building."

It's a miracle I'm able to keep a straight face. Activities? Is that how Granite describes what he gets up to at night?

A round of murmuring goes through the crowd, but I'm not paying attention to what's being said. I'm too busy trying to be certain my mirth stays suppressed.

Granite has his haughty face back in place, ignoring the responses. "I'll need you all to sign a release in case the camera crew films you while you're in the building. It's unlikely they would want to use footage of anybody but me, but still, you must sign the release. The forms are on Jeri's desk. Please sign and give them to Meredith."

"And if we chose not to sign?" A quiet voice rings out from the center of the crowd. It's Marco.

Granite scowls and rubs his head as though Marco's question has given him a headache. "I suppose you can work on days when I'm not here with the crew. Or you can find a new place to work."

My eyes grow wide. Granite has the indirect-threat technique down.

Granite claps his hands twice and bows dramatically. My upper lip curls from my revulsion, but I have it fixed before he can see.

"Back to work everyone," Granite says dismissively. "Or whatever else it was you were doing."

I start for my desk, watching as Granite stalks back through the front door and jumps into his black Jaguar. He even pulls out of his parking spot with a flourish. I look at Jeri, and we share a sigh of relief. She shakes her head and sits down at her desk.

I'm about to sink down into my own chair when someone behind me speaks in a warm voice. "Lila, it's good to finally see you."

Brandee walks around to the front of our desk and stands in front of me. She twirls her long blonde hair with a single finger, a habit I noticed when she was training me three years ago.

"Brandee, it's been so long. How are you?" My smile is genuine. Brandee has always been so nice to me. Plus she keeps our shared desk very clean, which I appreciate.

She lowers her head and leans in conspiratorially. I find myself mimicking her. We must look thick as thieves.

"Can you believe Granite?" she whispers. "A reality show?"

My tone is hushed too. "I know." I stick out my tongue and curl my lip.

Brandee continues. "I'm not happy about signing a release, but I guess I'll have to if I want to keep my job. Lord knows we need the money these days." Brandee reaches down to pat her belly and smiles like she has a secret.

"Oh my gosh," I mouth silently. "A sibling for little Aidan." My voice has turned to the quietest whisper.

Brandee nods happily, her blond hair shimmering. "I'm due in February."

"Ladies," Jeri interrupts our powwow. Her voice seems so loud after all the whispering. "Sorry to ruin your gossip fest, but here are the last two copies of the release. I'll hand deliver them, since you couldn't walk to my desk and get them." Jeri sets the two papers down with more strength than is necessary and stomps back to her desk, Granite Alexa style.

"What was that about?" Brandee asks.

I roll my eyes. "It's me, not you. She always wants to gossip, and I refuse. She's jealous. Ignore it." I grab one of the papers and push it toward Brandee.

Brandee takes the paper and holds her hand out for a pen. "Better sign this release. Who knows, maybe the camera will love me, and I'll get my own spin off reality show."

I laugh and hand her a pen from the silver mint julep cup on our desk. I don't have any qualms about signing the release. I'm not interesting enough for reality tv, and there's no way the American public would want cameras capturing my life. My face probably won't even make the final cut.

Alexa was busy today, but just before closing, I snuck in a quick run to the bakery next door for Jeri's favorite treat, a chocolate petit four.

Jeri hugged me when I gave her the sweet miniature cake on my way out. "Thank God you're not mad at me. I thought for sure you would be. I don't know what came over me."

"Lets just forget about it."

Jeri nods enthusiastically. "Bye, Lila. Thanks!"

"Sure thing. Bye, Jeri."

So Jeri is placated, but I don't know what to do about Jessica. My best friend won't be won over with scrumptious goodies, especially now that she's dieting again. I admire her discipline. The girl won't eat anything unless it's lean and/or green.

I'm on my way to meet Xavier for dinner, where I'll tell him about my plan to have coffee with Gigi. And once that's done, I can tell Jess to chill out. It's sweet of her to be so happy for me and to have my best interests at heart. But really, she can calm down. Xavier isn't going anywhere.

CHAPTER FIFTEEN

I spot Xavier's car as soon as I pull into the parking lot at the restaurant. I park, grab my bag, and climb out. It feels like it's been weeks since I've seen him, not just two days.

Xavier is out of his car already too, looking good enough to eat in his khaki shorts and navy blue v-neck. His hair is combed back in that preppy way that makes him look like a good ol' boy, Americana personified. He looks like he should be sailing a boat or, at the very least, in a Ralph Lauren ad pretending to sail a boat.

"Hello there, handsome," I say when I reach him.

Xavier grabs me and pulls me into him. He tips my face up and kisses me deeply.

"I have been waiting all day to do that." He says huskily.

I sigh against his chest. "Believe me, I needed it."

"Rough day?" He runs his hands through my hair. I luxuriate in the feeling, the now familiar electrical pulses running through my body.

"Something like that," I murmur. "Can I change in your car? Your windows are tinted darker than mine."

"Illegally dark."

"You're such a badass."

Xavier smirks as I move around to the passenger side and open the door.

He sits down in the drivers seat and I slip in beside him. I rifle through my bag and pull out the lavender sundress I've brought with me.

I start to pull my shirt over my head when I remember my audience of one. A blush steals across my face. I'm not sure why, considering what I've done with this man in the last month and a half.

"Are you going to watch me change?"

Xavier's green eyes sparkle. "Is that a problem?"

"I guess not. Not when I think of... Umm... You know..." I can't put my thoughts into a coherent sentence. It's too embarrassing.

Xavier runs a finger down my cheek, chuckling to himself. "Sweet Lila. You're brazen and funny and sarcastic, and under all that you're shy. Don't be shy. You're body is beautiful. I would know." Xavier wiggles his eyebrows playfully.

I smack Xavier's arm. He grabs my wrist and kisses my knuckles instead.

"C'mon, change Lila. Raw fish waits for no man."

I groan at the mention of raw fish. I've never had sushi before. I pull my shirt over my head, ignoring his gaze. When the dress is safely on, I shimmy out of my black slacks. I slip strappy summer sandals on my feet and turn to Xavier.

"Not fair, Lila. You skipped a part."

I bat my eyes. "Whatever do you mean Xavier? I changed just like a good girl. See?" My voice is sweeter than honey.

Xavier knows my game. "I seem to have missed the part where you removed your pants."

"Poor man. You should think about getting your eyes checked. If you're lucky, you'll get an encore later."

I exit the car and watch Xavier slowly step from his BMW.

"Ready for that raw fish?" I ask, my voice challenging.

Xavier's green eyes rake up my body, drinking me in. It's intoxicating, quite nearly making me request a second visit to his car.

"Raw fish... Yum." Xavier deadpans. He sounds anything but excited.

I smirk. "My sentiments exactly."

Xavier takes my hand and pulls me toward the front door of the restaurant. My feet are dragging.

"You'll love it, Lila. I promise."

My nose wrinkles. For the record, I don't believe him.

Ok, ok. I can admit when I'm wrong. Sushi is delicious. The salty soy sauce mixed with the spicy wasabi is to die for.

"Told you so." Xavier rubs it in as the server removes our last roll, aptly named the Las Vegas roll.

"Cool your jets." Someone has to rein Xavier in. He has this habit of thinking he is always right. The most irritating part of his habit is that he is too frequently right. It's a vicious cycle.

We've been having fun. Xavier's in a carefree mood, and that makes me happy. Now is as good a time as any to bring up my plans with Gigi.

"So, I got a text from Gigi this morning..."

Xavier's smile vanishes, and worry etches his face. He's silent. I know it's bad when he doesn't say anything. Xavier is never short on words.

I continue, hoping at some point this will turn into a dialogue. "She wants to talk to me. I'm not sure what about."

Xavier's anger breaks through his silence. "And you agreed to talk to her?"

"Yes." My response is quiet, totally opposite of his. Surely six weeks into a relationship is a little early to be fighting?

"I don't want you talking to her."

"Why not?"

"Why do you even want to talk to her?"

"Why don't you want me to?"

Xavier stares at me, his mouth a hard line. He seems torn between anger and fear, his hands clenched into tight fists. Mr. *In Control* looks like he's at a loss.

Xavier doesn't want me to know what happened with Gigi. Why else would he respond so strongly? I knew he was holding back, but a reaction this strong? He's hiding something, and it's big.

"Either you tell me now or Gigi will tomorrow."

Xavier's sullen silence persists.

I throw my napkin down on the table. I'm mad, and all Xavier has managed to do is increase my curiosity. I definitely won't be missing my coffee plans with Gigi tomorrow.

"This wouldn't be any of my business if your ex-wife wasn't so involved in your life. You know that, right?" I stand and walk out of the restaurant.

My trek home is silent, but the quiet is deafening. Each second my phone isn't ringing is a measure of time being counted in front of me. Xavier hasn't called, Xavier hasn't called, Xavier hasn't called.

After a night of tossing and turning I've finally accepted that Xavier isn't going to call me before I meet Gigi. He knows what Gigi's going to tell me, and he refuses to be the one who tells me first. What could be so awful that Xavier won't even say it? With a heavy heart I head to Roasters.

I'm five minutes early, so I order and find a seat. I'm trying to enjoy my vanilla latte when Gigi walks in. She's all flowing red hair and bare face, tight jeans and tank top. I feel a stupid stab of jealousy, picturing her and Xavier together. She's unique and I'm so, well, boring. Except for my green eyes. I love my green eyes.

Once Gigi has her order, she settles in front of me. It takes every ounce of my strength to stop picturing her with Xavier. Is this how most girls feel when confronted with their boyfriend's past loves? I don't like the feeling.

"Hello, Gigi." My tone is polite. I would rather skip the pleasantries and just demand the information I want. *Easy does it, Lila.*

"Hi, Lila. Awkward, isn't it?" Gigi's smile is wry.

I'm reminded of Gigi's direct nature. Perhaps this is how she prefers to communicate. Well, I have no problem with the direct approach.

"Awkward doesn't begin to describe it. The last time I saw you, you were verbally eviscerating my boyfriend." I say it coolly, as though it's no big deal.

Gigi blinks. She didn't miss my use of the word *boyfriend*. She clears her throat. Is she intimidated by me?

"Lila, first I want to ask you if there's anything you need to ask me? Any questions?" Gigi seems to have regained her strength and is peering at me, waiting with a quiet tenacity.

I smile sweetly. "You're the one who requested this meeting. Why don't you tell me what's on your mind?"

I may not be red tressed with a body that won't quit, but I'm not backing down. *You've met your match, Gigi Waters.*

"I highly doubt Xavier has told you about *our* past." She emphasizes the word, and it makes me want to leap across the table at her. Instead I control my impulse and take a sip of my coffee.

My voice is strong, my gaze level. "Xavier has been forthcoming, Gigi. But feel free to elucidate."

Please, please, elucidate. Please help me understand why Xavier still feels guilty about you and hasn't called me since I left him last night.

All at once Gigi transforms in front of me, from entitled ex-wife to brokenhearted woman.

"We were happy... At least I thought we were. Xavier had just become the assistant manager at a different club, and I was excited for him. I thought it meant we were on the road to having our own club. It's what we dreamed of doing together." Gigi's face looks crestfallen as she relives her tale. "I had no idea... I just didn't know. I was so dumb, so in love that I didn't see it. He'd been seeing her for fucking months when I learned I was pregnant. I mean, what the fuck? He seemed happy about the baby, and I was too. I was only ten weeks along when I went to the club one day to surprise him before they opened, and that's when I saw him with her. They were... well, you don't need the image. I turned and ran. Xavier came after me, and I just wanted to keep running. I tripped and fell, hard." Gigi pauses as the tears start falling. "I lost my baby and my husband."

Holy shit...

I expected the cheating. But a baby? My heart twists for her loss. I would have to be a robot not to feel something.

"Gigi, I'm sorry. I had no idea."

She laughs once without mirth. "I knew Xavier wouldn't tell you. I knew he wouldn't want you to know. But you deserve to know what you're getting yourself into." Gigi looks resolved. She truly believes I should know how she was wronged. Does she expect me to share her fate?

"Lila, I knew from the moment I saw you talking to Xavier that this wasn't going to end well for you. And you're too innocent, I just couldn't sit back and let it happen. If anyone knows what Xavier is capable of, it's me. He just doesn't have what you need. He loves the scene, the Vegas lifestyle. It's like he gets high on the adoration from the people coming into the club. Get out now, before he breaks your heart. Because he will." Gigi is resolute, her words spoken with such vehemence.

How am I supposed to respond to that? My mouth opens, but I have no words.

A surprise pregnancy, a cheating husband, a lost baby. Where do I start?

When I find my voice, it's soft, compassionate. "I'm so sorry you lost your baby. And your husband."

Gigi nods as she uses her napkin to dry her eyes and wipe her hose. "Thank you. I know that Xavier can be charming and easy to love, but trust me, you'll be much happier without him."

Ummm, what? This woman needs a reality check. Does she think she possesses an on/off switch to Xavier's relationships?

"Gigi, while I'm very sorry for your loss, my relationship with Xavier is separate from yours. I appreciate the depth of your concern for me and the well-being of my heart. Any choices I make in my relationship will be based on my own experiences and not Xavier's past choices." I gather my purse and drink, standing. There's nothing left to discuss with Gigi.

Gigi watches me, her mouth in a grim line. Between her red hair and the steely resolve I can see forming within her, she looks positively wicked.

"Good luck."

My stomach flips at her ominous tone.

"You're going to need it."

I opt for silence, turning around and striding through the coffee shop with my head held high.

Is it me or did Gigi just declare war?

CHAPTER SIXTEEN

Straight to Xavier. That's where I'm headed.

I would be lying if I said Gigi's words didn't shake me. Who wants to hear their boyfriend cheated on his ex-wife? *Once a cheater, always a cheater.* The saying is repeating in my head.

If I were listening to my brain, I'd be driving away from the strip, not toward it. But it's my heart doing the thinking right now. And my heart wants Xavier.

I won't let Xavier's past rule our future. My Xavier is caring and kind, he's considerate and invested in us. He's older now, and more mature. He isn't that man anymore.

I arrive at The Martin and toss my keys to a valet. He waves and smiles at me. I wave back with feigned cheer and hurry through the turnstile. It's amazing how this place has gone from a hotel to Xavier's home. I'm here so frequently that the throngs of guests have become background noise to me.

The elevator whisks me up to Xavier's floor. My head is swimming. What am I going to say? Too quickly I'm there, and the doors are open. I step out and into the hallway. Deep breath, squared shoulders. Hopefully he isn't still angry with me. I knock and wait, holding my breath.

Xavier opens the door, hair wet and a towel around his waist. *Wow...* I've seen his chest so many times, but it still disarms me.

"Hi," I say shyly. I flutter my eyelashes at him. Maybe it will soften him up. "You haven't called."

Xavier turns around and heads back to his bedroom. I follow, letting the door swing shut behind me.

"You walked out on me at dinner, remember?" Xavier says evenly, his back still turned.

I approach him and place my hands on his shoulders. I lean in, planting a light kiss in the middle of his back.

Poor guy. It's easy to see how scared he is. He's convinced I'll run for the hills if I know about the baby and his infidelity. *But I already know, Xavier, and look where I am.*

Xavier tenses but doesn't turn around. I sigh and back away. I'm not sure how to handle him right now. Fighting is new to us.

"I can't talk to your back, Xavier. I'll be on the couch when you're ready to talk."

And then I go to the couch and wait. And wait. The annoyance begins to flare inside me. If this isn't sulking, then I don't know what is. And I have next to no tolerance for sulking.

Twenty minutes of sitting on the couch waiting and now I'm pissed.

"Xavier Michael Townsend!" I yell. I sound way too much like my mother.

"Lila Jocelyn Mitchell!" Xavier strides into the living room and sits beside me.

I can't figure out his mood. We stare at each other, a stalemate. Who starts?

"Did you have your little coffee date with my ex-wife?" Xavier's mouth is turned down in disdain.

Does fear always turn you into an asshole? I don't ask the question, but damn, I want to. I nod my head.

Xavier's green eyes are wary. "What did Gigi want?"

There it is again, the fear. It's written all over his face. The anger is only a mask.

"Essentially, she wanted to warn me off you. Again."

"Is that all?"

I shake my head. "No." My voice is a whisper.

Xavier's fist comes down hard and lands on the couch between us, making me jump. He knows that I know.

I scramble onto his lap. My desire to soothe away his fear is strong.

"Xavier please, open your eyes. Look at me." I stare at him, imploring.

Finally his green-eyed gaze meets mine. Behind the anger and fear I see a third emotion, hidden deep within. Shame. *Oh no, Xavier.* I want so badly to remove it.

"I'm here, ok? I know about the baby and what happened with Gigi, and I'm here. And I will stay here. What happened with Gigi stays with you and Gigi. She's not a part of us." I take his hand and place it on my chest. "This is my heart. I'm giving it to you without any fear or reservation. Whoever you were back then isn't the man you are today. Today you're the man I've fallen in love with." The words are out of my mouth before I realize it. *What the...? No, no, no, no.*

It's too soon, too soon to be in love. Even if I feel it, why did I have to say it? Damn me and my foolish declaration.

Nervously I bite my lip and look away, at anything but Xavier.

I feel Xavier's finger under my chin, pulling my gaze back to meet his. I gulp once, hard.

Xavier's fingers run through my hair, stopping at my neck. He stares at my face, eyes open wide in wonder. My heart pounds watching the emotion on his face.

"I was furious when you said you were going to meet Gigi. I knew what she wanted to tell you, and the thought of you knowing what I did...it terrified me. How could you still want me if you knew all that?"

I shrug my shoulders once, quickly.

"And then I heard your knock. I thought you were coming to break up with me."

Nope, no break up plans, but an unexpected declaration of love. Ugh.

"I'm sorry. I really thought you would be finished with me when you learned what happened with Gigi. And the baby." There it is again, the shame and guilt, plain on his face.

It's my turn for an apology. "I'm sorry I walked out on you last night."

Xavier dismisses my apology. "It's ok. I know this is hard for you. Gigi isn't just your run-of-the-mill ex-wife. I'm sorry you have to deal with her."

I shrug, as if crazy exes are all in a days work. "I can handle her."

"I don't deserve you."

"Yes, you do. I would have kicked the old Xavier to the curb. But the new Xavier is welcome to stay." I lean in and softly rub Xavier's nose with my own.

When I pull back Xavier closes his eyes and sighs. "I love you, Lila."

Finally! Thank goodness he said it back.

"Xavier, this is kind of an opportune time to kiss me."

Xavier, with his fingers still entwined in my hair, pulls my face toward his.

"You're awfully bossy, you know that?"

I open my mouth to retort but his lips are on me, doing what he does so well. Almost instantly I'm lost, thinking of nothing but this man who holds such pain and regret deep down within him. He has completely stolen my heart.

I'm on my way home, happily humming along to the radio. I can't help my joyful thoughts. I know Xavier's secret, and it didn't break us!

Though it wasn't for lack of Gigi trying. I still don't completely understand what her deal is. Why does she want us apart so badly?

As much as I believe Gigi is a live threat, I don't want to waste another moment thinking about her. My happiness is too great to be tainted with any further thought of her tonight.

Besides, I still have to face Jess. I haven't talked to her since our spat on Wednesday morning. She was asleep when I got home from my disastrous dinner with Xavier last night. Yesterday I racked up fights with Jess, Jeri and Xavier. Three in one day, a record for me.

Tonight Jess and I can finally talk and I can tell her that everything is perfect with me and Xavier. More than perfect, actually. So she needn't worry any longer. I tap the gas pedal in my eagerness to get home.

Disappointment fills me when I arrive and see that Jessica's car isn't in the driveway. She must be out with Cade.

I need to see my best friend and make sure things are ok between us. Jess and I never fight. For that matter, she isn't usually as dramatic as she was yesterday morning, fleeing from the kitchen the way she did.

It's only eight o'clock, so I settle on the couch and watch television while I wait for her to come home. At eleven, when she still isn't home, I head up to my bedroom. I could call her, but I don't want to interrupt. I don't know where they could be knocking boots, unless they went to a hotel. Cade lives at home. He's milking the whole *recent college graduate with his first job* for all it's worth.

As I'm getting ready for bed, I send a goodnight message to Xavier. I know he's busy. Someone called today and reserved three tables, making the club sold out tonight. I don't expect to hear back anytime soon.

Hopefully I'll see Jessica tomorrow. I have a surprising ache to lay by the pool with her and drink her gross green juice. After a day filled with a grieving ex-wife, a baby shocker, and a declaration of love, I'm ready for some normalcy.

"Lila."

From somewhere in my sleep I hear my name being whispered.

"Lila."

The voice is more insistent this time. I groan and open my eyes. Jessica is sitting next to me on my bed. She's wearing one of Cade's Michigan T-shirts and a pair of shorts. Her eyes are red-rimmed and swollen. *Oh no, Cade broke up with her.*

I glance over at the clock as I sit up. It's only six forty-five. Are grocery stores open yet? I don't think we have enough cookies in the house for a break-up of this magnitude.

"What is it? You look like you've been crying." I stifle my yawn.

Jessica picks at an imaginary piece of lint on my comforter. With a small, shaking voice, Jessica says, "I'm pregnant."

Holy shit. Holy flipping shit. My stomach feels like it has dropped out of me, and my mind is scrambling to say something, anything supportive.

"Are you freaking kidding me? Jessica, please tell me this is a belated April Fools joke." I take a deep breath and try again.

"What I meant to say was, I support you and I'm here for you."

Jessica proffers up a small smile through her tears. "Visceral reaction first. That's ok. It's how Cade acted too."

Oh no. I'll kill him. He'd better support her in this.

"He was probably more shocked than I was. When did you tell him?" How am I speaking so calmly? On the inside, I'm anything but calm.

Jessica lets out a fresh round of sobs. "Last night," she manages, though her words are practically incoherent.

Thankfully I'm fluent in Crying Jessica.

"What did he say, sweetie?" I wait patiently as she plucks a tissue from the box next to my bed and blows noisily.

"He said that a pregnancy wasn't in his plan for right now. He said he was just starting his career. He kept going on and on about how young we are and how he still lives at home and I'm in college. He said in this really sarcastic tone, 'I'm sure my parents won't mind if I turn their living room into a nursery.' Can you believe that?" Jessica sniffles and runs the back of her hand along her nose.

I hand her a tissue and rub her back. My poor friend. I'm going to have Cade's balls on a platter. Hell hath no fury like the best friend of the woman scorned.

"What can I do for you right now?" My voice is gentle, masking my fury over Cade's dumb ass response.

"Breakfast. A big breakfast. After all, I'm eating for two now." Jessica pats her belly, the tears starting again.

My heart twists at the sight of her, so vulnerable and sad. *I'm going to kick your ass, Cade Blankenship.*

"Of course, Jess. You just lay down and rest. Let me take care of you and that baby." Did I really just say those words?

Jessica is snoring softly before I can even cover her with a blanket. The poor thing is exhausted. I look at her belly, marveling that she has a person growing inside her.

I walk on soft feet to my closet. Quietly I pull on a pair of pants and a T-shirt. I tiptoe into my bathroom, where I barely make a peep brushing my teeth and hair.

Breakfast can wait. I have an ass to kick.

Jessica has mentioned on more than one occasion that Cade likes to get to work by eight. He's still learning the ropes at Scion Financial Advisors and likes to arrive early. Something about getting familiar with their extensive client list. This morning Cade will be lucky if he doesn't get too familiar with my fist.

Thanks to that annoying house party I attended a few months ago, I know where Cade lives. I also know that he only has a five minute drive to work. So when I pull up at seven-fifty, I catch Cade just as he's walking to his car.

The navy blue pants and white collared shirt scream businessman, but the slump in his shoulders says he's under some serious stress. For a moment I soften. He looks rough, like he didn't sleep well. *Yeah, well, neither did your pregnant girlfriend.* My resolve hardens again.

"Hey, Cade." My voice rings out loudly. I even sound confrontational.

Cade looks at me and sighs. He doesn't look happy to see me.

I scowl at him. "I'm not happy to see you either."

Cade raises his hands up, palms facing me. "Look, Lila—"

I interrupt him, waving away his words with my hand. "I'm not interested in your excuses."

Cade eyes me warily. "This is between me and Jessica."

Oh, really? Why didn't you keep the sounds of all your baby making practice between you and Jessica?

I challenge him. "What's between you and Jessica? Your cowardice? Your bad reaction? Your selfishness?"

Cade hangs his blond head.

"You should be ashamed, Cade Blankenship. The best woman in the world is doing you the honor of having your baby, and you act like a grade-A, third degree asshole. You're college educated with a good job. Jessica is graduating in December, and she'll probably be offered a job with the company she's interning for right now. Of all the things that could happen, this isn't the worst of them. So quit being scared, or whatever the fuck your problem is, and get on board."

Cade looks like he's in shock. Hasn't anybody ever given him a proper tongue lashing?

Without another word I climb into my car and drive. I need to get home to the pregnant woman who wants a very large breakfast.

CHAPTER SEVENTEEN

"Baby, it's so good to see you. Last night was ridiculous." Xavier sweeps me into a hug the second he steps into my house.

I lean in to him for a kiss. He's so warm, and he smells amazing. Must be the body wash he uses. Where we're headed, he doesn't need cologne.

"Follow me. We need to eat lunch quickly if you want to make it to that class on time." I lead the way into the kitchen.

Xavier follows. "Mmmm, Lila, I love the way your ass looks in those yoga pants."

Playfully I shake my behind for my party of one, dancing out of Xavier's reach. If we start now, we'll never make it to hot yoga.

"Simmer down, Mr. Townsend. We have somewhere to be."

I pull the lettuce cups out of the crisper and spoon the prepared chicken mixture into them. A little sauce, and they are ready.

Xavier eyes them cautiously. He knows the kitchen is not where I should spend my time.

I roll my eyes. "Jessica made it a little while ago. She took a half-day."

Xavier looks visibly relieved. Frankly, I would be too.

"Eat up." I urge, pushing his plate across the table. Xavier digs in.

"Tell me about your night," I say between bites.

Xavier chews and swallows. "The person who bought the three tables was pretty wild. I think it was a guy."

I can't help but chuckle. "You think?"

"The Adam's apple gave it away. Other than that, it could have been a woman. Same goes for most of the people that he...she...the person was with."

I'm doubled over in laughter. Xavier laughs with me.

"You know, my male boss becomes a woman sometimes."

Xavier snorts. "That's a normal sentence."

"It is in this freak-ass town."

"You're the one who moved here."

"I got a scholarship," I remind Xavier. "Not because I was dying to live in Las Vegas."

"We all know how you love to party." Xavier's tone is ironic. How can the club owners girlfriend never want to go to the club? We've had this discussion before.

Xavier takes our plates to the sink and sets them down. "I'll deal with those later. Let's go. Being late to yoga is a no-no."

I pick up my newly acquired hot pink yoga mat and lead the way to Xavier's car.

Who would have ever thought that I, hater of all exercise, would enjoy hot yoga?

The stretching alone is great, and necessary, thanks to the extracurricular physical activity I've been engaging in since meeting Xavier.

Beyond the stretch is the way it's changing my body. I'm developing actual biceps. And my back is getting toned, or so Xavier says. If I listened to Xavier, then apparently my behind is getting rounder too. But that may just be Xavier and his borderline obsession with my ass.

Yes, hot yoga does a body good.

Our instructor today is different from the usual friendly, petite blonde. Brandon is young, maybe twenty-six or twenty-seven, and gorgeous in that peaceful, kumbaya kind of way.

"Ok, everyone, lets start in child's pose." Brandon's voice is deep, reaching us at the far end of the studio. "Whatever you've brought in here today, make peace with it and allow yourself to enjoy your practice."

I do as Brandon says, pushing aside Gigi's threat, Jessica's pregnancy, and even my harsh words toward Cade. This is why I really love yoga. Forgetting about life for an hour and focusing entirely on my body.

The class flows so nicely that I hardly notice when we come to the end. My clothes are soaked with sweat, yet my body is still producing more, the beads perched on my skin before rolling off me fluidly. We're in pigeon, my favorite stretching pose, when I feel hands on the small of my back. Brandon is pushing his hand down the length of my spine, allowing me to stretch forward further.

He moves on from me and moves us into our next pose. Too soon, the class is over. I reach for my ice water and chug. By now I know I'll need at least one more refill of my water bottle and maybe even a coconut water to rehydrate.

I roll up my mat and look over to Xavier. He's in the middle of rolling his mat up too. A bead of sweat rolls down his back and curves around his oblique, disappearing into the fold of his shorts. I gulp. I've been beneath him, on top of him, and everywhere else on him, but that one bead of sweat has my insides twisting again. I want him. Right now.

"What?" Xavier whispers. He doesn't look concerned, just confused.

I clear my throat. "Nothing." I can at least wait until we get home.

"Lila…"

He winks at me, rolling on his heels and standing. I grab his extended hand and rise.

He leans down, putting his lips against my earlobe. "You had that look on your face. The hungry one."

I position my body so that my side is pressed up against his front, blocking us from the view of the other yogi's. One fingernail starts at his belly button and slides up to the base of his throat. I feel the hiss of breath.

"Not hungry. Starving." I look up into his eyes.

"Stay here," he commands, his voice low.

Oh my. What did I just get myself into?

Xavier busies himself with putting the straps on our new mats and makes a show of gathering our towels and water bottles. The last person leaves the room and the instructor is long gone. And there isn't another class for two more hours.

Xavier walks quickly to the door and locks it. He turns around, coming toward me, pointing at me. "You."

My chest heaves. How can just one word do that to me? It must be the excitement of what's about to happen. But deep down, in my heart of hearts, I know what it is. I love Xavier, deeply.

The windows are clouded with humidity, the heat, and the collective breath of the class. Water droplets drip down the mirror, leaving streaks of exposed glass in their wake. Xavier is in front of me and reflected back at me. So many Xavier's, all coming toward me with a common goal.

"You want me."

"Yes." I pant the word.

"What made you want me?"

I blush, but he won't see it, because I'm already red faced after the class. I lift up my face boldly and meet his gaze.

"There was a sweat droplet that slid from your back, across your waist and into your shorts."

Xavier's eyes crinkle when he smiles. "So it's the little things that turn you on."

"And the big things too," I say with a provocative grin.

He grabs my thighs and lifts me into the air. My legs wrap around his waist as he walks, then I feel the cool smooth mirror against my back. My sweat mixes with the water drops on the mirror and creates the perfect surface for sliding.

Xavier's mouth is on my neck and moves to the top of my sports bra. "You taste like salt. And Lila."

My fists curl in his hair as sensation takes over. The heated room, our heated bodies, slick with sweat. The sensuality of it overwhelms me.

Xavier pins me to the mirror with one arm and his upper body, while his other hand manages the task of ridding us of our bottoms.

He brings me back down on him, a happy growl coming from low in his throat. "You. Are. Wild."

I can't form a response. I'm too busy sliding up and down the mirror.

"I fucking love you, Lila."

I bring my eyes down from the ceiling and meet his steady, lustful gaze.

"I love you too."

And I do. Oh, how I do.

"That was an awesome class," I smirk as I get in Xavier's BMW.

"Are you just saying that because the instructor gave you a back rub at the end?" Xavier's voice is teasing. He checks his mirrors and pulls from our space, heading back to my house.

"Well… Brandon's back rub was incredible."

"You better be kidding."

I roll my eyes. Of course I'm kidding. "I think it had more to do with the sating of my hunger."

Xavier grins. "Are you full?"

I look at his strong hands gripping the wheel, the arrogant lift of his chin, those green eyes that have turned my life on its head. "Never," I say.

He reaches over to squeeze my thigh. "Good." He turns his attention back to the road.

I watch out the window as the stores fly by us, until a baby store catches my gaze and I think about Jess.

"Jessica is pregnant." I blurt out.

Xavier turns to stare at me. His mouth forms an O.

I point at the road. "Drive."

"Holy shit, Lila. That's huge."

"Yeah, and Jessica said Cade didn't take it well."

Xavier nods knowingly. "When something like that happens unplanned, it can really rock you."

Right... how could I have overlooked that Xavier would know how Cade feels right now? The pang of jealousy I feel is ridiculous. So what if Xavier has been here before, if only for a short time? His past is in the past. Except when his ex-wife is inserting her nose into our relationship.

"Well, hopefully I talked some sense into him."

Xavier sighs. "What did you do?"

My arms cross. "I went to see him this morning. I'm not going to let Cade make Jessica feel like that. He made a baby with her, and he can't treat her that way. She was sobbing in my bed before 7 a.m.. I won't sit on the sidelines while my best friend is mistreated."

"It's Cade and Jessica's business, not yours."

"You sound like him."

"Who?"

"Cade."

"What did you say to him?"

I shrug, like it's no big deal. "I reminded him of what they have going for them." There *may* have been some stronger words sprinkled in here or there.

"What else did you say?"

I sigh. How does Xavier already know me so well?

"I told him to get over whatever he has a problem with and man up."

Xavier chuckles. He reaches over and lightly tugs on my ponytail.

"Birthday Girl, you sure can breath fire when you want to. It's one of the things I love about you."

I beam back at him.

Xavier was certainly enthusiastic when we got back to my house. He was so ready for round two it was all I could do to get him into the shower first. And now I'm grinning to myself like an idiot as I think about how we spent our time post-yoga…both times. Sex with Xavier makes the sex I had with my first boyfriend look like amateur hour.

After my romp with Xavier and a nice leisurely nap, Xavier has just informed me that he isn't going to the club tonight. A Friday night with my boyfriend? Yes, please!

"Not that I'm arguing, but why are you taking tonight off?" I roll over and snuggle into Xavier's chest. My fingers trace patterns across the wide expanse.

I feel his kiss on the top of my head. "Because I would rather spend Friday night with my girlfriend, like a regular couple. And I think I've had enough of that place after last night."

I giggle. Maybe Granite Alexa was part of the cross dressing crew. My phone starts buzzing on the table beside me. With a groan I pull myself away.

When I see who it is, I haul myself off my bed.

"It's my mom."

Xavier grabs my hand. "Stay."

I shake my head. "No way. I can't have a conversation with my mother while I'm sitting in bed with you. That's too weird."

"I promise to behave." Even as he says it his eyebrows are wiggling.

"See you later, alligator." I flutter my fingers as I sail through the door.

"Mom, hi." I answer my phone on the last ring.

My mom sounds surprised. "Oh honey, hi. I thought I was going to have to leave a voicemail."

"Nope. What's going on?" I make my way downstairs and into the living room.

"Can't I call you for no reason?"

"You can call Hannah for no reason. And she will talk for no reason." It's true. Hannah will talk to someone until they fall asleep. And then she will keep talking and call it a lullaby. Hence, I don't call Hannah.

My mother laughs. "Oh, Lila, my little introvert. Always the one who says it like it is and prefers the company of her camera."

I clear my throat, feeling suddenly guilty. My camera hasn't seen much action since Xavier walked into the picture. I haven't told my parents about Xavier yet. It's not a secret, I just haven't talked to them. Here goes nothing…

"Actually, mom, there's someone whose company has bumped my camera to second place."

"What!" my mother shrieks.

Oh, Lord. Does she have to overreact? I switch my phone to speaker to protect my hearing. She may not be done shrieking.

"Mom, calm down."

My mother is so excited, she can barely contain herself. "Who? How long? When can I meet him?"

Never if you keep acting like this.

Suddenly my phone is plucked from my hand. Xavier takes it off speaker and puts it up to his face. His look is mischievous.

"Mrs. Mitchell, this is Xavier Townsend. I hope I'm the person Lila is referring to." Xavier's voice is smooth without being slimy.

Whatever my mother's response is, I can't hear it. Xavier is so charming that my mother doesn't stand a chance. I shake my head at Xavier, grinning. Despite having my phone snatched from me, I'm in good humor.

"I own a nightclub here."

Pause.

"Yes, the one Lila went to on her birthday. We met that night."

Pause.

"Since roughly one week after that."

Pause.

"I'm not sure why she was hiding me. Maybe she's embarrassed about me."

Pause.

"Please let me know when you're planning your next visit to see Lila. I would love to have you and Mr. Mitchell as special guests at my club."

My parents at Townsend? NFW.

Pause.

"Lila has become very special to me. I'll take nothing but good care of her."

Xavier looks down at his pocket, where I presume his phone is. I can hear the vibration of the incoming call.

My hand stretches out for my phone. "I believe your pocket is ringing."

"I look forward to meeting you and Mr. Mitchell. I'll give you back to Lila now."

Xavier hands the phone back to me with a smirk, then exits the room just as quietly as he entered it. I hear him say hello, and then the door to the backyard shuts. Why is he taking a call outside? It's flipping hot out there.

I resume my conversation with my mother. "So, now you know Xavier."

"Now I know *about* him. I'll reserve judgment for when I meet him. But knowing you he is a good guy. I know my Lila. You don't suffer fools gladly. He wouldn't be in the picture if he wasn't good enough for you."

"Aw, thanks mom. Now that the cat is out of the bag, why don't you tell me why you called?" I peer around the wall of the living room and through the open kitchen. I can only see a portion of Xavier's body, but enough to see he has his back facing the house. The phone is still up to his ear.

"Honey, don't you have anything to say about this?" My mother sounds worried.

Crap. I wasn't listening.

"Sorry mom, I was distracted. Can you say that again?"

"Tell Xavier to leave you alone long enough to talk to your mother. He can have you after we're off the phone."

"Mom! Don't say things like that. And Xavier isn't even in the room."

He may not be in the room, but he's definitely the reason for my distraction. Why did he take the call outside? And why does he still have his back to the house? And why am I so damn suspicious?

"Lila, your dad and I have decided to sell the Vegas house after you graduate in December."

Ok, now she has my attention.

"Where am I supposed to go?"

"Wherever you want. Back here, hopefully."

Newport Beach is incredible, but it doesn't feel like home anymore. And Las Vegas doesn't feel like home, either.

"Are you mad?"

"It's your home to do what you want with."

"Lila, we—"

"Mom, really, it's ok. I'll figure it all out. There are just some other things going on right now that need my attention. I have a few months before I need to start thinking about where I'll go after graduation."

"Do you know what kind of job you want? Because I have a friend who's looking to hire a new photographer. Between all the weddings, babies, and families out here she can't keep up. I'm sure she would hire you on the spot."

I groan. I don't want to take pictures of posed people. I want to catch the moments when they are real. That's where the magic is.

"Thanks mom. I'll think about it." It's the first step in the direction of letting her down easy. Family pictures are her thing, not mine. I would rather forget the days of braces and center parts. And I sure as hell don't want to memorialize them for other people.

"Everything ok back there? What needs your attention?"

I hesitate. Should I tell her about Jessica's pregnancy? Mom has always had a soft spot for Jessica. "Mom, this is very new. As of this morning, actually. Don't freak out, ok?"

"Spit it out."

"Jessica is pregnant."

Her shock is evident in her silence. I'll just give her a moment to digest.

"Whoa. That is something that would need your attention. And the father?"

"It's Jessica's boyfriend, Cade. I'm sure I've told you about him."

"Honey, you haven't called me since your birthday."

Whoops. I've been…busy.

"Anyway, so Jessica and her boyfriend Cade Blankenship are having a baby. It's very big, very new news. Everyone's still processing it. So welcome to the processing club."

"Oh my. Ok. Well, this has been quite a phone call. You have a boyfriend and Jessica is pregnant. I might need a drink after I pick up your brothers."

"Have a glass of chardonnay, and one for Jessica too. Everything will be all right with the house and all the other stuff we talked about. Give Dad and Jackson and Colin a hug from me." After we finish the conversation, I put down my phone and head out to the backyard. Time to find out who my boyfriend is talking to.

CHAPTER EIGHTEEN

I'm totally embarrassed. How could I have gotten so worked up about Xavier's mysterious phone call? The disappointment was evident on Xavier's face when I asked him who he was talking to.

"It wasn't the question, it was the way you asked it," he explained.

I know what he meant. I heard my own voice. What my words didn't say, my voice had written all over it. So much accusation in that one seemingly innocent question.

Xavier had just ended his call when I walked outside. He looked at me and smiled, and I hurled my question and silent incrimination.

Xavier, green eyes stunned and hurt, knew immediately what I was really asking. *Are you being unfaithful?*

Instead of getting angry, Xavier took my hand and led me to the patio chairs.

After we sat, he scooted his chair in front of mine. With his hands on either side of my face, he spoke softly. "This is what Gigi wants. She put her words into your head. She didn't want to just tell you what happened. She wanted to plant doubt. Don't let her hurt us. Please."

Xavier is right. Damn her! Planting doubt was her first assault. What will be her next? Her final words from our coffee come back to me.

"Xavier, something Gigi said to me yesterday has really been bothering me."

Xavier raises his eyebrows. "Clearly." The word is acerbic.

My cheeks warm. Xavier reaches for me. Our hands, intertwined, come to rest in my lap.

"Sorry," he mutters. "I'm mad at her, not you. Continue."

"Gigi told me, 'Good luck. You're going to need it.' At the time I thought she was referring to you. But now..." I'm too busy imagining the possibilities to finish my sentence.

"Fuck," Xavier growls the swear word. "Gigi can be such a bitch."

I cease my imaginings long enough to glare at Xavier. I detest the word 'bitch.' Xavier knows that already, having received my lecture on the use of the pejorative term.

"I know, I know. Sorry. I'm too intelligent to use the generalized word on her. If I took a moment I could come up with a better label."

I nod proudly. *He was listening!*

'Look, I haven't said it yet, but I'm sorry I was suspicious. I let Gigi into my head, even though I didn't realize it." The apology sounds light, even to my ears, but what am I supposed to do?

Xavier locks his green eyes on mine, so serious as he speaks. "Gigi is underhanded and conniving. Believe me, I learned the hard way. I know she painted you a sad picture of a sweet pregnant wife who learned her husband was cheating on her. It's not an excuse, but she wasn't exactly pleasant to be around. We were both very unhappy."

I don't want to hear all the dirty details. It's clear Xavier has residual feelings of guilt over their issues and what happened, and rehashing it only makes him feel worse.

I clamber onto his lap and gaze into his face. Behind the emerald eyes, the strong jaw and perfectly straight nose lies a man whose soul is even more beautiful than his outside.

My voice is soft, overcome with the love I feel for this man. "We don't need to talk about this. Let's just agree to be on the lookout for her next onslaught, ok?"

Xavier leans his forehead in and touches mine. "Deal. I love you, Birthday Girl."

"I love you, Xavier."

And then he kisses me, and it's so sweet, tender, and filled with love.

This is how Jessica finds us, kissing and canoodling on the patio.

"Get a room," she jokes as she walks outside.

"Gladly," I whisper into Xavier's ear as I climb off his lap.

He turns to Jessica. "Lila told me your big news. Congratulations."

Jessica looks pleased for a nanosecond, then her face darkens. "If only everyone thought it was cause for celebration."

"Cade will come around." *And if it's not soon, I'll pay him a second visit.*

"And my parents too?" Jessica asks dejectedly.

I stand and pull her in for a hug. Poor Jessica. A baby announcement is supposed to be an exciting thing.

"Yes, them too. And in the meantime, you have us."

"Thank God for you, Lila. I have my best friend and a roof over our heads." She reaches down to pat her belly.

Oh no. A roof over *our* heads. Now isn't the time to tell her about my parents' plan to sell after we graduate in December. She doesn't need the added stress.

"So," I say brightly. "Let's get you and that baby some dinner."

Jessica nods. "You wouldn't believe how hungry I am. Fighting with your parents over whether or not having a baby out of wedlock makes you a slut can be so taxing."

Xavier shakes his head. "I'll meet you ladies inside. I'm going to water the rosebush. Apparently Lila doesn't know how." Xavier narrows his eyes at me.

I glance over to the rosebush and see the sad, drooping and curling leaves.

"Oops," I mouth at Xavier.

"We will go over proper care and watering. Again."

"Can't wait for that lecture." I grin and kiss Xavier's cheek.

He chuckles, and I know I'm forgiven for being a deadbeat gardener.

"C'mon, Jess. I'll let you put make-up on me while we wait for Mr. Green Thumb to resuscitate my roses. Then we'll get dinner."

Jessica smiles and inside I rejoice. Her smile is definitely worth a dreaded make-up application.

The 50's style diner couldn't be any cuter. And Jessica couldn't look any cuter as she shoves onion rings dripping with ranch into her mouth.

"So much for yoga today," I say as I cheerfully eat another fry.

Jessica taps her finger against her lip as though I've made her think of something. "What kind of exercise can I do now that I'm pregnant?"

I shrug. "I don't know. We could look for some prenatal yoga. I know I've heard of that. You can still go for walks."

Xavier intervenes, enlightening us both. "Actually, you can do whatever you were doing for exercise before getting pregnant, just with some modifications."

There it is again, that stab of jealousy. Irrational, I know.

"How do you know so much?" Jessica asks.

Xavier shifts uncomfortably. I haven't told Jessica about Gigi's pregnancy. I would have, if I'd seen her last night. And this morning her baby drama definitely took precedence over my baby drama.

"It's something I've dealt with before. How about milkshakes for dessert?" Xavier motions to the server.

The subject change couldn't be any more obvious. I look at Jessica, who's looking to me for understanding. *I'll tell you later,* I mouth at her.

She nods, appeased.

We order our milkshakes, and the banter returns to normal. Nobody mentions Cade, and frankly, it's hard not to. We've been on so many double dates together that it's glaringly obvious who's missing from our group. It's like a big blond elephant is sitting in the empty spot beside Xavier.

Conversation flows freely between me and Jessica, but Xavier is quiet, randomly looking at his phone. With Cade absent, there's no one for Xavier to toss ideas around with. Usually the guys would be discussing the recent reports out of Wall Street, the discovery of yet another exoplanet, or people they knew way back when.

Xavier pays the tab amid protests from Jessica. I don't even try. I've endured his lecture on paying for dates. How I feel about the word 'bitch' is how Xavier feels about girls paying for dates.

Jessica's relatively good mood has soured on our drive home from dinner.

From the backseat of Xavier's car I hear sniffling.

"You ok, Jess?" The concern in Xavier's voice is touching.

"Why is he doing this?" Jessica's voice is small.

"He's scared," Xavier says with absolute certainty.

"Me too." Jessica whispers despondently.

My heart lurches. I've seen Jessica through painful break-ups and never heard her sound so dejected. I turn around and reach into the backseat. When I find Jessica's hand I give it a strong squeeze.

How much longer will Cade keep this up?

I have no desire to be at The Pain Shoppe today. Jessica's intermittent crying woke me up multiple times throughout the night. I got out of bed at three a.m., leaving a sleeping Xavier behind, and went to console Jessica. With my arms wrapped around her, Jessica finally fell asleep.

Now I'm headed into work and I'm totally exhausted. When I pull up I see two large white vans parked out front.

Crap. I forgot about the television crews. They start filming today. Granite gives me a dirty look the second he sees me, staring in disgust at my unkempt bun and no make-up face. I don't know why he cares so much. It's not like I'm even going to be on his stupid show.

I had absolutely no time to get ready for work. After waiting all night to fall asleep I ended up oversleeping. Luckily my work clothes were clean. I would've forgotten deodorant if Xavier hadn't tossed it to me while I was dressing.

I wish I were staying home with Xavier. Instead I have to watch Granite run around like a fool. Is it just me or has he turned up the volume on his hip switch? Something tells me this whole reality show thing is going to make Granite more manic than ever. *Greeaat.*

Marco appears at my desk and motions for me to follow him. With an armful of hair styling implements and a make up bag, he leads me to the break room.

"What's going on?" I ask when we arrive.

Marco points to a chair. "Sit." He orders. "Granite has asked me to do your hair and make-up, on the off chance the camera catches you."

Oh Lord. My eyes are rolling, my head is shaking. I don't look that bad.

"Do what you must," I mutter, crossing my arms in defiance. I don't have to like it.

In just ten minutes my bun looks perfectly round and big, like I have way more hair than I actually do. It's teased beyond measure, but somehow it still looks sleek. My make-up is understated, the way I would actually wear it. Marco knows me well enough by now. No bright Jeri lipstick for me.

"There, you're perfect." Marco steps back to admire his handiwork.

"Thanks." It irritates me that Granite has ordered this make-over. There are a few things I'd like to re-do about him.

The camera crews are more annoying than I ever believed they could be. Every time I turn around, one of them is in my way. I was picturing two guys and a camera, but this is ridiculous. Seven guys are crowding up the walkways, following Granite Alexa around. And Granite cannot get enough. Not only has he increased the sway of his hip switch, he also has his chin higher than usual. It's like he has been practicing in a mirror. It's more dramatic than I've ever seen him, even in his haughtiest moments.

None of this matters, because in twelve minutes, Xavier will be here to take me to lunch. One hour away from this madhouse sounds amazing.

I'm checking out a client when Granite approaches my desk. I ignore him while I smile at the guest warmly and send her on her way. *See what a good employee I am?*

"Lila, have you had a chance to meet the crew yet?"

"Not formally."

Granite turns to the group of men standing behind him, pointing to each person as he ticks off their names. "Roberto, Will, Chase, Markusen, Cooper, Alfie, and Bob."

I resist the urge to roll my eyes. I refuse to be held accountable for remembering their names when they are introduced to me in such an asinine way.

I smile politely in their direction. "Nice to meet all of you."

Two of the men are looking at me like they are enjoying the view just a little too much. If I weren't at work, I would tell them where they could put their eyes. I settle for curling my lip at them.

Granite looks over my head and turns to mush before he can get to the point of why he has singled me out. He pushes past me, eager to greet whoever has caught his eye. A guy from the crew presses a button on his camera, and they begin filming.

"Xavier Townsend. Granite Alexa."

I turn at the sound of my boyfriend's name. Xavier is just in time.

Xavier looks at Granite. "Hello," he replies. He reaches to shake Granite's waiting hand.

"We met at your club the other night. You probably don't recognize me in my day time clothes." Granite winks conspiratorially at Xavier.

My mouth opens, stunned. Granite was one of the cross dressers at Xavier's club a couple nights ago. Holy crap! Xavier somehow remains professional, nodding evenly. *How does Xavier do that?*

"I remember now. Did you enjoy yourself?" Xavier's voice is pleasant, detached. The club owners voice.

"Immensely." Granite gestures around the expansive salon. "I hope you enjoy yourself here today. I would be happy to comp whatever service you've booked."

"I appreciate that, Mr. Alexa, but I'm not here for a service."

"Granite, please. What brings you in? Is there something I can help you with?" Suddenly Granite's voice has a flirtatious lilt to it. *You have got to be flipping kidding me!*

Xavier either doesn't hear the change in Granite's voice or chooses not to acknowledge it. "I'm here to take my girlfriend to lunch." Xavier peers past Granite and makes eye contact with me. "Lila, are you ready, baby?"

I sail past a surprised Granite. As hard as it is, I ignore my desire to elbow him.

"I'll have her back on time." Xavier jokes as though he's talking to my father.

Granite holds up his hands, and for the first time I notice his nails are painted black. "Take all the time you need." The man—and I use that term loosely—is simpering.

Ugh, I don't know who I dislike more, caustic Granite or fawning Granite. I find myself vowing to start thinking seriously about what I'll do after graduation. I must get away from this crazy person.

With Xavier's arm around my waist, we head for the exit. Jeri stares as we leave The Pain Shoppe. I can't blame the poor girl. I was struck dumb the first time I saw Xavier too.

"You aren't going to Townsend again tonight?" I stare at Xavier in shock.

"No. I need a break from that place. And, uh, there's something that I have to do." Xavier looks furtively at his watch.

"Do you have somewhere to be?" I'm starting to feel annoyed. It's the fourth time Xavier has checked his watch since I got home from work.

"Not yet."

I finish changing out of my work clothes and put my hands on my hips.

"What's going on, Xavier?"

Xavier sighs. "Nothing, Lila. Can you just quit asking questions?"

"No. You're being weird."

Xavier ignores me and walks to my bedroom door. "Find Jess. Let's go get something for dinner."

I stomp past Xavier and into Jessica's room. Behind me I hear Xavier's faint chuckle.

By the time we're finished with our meal I've forgotten about Xavier's odd behavior. He has been so funny and engaging during dinner, making Jessica and I laugh with his stories of Granite Alexa and his crew at Townsend.

Xavier glances down at his watch again, suddenly antsy. "Lets go, ladies."

I raise my brows. "Late for something?"

"You'll just have to wait and see." Xavier looks like he has a secret. And whatever it is, he's excited about it.

Why has Xavier brought us to a sports park? Is he expecting me to get on the track and run off the calories from dinner? Not happening.

Xavier still has that stupid grin on his face, and he isn't giving anything up. I would know, since I badgered him the whole ten minute drive here.

"A park?" Jessica asks in disbelief.

"C'mon." Xavier gets out of his car. Even his walk is excited.

Jessica and I stay in the car, giggling as Xavier starts walking. In his excitement, he hasn't noticed that we aren't with him.

A few more steps and Xavier turns around, eyes narrowed. He probably can't see into the car anyhow, since it's nighttime and the windows are tinted so dark.

"Now." I can't hear him, but I can read his lips, and he looks all *Mr. Boss Man*.

"Ok, ok. Keep your pants on." My response sends Jessica into a fresh round of giggles. She has cried so much in the last two days, it's nice to hear her laugh.

Xavier gives me his stern look when we join him outside the car. For the hundredth time I feel thankful that I don't work for him. Though Granite Alexa isn't a breeze either.

"Follow me." Xavier leads the way, giving me an opportunity to admire his physique. Will I ever tire of those strong shoulders?

Jessica grabs my hand and whispers, "I think your boyfriend is craaazy."

"Certifiable," I whisper back, giving Jessica's hand a squeeze.

We walk around a brick building, past all the sports fields, and head toward the children's playground. In the distance I can see light, but it looks like the light is moving. What the heck is going on?

We get closer and the picture becomes clearer. The moving lights are the flickering flames of at least fifty candles. And there's Cade, standing front and center in front of the playground. *Oh my God. Is this what I think it is?*

Beside me I hear Jessica's gasp.

Cade's eyes, looking so contrite, are for Jessica only. He holds out a hand, and she goes to him.

Cade clears his throat. "Jessica, I'm so sorry. We made this baby together, and I didn't act like that. I was stupid, and scared, but I'm not anymore. I want us to be a family. I want our son or daughter to play on this playground. And play soccer on those fields. Jessica, I love you, and I would be doing this soon anyway. Our baby just bumped up my timetable." Cade gracefully pulls a box from his pocket and sinks down on one knee in the sand.

"Jessica, will you please be my wife?" Cade's face looks hopeful in the flickering light.

My best friend is so overcome she can only nod. Finally, in a teary voice, her answer comes out.

"Yes."

Cade slips the ring on her finger, and before he stands upright, he kisses her stomach. He whispers something to the tiny baby, but it's too quiet to hear.

Xavier winds his hand around my waist and guides me away, giving the happy, newly engaged couple a little privacy to celebrate.

"You knew?" I ask in wonder, looking up at Xavier. I'm overwhelmed. My best friend is pregnant and engaged. Three months ago, we were drinking green juice and going to classes like non-pregnant, single college girls.

"Lila, you're crying."

"No I'm not," I argue. "There must be a cat nearby. I'm terribly allergic." Not true. I'm not allergic to anything. Hastily I wipe the evidence off my face.

Xavier smiles. "Birthday Girl, you're not as stoic as you pretend to be."

I lean my head against his chest. "Don't be so proud of yourself. You haven't unlocked any secrets."

I feel, rather than hear, Xavier's chuckle. It makes me want to snuggle in closer, if that were possible. I sneak a peak at the couple standing in the sand. Cade is hugging Jessica, holding her as though she's the most delicate flower.

Oh Jess, how did we get here? You're starting a family, and I'm in love.

"Coffee for my lovely Lila."

Xavier's soft voice wakes me gently, his breath tickling my ear. I sit up in my bed, stretching. Xavier waits patiently for my stretch to be over, then hands over my coffee.

"It's cashew milk." Xavier assures me.

I smile up at him. The man knows how I like my coffee. *A girl could get used to this.*

I sip the steamy liquid, noticing that Xavier doesn't have a cup. "Aren't you having any?"

He shakes his head, brown hair still tousled from sleep. "I had a cup downstairs with Cade. Jessica's still sleeping."

I nod, happy to hear it. She needs her rest. "I still can't believe you helped Cade put all that together last night."

Xavier looks at me pointedly. "Now you know why I took that phone call outside. It was Cade. He needed someone to talk to."

My face flames. I feel beyond embarrassed about the way I acted. Of course I trust Xavier. It was silly of me to be suspicious. Stupid Gigi and her mind games.

"Hey," Xavier warns. "Don't start. Everything is fine."

I nod. "I'm relieved Cade came around. Maybe my ass-chewing did some good."

Xavier eyes me. "Wouldn't you rather think he came around on his own?"

I pout. "I guess so."

"Lila, Lila full of fire," Xavier says in sing-song.

I stick out my tongue at him.

Xavier laughs. "You better put down that coffee."

"Or what?" I challenge.

Xavier rears back, ready to attack. "Or you'll be washing your bedding."

I get my coffee on my nightstand with less than a second to spare before Xavier jumps on me.

CHAPTER NINETEEN

Dinner is a family affair tonight, our little family of four. We sit at the dining room table, keeping Cade company as he whips up the lasagna that was requested by his lady love. Jessica isn't shy about her hunger.

"I eat first," she warns us, pointing her fork at me and Xavier.

Cade sets the hot lasagna on the top of the stove and looks at Jessica with concern. "Wait for it to cool, ok? I don't want you to burn your mouth."

Oh gag, Cade. Why don't you blow on it for her?

"Fine," Jessica says with impatience. "Lila, tell me more about this film crew. You had to sign a release?"

Xavier interjects. "Yeah, what was that about? Nobody told me those bozo's were going to be hanging around you."

I choose to ignore Xavier's comment.

"They are there to film Granite's life for a reality show. You know, Pain Shoppe owner by day, cross dresser by night."

"So why do you have to sign a release?" Jess presses.

"In case I make it onto the final product. Highly unlikely, I'm sure." I wave my hand dismissively.

"That's wild," Jess says. "I'd watch a reality show about Granite's life."

"You'd watch a reality show about anything."

"True," Jessica agrees.

I turn to Xavier. "By the way, Granite wants me to ask if you'd be willing to sign a release too. The cameras were rolling when you came in yesterday. He was all kinds of starstruck. Something about being associated with someone like you."

Xavier shrugs. "I guess, but I don't think my conversation with him was that exciting."

"It wasn't. But just in case. I have the release with me, at Granite's request."

The conversation comes to a halt when Cade carries the lasagna pan over and places it in the middle of the table.

"Dig in."

We all sit back and watch with poorly suppressed laughter as Jessica takes a massive piece.

"Kiss my ass," she announces without looking up at us.

The flood gates open, and we're all in hysterics. Jessica's appetite is to be admired. I'm not laughing for long. One bite of my lasagna shuts me right up.

"Cade, this is flipping amazing. You're officially the cook." I smile at him, my first genuine smile in his direction since I accosted him outside his house. Was that only Friday morning? I feel like so much has happened since then.

Cade nods politely. "Position accepted." He sounds so serious.

I don't think Cade knows how to act around me yet. Maybe I scared him. *Well, that's fine.* Hurt my best friend, and I'm going to rain down on you. It's a good lesson for him to learn.

Xavier takes control of the dinner conversation. Jessica has barely come up for air since she began eating, and it's obvious Cade and I have a weird vibe going.

"Cade, Jessica, I know you guys just got engaged last night, but do you have any thoughts regarding wedding planning?"

Cade looks to Jessica, but she's chewing. "We discussed it today. We'd like to do something quickly. Small, but special. Right, babe?" He reaches over to squeeze Jessica's hand. The small diamond on her ring finger sparkles in the overhead light.

Jessica swallows her bite. "Yes, small but special. Lila, when can you get a Saturday off from Alexa?"

"Whenever you need. I'll switch a day with Brandee. Who's also pregnant, by the way."

"Awww. Cool. Maybe you're next?"

Xavier sputters on his water, coughing hard. Jessica giggles.

My head is shaking adamantly as I smack Xavier's back. "Um, no. I take my birth control at the same time every night. No error."

"Ladies." Xavier clears his throat, recovered from the coughing fit. "Please don't make me pass out. I have a proposition for the betrothed."

I gesture out to the space across the table. "The floor is yours."

Xavier speaks eagerly. "I talked to my mom today and told her about you guys. She offered to host your wedding."

"In Tahoe?" Jessica screeches. Her blue eyes light up with excitement.

Xavier nods. "Have you been there in the summer? It's incredible. And that way, Lila can meet my parents."

Wow. I'm stunned.

Jessica actually puts down her fork. "Are you sure? I mean, your parents don't even know us."

Cade clears his throat. "That's not totally true," he corrects Jessica, his face somber. "They know my family."

Xavier closes his eyes. It weighs heavily on him that Brent was killed. Ultimately Brent made his own choices, but Xavier knows how he influenced Cade's big brother. Just like Gigi and their baby, Xavier lives every day with his guilt over Brent's death.

"My parents would really like to do this for you." Xavier's voice is quietly hopeful. He's looking right into Cade's eyes as he speaks.

Cade is quiet for a beat, then nods his head. "I certainly can't pass up a wedding in Tahoe. It's been long enough. My parents will be fine with it."

Xavier reaches his hand across the table, offering it to Cade. Cade takes it, and they shake.

"I wish you didn't have to go to work," I whine to Xavier. I give him my best pouty face.

Xavier looks annoyed, but I know it's not at me. "Me too. You know who will be there tonight."

Gigi... Xavier hasn't seen or heard from her since our tell-all coffee date. *I hope she goes away.*

"Keep her in the cage tonight. Lock her in there."

Xavier laughs. "Lila, you're very funny."

"I wasn't joking," I murmur irritably. The thought of Gigi and Xavier spending Saturday night together makes me uneasy. I keep thinking about her threat and wondering what her next offensive will be. Xavier swears she has one.

He takes a step backward towards the front door, but I follow him instead of releasing him.

"Lila, I have to go." Xavier's tone is reluctantly chastising.

I press into him, letting my breasts rub against his chest. He inhales sharply.

"Are you sure?"

His exhale is deep, long. "Yes," he growls.

I back away. "All right, fine." I know he needs to go. He's the owner, and he hasn't been there for the past two nights. "You can come over when you're finished." I know he won't take me up on my offer.

Xavier's brown hair moves as his head turns with his silent declination. "I'm not waking you up at four a.m., Lila."

"Thought I'd offer. I wouldn't mind, you know."

Xavier leans in to kiss my forehead. "I love you, Birthday Girl."

"Love you too. Now go be the big boss man."

Xavier turns, and I swat his butt as he walks through the door. He looks back at me with a smirk and climbs into his BMW. I shut the door and go in search for Jessica and Cade.

"So you met her for coffee. What happened?"

Jessica and I are seated on the couch in the living room, sipping cups of pear and ginger tea like old times. It feels familiar and oh, so welcome in this time of drastic change. Cade has gone to bed, giving Jessica and me some time for girl talk.

"Well, for starters, she told me what happened to end her marriage to Xavier."

"Oh, oh, is this where you tell me what you said you would tell me later?"

I nod my head. "Yes. Ok, just remember, Xavier isn't the person he was when he was with Gigi."

Jessica looks exasperated, pointing back at herself with one finger. "Do you remember who you're talking to here?"

I nod. "His number one supporter, I know. How could I forget?" I take a deep breath, the feeling of reticence strong. I accept Xavier's past, but it doesn't mean I enjoy retelling it. "Ok, here goes. Essentially, Gigi was newly pregnant and found out Xavier was cheating on her. She saw it happening, ran away from what she saw, fell, and miscarried the baby."

Jessica gasps, wrapping her arms around her stomach protectively.

"I know, not a super great story for you to hear right now."

"No, it's ok. It's a good reminder that I need to find a doctor. Add that to my to-do list." Jessica writes in the air on a pretend list. "So is that all? Was there more? Did she hit on you again? Try to steal you away from Xavier with that hot body of hers?"

"I can't believe that was going on when I first met her." I'm still not sure how I missed the signs.

Jessica's expression is apologetic. "I didn't catch it either. But it does explain how she was toward me that first night at Townsend and the breakfast after."

"I guess that should have been our clue. Who knows? Xavier says she's underhanded. I feel like I need to be on the look out for her now. She said the oddest thing right before I walked out on our coffee. She said—"

Jessica interrupts me, overcome by her intrigue. "You walked out on her?"

I nod. "Apparently it's my thing now. I walked out of dinner with Xavier the night before too."

Jessica's eyebrows are raised. "Because?"

My voice is small. I hate admitting someone else was right, and Jessica certainly was. She called it. "Xavier didn't want me going to see Gigi."

Jessica is smug. "I won't even say 'I told you so.'"

I ignore her. "I walked out on *Gigi* because she was so arrogant, so certain that she had ended my relationship with Xavier by telling me what he did in their marriage. It was like she owned him, and he was her pet and needed to be put back in his cage. I told her that I was sorry for her loss but my relationship was none of her business. And then, right before I walked out, she looked at me and said, "Good luck. You're going to need it." How ominous does that sound?"

Jessica smacks her forehead lightly. "Lordy, this woman is batshit crazy."

"No kidding."

"It sounds like she's still in love with him."

I look at Jessica, my mouth agape. "Now you're the one who's crazy."

"Think about it. She warns you multiple times. She goes out of her way to make sure you know what Xavier has done in the past. Why would she go to these lengths? Haven't you wondered?"

"I don't know. She always seems like she hates him."

"There's a thin line between love and hate."

I groan.

Jessica smiles. "Sorry, I had to. It was too easy."

"Well, my dear Jessica, I'm exhausted. And you have given me much to think about." I rise from my place on the couch. "Are you coming?"

"No, I have some wedding planning to do. I need to get a dress, and so do you."

"Ok. Talk to Xavier tomorrow. He can coordinate things between you and his mom."

"Get a dress, Lila." Jessica's voice is stern. She knows shopping is not my favorite pastime.

I lean down and kiss the top of Jessica's head. "Don't tell me what to do. Goodnight."

Xavier has worked all night and now, at eight a.m., he's probably sound asleep. I, on the other hand, am wide awake and ready for the day. I could go downstairs and be the third wheel for breakfast *again*. But I'd rather not.

I sit up and survey my room. The tree outside my bedroom is tall enough that I can hear birds chirping from their perch on the branches. The homeyness of it makes me sad. Where will I be in six months? This house will probably sell right away to the parents of another college student or a young couple.

Photography is my passion, but how can I really make a life on that? Definitely not on Day One after college. Most photographers are in it for a long time before it becomes their main job. And for some it never does.

My father's warnings about choosing photography as my major are coming back to me. I can still hear his stern voice. "Your camera is a hobby. Not a career." But that was four years ago, and graduation and real life seemed so far away. I had won a full ride to college based on my skills with my camera, so picking photography as my major was a natural choice. I wrote his words off as nonsense.

Panic begins to rise as I think through all this. I can't make it on my hourly wage from Alexa. That job is part-time. And I can't go full time, because Brandee is there, and with one kid and another on the way, she needs the money more than I do. Going back to Newport Beach wouldn't be the worst outcome, but what about Xavier? Where does my boyfriend come into play? Just thinking about all this is giving me a headache.

Across from me on top of my dresser is my camera. It has been sitting practically unused since I met

Xavier. For years my camera was how I chose to experience emotion, and then Xavier came along. With his charming smile and green eyes, he has become my outlet for emotion. But Xavier isn't here this morning, and my mind is full of worry. I need a way to work through this distress without him. I need my camera.

I get up, the idea of going off, just me and my camera, making me rush. Suddenly I need my camera, desperately. And I know exactly where I'm going with it.

Fulton Gardens is as beautiful as I remember it, even without the excitement of a first date to add to its magic.

I arrive ten minutes before it opens and take the opportunity to shoot the house, in all its old-fashioned splendor, with the sun rising behind it. The sun hasn't gone above the house yet, and I capture the lens flare. It reminds me of somewhere in the South, a house that Scarlett O'Hara would have lived in. Stepping back, I re-position myself and take more pictures with the little wooden Fulton Gardens sign in the bottom corner of the lens.

The front door opens, and Mrs. Fulton walks out. Her gray hair is in that bun again, and her voice reaches out to me softly.

"Hello, dear. We don't open for a few more minutes, but you can come inside anyway." She smiles kindly at me and gestures into the house.

I stoop and gather my camera bag. The camera bounces on my chest as I hurry forward. Mrs. Fulton looks so old and frail, I don't want her holding the door for me any longer than she has to.

"Thank you, Mrs. Fulton." I say when I reach her, reaching out to hold the door for her. She shuffles in and goes to the tea station next to her desk.

"What is your name dear? You seem to know mine. I'm sorry if we've met before and I don't remember. Old age is a pesky thing."

"That's all right. I don't expect you to remember me. We met almost two months ago when I came here on a first date. You may recall the man I came here with. Xavier Townsend?"

Mrs. Fulton's eye are alight with recognition. "Oh yes." She claps her hands together with happiness. "He's a very nice young man. His dad was a nice man too, back in the day. Would you like some tea, dear?"

"Please. I can help you with that." I go to Mrs. Fulton's side, where she is setting two cups in their saucers.

"You pour," she instructs, pointing to the carafe of hot water sitting on a portable burner. Her finger shakes a little as she points. I see why she would prefer I pour. "What kind of tea do you like?"

"I'll have what you're having," I reply, focusing on pouring the steaming water without spilling.

Mrs. Fulton leads me to the yellow flowered couches in the middle of the living room. She pats the space next to her, gesturing for me to sit beside her. I set down our cups on the coffee table and remove my camera and bag from my shoulder, gingerly setting them on the table beside my cup.

Mrs. Fulton hands me a packet. "I hope you like chamomile."

"That's lovely, thank you." I take the packet and rip it open, remove the tea bag and dunk it into the hot water. I hold my hand out for Mrs. Fulton's tea. "I can prepare yours, if you'd like."

Mrs. Fulton sighs, the sound not altogether unhappy. "I wish I could say no thank you, that I can prepare my own tea, but that's just not the case anymore." She hands me the packet and smiles wistfully. "If it were right in front of me, I could do it, but reaching that far makes me afraid of falling." I hand her the tea, and she says, "Thank you."

I smile at her, so happy to have been of help to her. What is it about this old woman that makes me want to take care of her?

"What is your name again, dear?" Mrs. Fulton looks at me apologetically.

"My name is Lila Mitchell."

"Oh, that's right. Such a lovely name. What brings you here to Fulton Gardens so early on a Sunday morning?"

"I wanted to take pictures. Photography is my major and my passion. The first time I was here, I didn't have my camera, and I knew I wanted to come back. There's just too much beauty here for me to pass up."

"I agree with you. There is much to be seen beyond those doors. If you don't mind me asking, was there a second date with Mr. Townsend?"

I grin and nod. "Yes. And many dates since. We're serious." The smile on my face must give it all away, because Mrs. Fulton looks delighted.

"I knew he was smitten with you. In all my years here, I've never had a young man call ahead of time and request his date be allowed to choose a rose bush from our garden. Normally we sell those to nurseries."

My sweet, romantic Xavier. Of course he would do something extraordinary.

I know my grin is lovesick. "Xavier is certainly one of a kind. We planted the rosebush in my backyard."

"And how is it doing? It can be very difficult to grow roses in the desert."

Simply put, the rosebush is not thriving. Is it my black thumb or the harsh desert it's trying to live in? Briefly I contemplate lying to her, but I can't.

"Well, let's just say that you're right, it's difficult to grow roses in the desert."

"I find the closer you are to the city, the harder they are to grow. Who knows, perhaps the native soil is tainted with all the debauchery," muses Mrs. Fulton with a grin.

I laugh out loud. "Does that mean I can blame the struggling rosebush on Xavier? He owns a nightclub on the strip, and he planted the bush. Maybe he inserted debauchery right into the soil."

Mrs. Fulton laughs with me. "Maybe so. My only advice is to keep feeding and watering it."

I nod. "Will do."

Mrs. Fulton pats my knee. "Well, dear, I should let you get to your picture taking. Thank you for stopping your busy life to have tea with an old woman."

"The pleasure was all mine. It has been wonderful spending a little time with you." An idea dawns on me. "Would you mind if I took your photo?"

"Why would you want to capture these wrinkles on film? Oh, Heavens." Mrs. Fulton smoothes her pulled back hair and straightens her shirt.

I grin. "Is that a yes?"

Mrs. Fulton winks at me. "I suppose."

I beam at her. I have an idea. I gather my camera and bag from the table and switch lenses. A couple adjustments to the camera settings, and I'm ready.

"Mrs. Fulton, look at the camera and tell me what advice you would give to me on my wedding day."

The old woman is quiet, pondering the answer to my question. The wisdom is there in her twinkling eyes, her deep wrinkles, her serene face. This is what I'm after. I shoot quickly, taking multiple shots before Mrs. Fulton has the chance to change her expression.

"Lila, I would tell you that love is shown in many, many different ways. Look for the love in your husband's actions and words."

Mrs. Fulton has just given me the best advice I've ever heard. An uncharacteristic burst of emotion hits me. I set my camera down on the couch and lean over, gently folding the sweet, old woman into a hug.

CHAPTER TWENTY

These last ten days have been a flurry of activity. Who knew wedding planning was such a strenuous task? Jessica's dress alone took three separate appointments before it was perfect. Apparently the Townsend name carries some weight in Vegas, because the bridal shop was only too happy to cater to us on such short notice. Jessica has herself a new best friend in Mrs. Townsend. They are on the phone constantly, discussing details. Color? Theme? Time of day? Arch or no arch? Flowers? Cake flavor? Should there be flowers on the cake? Thank goodness this wedding is being planned in two weeks, because I don't think I could handle this for much longer.

I was actually relieved on the days I had to go into The Pain Shoppe. Granite has been in more than usual, thanks to his annoying reality show. They want plenty of footage of him at work, so they can draw a real comparison to his nighttime activities. It's not like he works anyway. Mostly he just stalks around the place and irritates the living crap out of people. I'm beyond envious of the spa staff who are busy in their quiet, babbling brook music treatment rooms. They are totally removed from Granite and his alligator loafers.

Granite has been way nicer to me now that he knows who my boyfriend is. He was like a kid at Christmas when I gave him Xavier's signed release form. Granite sees Xavier as some kind of Vegas royalty. I'm sure he wonders how the hell an underwaxed commoner such as myself landed the high and mighty Xavier. As long as I'm on Granite's nice list, I couldn't care less what he thinks. And pretty soon I'll get away from The Pain Shoppe and its bizarre owner for a whole weekend.

Jessica and Cade's big day is nearly here. I'm thrilled for them and my three day weekend with Xavier. It's quite the perk that it'll be in Tahoe, a place I've never been. Meeting Xavier's parents is another perk. I feel like I'll know Xavier even better after seeing him around his parents.

As if whirlwind wedding planning wasn't enough to excite emotions, I had to break the news of my parents' plan to sell our house. Jessica looked completely distraught when I told her, but dependable Cade didn't blink an eye. He took out his phone and began punching numbers on his calculator, asking me questions along the way. I didn't know the asking price but Cade was able to find the area comp's and estimate. Something about multiplying the size of the house by dollars per square foot. Just hearing him talk about the math problem he was working on so excitedly was making my brain hurt. Photography is where my brain lights up. Math? No thanks.

Cade, armed with his phone calculator and a wide, trusting Cade-like smile, announced that he and Jessica could buy the house. I put Cade in contact with my mom, and that was that. Now they're in talks, not that there's too much to be said. Cade's dad is a realtor and will be representing both parties. My parents set an asking price and knocked 10k off it as a wedding present. Then Cade's dad waived his commission as *his* wedding present to the happy couple.

I love when loose ends are tied up. The wedding is planned, the house is being purchased, and Jessica and Cade have a place to raise their little one. Of course, this leaves me homeless after graduation. Jessica insisted that I don't need to move out right away, but I don't want to rain on her married with a baby parade. It's something I'll have to start thinking about soon.

Everything is just about perfect. Now it's time to pack and embark on our wedding weekend in Tahoe.

Xavier finds me in my room, assembling outfits for our getaway. Clothes are strewn all over my bed, including all the new clothes Jessica and I went shopping for yesterday after we got off work.

"Hey you," Xavier comes up behind me and nuzzles my neck.

"Hey yourself," I murmur, turning around and going straight for a kiss. I haven't seen him in nearly two days, thanks to our opposite schedules on Tuesdays and my outing with Jessica last night. Our kiss deepens, and I want him now, on top of all the clothes I plan to wear this weekend. Without breaking our kiss we stumble together toward my bed.

"Well," Xavier says after, sitting up and straightening his shirt. I bound half-naked off the bed and toss Xavier the rest of his clothes.

"Put these on. You're leaving an ass print on all my clothes."

"Oh no," Xavier says in mocking. "An ass print? Everyone will know what you were up to."

I laugh as I pull on my jeans. "You mean what *we* were up to."

Xavier stands and dresses his bottom half. He turns around to my bed and attempts to unsnarl all the clothes we've just made a mess of.

I join him in the task. Xavier comes across my new flannel shirt and holds it up. "Are you planning on chopping some wood while we're there?"

"Haha. No. Jessica insisted I buy it. When it comes to fashion, I usually take her advice. You don't like it?"

Xavier tosses the shirt aside. "I like your fashion sense."

I smirk. "That was an artful answer."

"I love your tight jeans and t-shirts, Lila. And that little red dress you wore the night we met."

I wiggle my eyebrows suggestively. "Maybe I'll wear it for you again sometime."

"I'm going to make sure you do." He says it authoritatively.

Oh, boss man Xavier. I kind of like when he acts so commanding. *Speaking of boss man...*

"How was work the past two nights? You haven't said much about it."

Uh-oh. Xavier's open face shuts down, and his shoulders slump as if something heavy has been placed there.

I toss down the shirt I was folding and grab Xavier's wrist. "What is it?"

Gigi. It has to be. *This is it. This is what I've been waiting for.*

Xavier sighs and rubs his forehead. "Maybe we should just drop it. I took care of it. No big deal."

Who are these words meant to reassure, me or him? They aren't working either way. I watch as Xavier trembles. *What the hell happened?*

"Xavier, you need to start talking. Now." My voice is calm, though I'm anything but. My stomach is starting to feel hot. *Lila, Lila full of fire.*

Xavier makes space on the bed for me to sit. I do, then wait while Xavier stands in front of me and shuffles his feet nervously.

"Spit it out." My voice has raised a few octaves. My imagination is taking off, and I need the truth so I can pull it back in.

"Let me start at the beginning. It's a normal Tuesday night, except Gigi is working and she usually doesn't. Unless there's big money in the booths, I haven't been spending too much time walking the floor. Mostly I help the bartenders or hole up in the office and do paperwork, liquor orders, whatever. I'm in the office when Gigi comes to find me. She has a key to the office, of course, because she's part owner. Only the owners and managers have keys."

My stomach is rolling, waiting for the next part.

"Gigi had been in the sky. I promise, I ignored her." His green eyes are wide as he proclaims his innocence.

"Finish the story." My voice is a whisper. *So this is how we will end. Gigi was right. Xavier will break my heart.*

Xavier is running his hands through his hair now. "Gigi comes over and stands next to me. I feel rude, ignoring her, so I try to make small talk. And then she just starts crying. She says, 'Don't you know what today is?' And when I don't, she cries even harder. Then she says, 'Today is the day our baby died.' And what the fuck was I supposed to do? It makes me sad too, you know? So I hug her. I'm thinking, Lila wouldn't mind a hug. It's just a hug between two people who are remembering something really sad. But then Gigi sees it as more and pushes me down, back into my chair."

I drop my head into my hands. *Oh God, oh God...* This is it. In my mind I see Gigi in her hot pants and bra top, having just come from the cage, throwing herself at Xavier and knowing he will succumb. I force my gaze back up. I'm strong. I can take this.

Xavier pushes on, even though he looks like he might throw up. "She climbs on top of me and tries to kiss me. I grabbed her by the shoulders and told her no. I said, 'I love Lila.' She just laughed and took off her top. 'You used to love these.'" Xavier shudders at the memory.

I picture the scene as he describes it. Gigi sitting astride Xavier, the only thing keeping her from being completely naked are those skin tight hot pants. Xavier promised he was horrified but in my imagination he looks intrigued at Gigi's big breasts bouncing right in his face.

Xavier's disgusted voice breaks through my disturbing mental images. "I told her to get off me, that I was serious and I didn't want her anymore. I said, 'We're divorced and I love Lila.' She was mad. So mad. She grabbed her top and said, 'You loved me too. Don't worry, one day you will fuck up.' She said it like she was absolutely certain. Then she left the office."

Xavier looks scared and sad, like a small child who needs reassurance after a bad choice. He sits next to me, looking for that reassurance. I'm frozen, unable to offer what he needs.

My heart is hammering in my chest, gratefulness filling my body. *He didn't do it.* The joy and elation I feel is paramount to any other happiness I've ever experienced. I turn to him.

"Xavier, oh my God. I thought the ending to that story was going to be totally different. I'm so happy it wasn't." The relief feels so real as it floods through me. I jump into his arms, my hands running over his body as I try to erase the image of Gigi throwing herself at him. This man is mine. Not hers.

"Lila, I would never cheat on you. Don't you know that? I love you so much. You're the most important thing to me."

"I know, I know," I croon, my hands in his hair. "The way you told that story, and she's your ex-wife, and you made a baby together, and she was practically naked." I'm nearly panting as the words come tumbling out. "It all sounded so bad when it was combined. Why didn't you tell me sooner?"

I feel Xavier's shrug. "I was trying to process it all. It was so shocking, you know? Gigi hasn't cared about me in a long time. I don't understand why she does now."

Suddenly it all makes perfect sense. "It's because of me."

"What do you mean?"

I draw back so I can look Xavier in the eyes. "Have you loved anybody else since her?"

"No."

"She doesn't want you to love me. I'm a threat to her. Xavier, she's still in love with you."

Xavier looks blown away. "No way."

I nod my head slowly. "No question. It makes so much sense now. I couldn't figure out why she kept warning me, why she was so persistent. At first I thought it was because she was trying to be my friend." I pause to shudder. Some friend. "Then I thought it was because she wanted to date me herself. When it became clear that I'm hetero and only interested in you, she still kept on with her warnings. That's when I couldn't understand her anymore. Why keep warning me?" I bring my hand up to my forehead, astonished. "Duh, how could I have missed it? How could *you* have missed it? You have way more experience than I do. Of course she's still in love with you."

Despite the situation, I feel weirdly proud of myself for finally figuring this all out. The many layers of Gigi Waters. The girl is like a damn onion.

"Why are you smiling?" he asks.

"Because we've solved the puzzle. Now we know what her angle was."

"Was? You think it's over?"

"Hopefully. I mean, how much more rejection can a person take? She was topless on your lap, and you told her no. That would be beyond humiliating. She would be just plain stupid if she didn't get the message."

Xavier's hand runs through his hair anxiously. "I hope you're right."

"Me too. Now listen to me." I bring my hands up and hold Xavier's face. "You did everything right. I'm so sorry that she used your loss to manipulate you. And you were right, I wouldn't have had a problem with you hugging her. But I will now. What's done is done, and we have to move forward. Let's focus on our trip to Tahoe. We're going to have a great time, ok?" It makes me sick inside to think of what happened with Gigi, but I know that right now I need to be the strong one.

Xavier nods quickly, eager to accept my words. This is the first time I've seen him so shaken. It must have been killing him.

Suddenly I feel protective of my big, strong, handsome, charming, arrogant, and bossy man. I will protect him, and us, from his conniving ex-wife.

"Tahoe, baby!" Jessica bursts into the kitchen, fresh from a ten hour sleep. She looks gorgeous, all soft, glowing skin and curled strawberry blonde locks. The white sundress she picked out as her traveling outfit looks amazing on her.

Jessica isn't the only person who's excited. I woke up before my alarm and couldn't go back to sleep. I'm dressed in my own newly acquired red sundress and my long brown hair has been brushed to shiny perfection. I added a little make-up because, truth be told, I want to impress Xavier's mom. I can't show up looking like a frump, especially beside my beautiful best friend.

I leave my coffee for a moment to do a happy dance with Jessica. When we finish she wraps me in a huge, warm hug.

"Oh, Lila. I'm so happy."

"I'm so happy for you. And I have an idea that might make you even happier. You know how you've been having some trouble getting a photographer for tomorrow?"

Jessica lets me go and stands back, stress clouding her face. "We will just have to improvise somehow. Mrs. Townsend suggested giving all the guests cameras and then having them leave the cameras so we can upload their photos. I guess that will just have to do."

The crestfallen look on my best friends face tells me that's not good enough. Lila to the rescue!

I rub my chin thoughtfully. "If only you knew a photographer who already has their camera packed and was planning to be in Tahoe this weekend."

"What? You would photograph my wedding? I thought you despised wedding photography?" Jessica looks genuinely perplexed.

"I do, in general. But I like capturing beauty. And because I know you, I know I'll find beauty in your special day."

Tears spring to Jessica's eyes. Oh geez, pregnant women and their tears. She's like a faucet these days.

And then she's jumping up and down again. "Yes, yes, yes!"

Jessica grabs my hands and I jump with her, our second happy dance of the morning.

Cade and Xavier choose now to make their appearance. Both men eye us with surprise.

"What's going on?" Cade asks in his serious Cade way.

Xavier watches with a smile. He likes when I act goofy.

Jessica goes to Cade and throws her arms dramatically around his neck. "My photographer woes are over. Lila's going to do it!"

Cade looks surprised. "I didn't know you were a photographer."

Jessica defends me to the objection hidden in Cade's tone. "I've told you before that photography is Lila's major. And she's amazing. She won a full ride to UNLV, thanks to Smiles by the Sea. It's a series of photographs she took when she was still in high school."

Xavier looks astonished. "Why didn't I know that? I assumed your scholarship was for good grades." He's using his demanding voice.

I shrug, feeling uncharacteristically shy. I'm not big on self-promotion. I head to the sink, rinsing out my coffee cup and placing it in the dishwasher.

Jessica answers for me. "Because Lila doesn't brag. Ever. But it's true."

I hold up my hand. "Enough about my talent, or whatever. We have a plane to catch."

"Don't forget your camera." Cade's reminder is meant nicely, and said in a very Cade-like way, but it's still annoying.

"It's already packed." I respond in a voice that is too pleasant to be genuine. Of course, Cade's ear isn't trained to disingenuous responses. He grew up in a house with Sunny, for God's sake. She's like a cheerleader at state finals with too much Vaseline on her teeth.

We head toward the front door, where all our suitcases are lined up. I see Cade's point in putting them there, even though last night I thought he was being ridiculous when he made the suggestion. Now nobody has to take the time to go back upstairs and retrieve them.

I'm the last one out the door, double checking the locks while Xavier puts our bags in his car.

Cade's waiting in his car but Jessica is next to the passenger side of the BMW, waiting for me.

"What's wrong?" I ask as I walk around the car.

"Wedding weekend!" Jessica explodes with exuberance, taking my hands and jumping up and down again.

Three happy dances before seven a.m.? Oh, fine.

CHAPTER TWENTY-ONE

Tahoe is breathtaking. The drive up the mountain, before the lake even came into view, was incredible. So much forest, such lush greenery. I'm in love.

Jessica is practically bouncing up and down in her seat like a girl on her way to Disneyland. Thank goodness for seat belts.

Xavier is concentrating hard on driving our rented SUV. All the twists and turns on these mountain roads makes me nervous too. Clearly Xavier was choice for driver. He's navigated these roads a dozen times since his parents moved here five years ago. Even Cade, control freak extraordinaire, agreed. That was his practical side coming into play. I'm glad Cade makes Jessica happy. He'd drive me crazy.

"How much longer?" Jessica whines from the backseat.

Xavier smiles. "Twenty. Look for signs for Incline Village."

Jessica nods, not that Xavier can see her. His eyes never drift from the road, but he looks happy. His grin is so cute, I wish I could reach over and hug him. Instead I settle for remembering how he woke me up in the middle of the night...

Jessica interrupts my reverie. Probably a good thing, considering soon I'll be meeting Xavier's parents. Hot and bothered isn't the state I want to be in for my first introduction.

"Lila, how irritating was that flight attendant? It was like she couldn't get enough. Ugh."

"I know." I mirror her tone, but honestly, I don't care. Women look at Xavier all the time. He's gorgeous. And Cade, for all his seriousness and pragmatism, is very easy on the eyes. Besides, leering flight attendants are the least of my problems. I have a scheming, red-haired ex-wife who tries to seduce my boyfriend. She's way more trouble than any flight attendant ogling my man.

Xavier, our unofficial tour guide, speaks up. "This is Incline Village. My parents live just off Lakeshore Boulevard."

We're all quiet as we take in the beauty of the place. It's extraordinary. Xavier makes a left and pulls up to a black wrought iron gate, then leans out the window to punch in the gate code.

I'm busy looking at the shrubbery that crawls up the walls, meant to provide the home privacy from the road. The gates open and Xavier pulls through, driving along the stone driveway toward the mansion before us. The home is sided with a reddish-brown wood and river stones. Beautifully landscaped flowers line the front of the house. Xavier parks and get out, but the three of us sit, frozen. I knew Xavier was well-off, though I never asked him about it. His clothes and car tell me he earns well. But this? This is mega-wealth.

"Come on guys, we need to get out."

I'm just stepping from the passenger seat when two people emerge from the house. I take a deep breath and walk forward. Here goes nothing.

Mrs. Townsend reaches me first. She is dressed beautifully in a cream sweater and gray silk lounge pants. Her blonde hair is pulled back in a ponytail at the nape of her neck.

"Lila, it's so good to finally meet you in person," she says as she approaches.

I reach my hand out. "It's very nice to meet you, Mrs. Townsend."

She surprises me as she bypasses my extended hand and pulls me in. "I need a hug from the girl who has stolen my son's heart. And no more Mrs. Townsend. Call me April."

As I return April's hug, I can't help but notice how tiny her frame is. I realize now that her sweater is making her look bigger than she actually is. Is it on purpose? Perhaps she's just one of those people who are naturally extremely skinny.

"Mom." Xavier's voice sounds behind us. "When do I get my hug?"

We break apart as he approaches, my suitcase in one hand and his brown leather duffle in the other. He drops them on the stone driveway and hurries forward. He smiles and reaches for her. I watch his face as he registers her diminutive size. Worry creases his eyebrows, and he pulls back to look at her.

April continues on as though she hasn't noticed her son's concern. "It's wonderful to have you home, Xavier. Now let me at the soon-to-be wedded couple."

Jessica and Cade walk forward, eager to meet their wedding planner.

Mr. Townsend is still standing on the porch, watching his wife greet everyone, an odd look of longing on his face.

Beside me Xavier raises his hand and waves. "Hi, Dad."

Mr. Townsend nods. He looks so serious in his black slacks and white collared shirt. "Hello, son. How were your travels?"

"They were fine, thank you."

And that's it.

Xavier never told me his father was so austere. Come to think of it, he hasn't said a whole lot about either of his parents. I know the basics, like what their careers were, but I have very little knowledge of the landscape of Xavier's childhood. If his father was always this cold, I can guess why he hasn't said much. And I can empathize too, at least a little. My dad isn't exactly the warm-and-fuzzy type.

April turns to her husband. "Grant, what are you still doing up there? Come down here and greet our guests." She shakes her head and clucks her tongue.

I'm the first to go to him, extending my hand just like I did with Xavier's mom. I can see where Xavier gets his green eyes. Unlike the warm and open-hearted April, Mr. Townsend is fine with just a handshake. What would he do if I hugged him? Not that I actually would.

"Hello, Lila. It's nice to meet you." Mr. Townsend's voice is deep and very formal.

"Likewise, Mr. Townsend." Also unlike his wife, Mr. Townsend prefers a proper greeting.

He shakes hands with Xavier. Not even his son gets a hug? What is it with this man? My dad's hugs are half-hearted and uncomfortable, but hey, at least he can stand touching me.

Mr. Townsend moves on to shake hands with Cade and Jessica. Cade thanks him profusely for hosting their wedding.

"It's no trouble." Mr. Townsend looks at his wife. "April has been having quite the time planning it."

Was it just me, or for a brief moment did I see wistfulness in Mr. Townsend's eyes? This man is a mass of contradictions.

April claps her hands and heads toward the front door. "Come on inside, everyone. Lunch is ready. We'll eat out back after you've put your things in your rooms. And don't worry, I don't expect you to have separate rooms. Couples are together."

April leads the way into the palatial cabin, and we all file in after her.

Our room is enormous. And the view is spectacular. With floor-to-ceiling windows, it overlooks the lake. A fireplace sits in the corner and a seating area is in the opposite corner, but it's the humongous four poster bed that has my attention.

Xavier notices. "You like the bed? It's very comfortable. This is always my room when I visit. Something tells me it'll be more fun with you in it."

225

He walks toward me casually, but I know his intentions are anything but casual. I walk slowly backward and soon I bump into one of the windows.

Xavier smiles languidly, slowing his attack. "I do believe my prey has been captured."

"Your mother expects us downstairs for lunch." I glance down through the window to the terrace. The table is set, and Jessica and Cade are already down there. I'm sure their promptness can be blamed on Jessica's appetite.

"See?" I point down. "We're the only ones missing. Little obvious, don't you think?"

Xavier looks through the window and sighs. "Fine. But you won't be so lucky next time." He runs his finger down the length of my face, making me tingle.

"I hope not," I whisper.

April has prepared a delicious lunch for us. I fully enjoyed the chicken salad wrapped in lettuce cups, fresh fruit, ribboned carrot and zucchini salad, and crisp white wine. April and Jessica's wedding conversation has dominated most of the meal, which is fine by me. I'm busy studying the impressive rosebushes that create a hedge on one side of the yard. There are pinks, whites, and yellows, but it's the red one in the center that has my attention. My rosebush will never look that lush, and now I understand why. The desert just isn't the right place to grow a healthy, vibrant, deep green bush with blooms that look waxen and silky. And since when have I ever cared about growing anything? I associate my rosebush with Xavier. It's silly to be afraid, but I can't help wondering if a dying rosebush is a bad omen for our relationship.

Xavier rubs my arm, breaking me from my maudlin thoughts. I look into his eyes and find curiosity there. Was my face betraying my emotions?

April pauses her wedding discussion with Jessica to go over the schedules for the rest of today and tomorrow. All of the guests are flying in at various times throughout today and staying somewhere in the village. There will be a dinner here this evening for all the guests, and the wedding begins at three p.m. tomorrow.

"The caterers will arrive in a few hours for dinner tonight, but first I have a surprise for the ladies." April claps her hands together in her excitement. "Every bride and her maid of honor need to have well manicured feet and hands. Your appointments are at the Stillwater Spa, and they start in half an hour."

Jessica and I share a look, grinning. Although this does mean Xavier and I can't finish what we'd started upstairs. I steal a quick glance at Xavier. The corners of his mouth are turned down. My shoulders give s small shrug, and he mouths the word *later*. I'll hold him to that.

April touches her son's arm. "Would you please drive the girls to the hotel where the spa is? They should go early and get a few minutes in the relaxation room before their appointments. You can take my car. The keys are in the kitchen drawer." April points back to the house.

"Mom, I can drive the rental."

April smiles and winks at me. "Twenty-eight years old and he still doesn't do what he's told."

Xavier stands and tosses his napkin on his plate. "Ladies, I'll be waiting out front. In my mom's Land Rover."

I watch Xavier stride across the stone terrace and back into the magnificent house. He seems so comfortable here. No stress from running Townsend, no crazy ex-wife. He's carefree, playful, charming. I love Tahoe Xavier.

Jessica and I leave our al fresco lunch amid a chorus of *thank you's* and *have a good time's*. We scoot out front where Xavier is waiting. He opens the two passenger doors of the Land Rover and bows dramatically.

"Your chariot, Ladies."

Jessica and I hop in, giggling in our excitement. The weekend has just begun, and it already feels magical. The opulent cabin, the delicious fresh air lunch, and now a trip to the spa. And we still have so much in store in the next forty-eight hours.

After a long siesta and an hour in Jessica's room getting tortured by her curling iron and make-up bag, it's time for the dinner. I can hear the sounds of the first batch of arrivals from our room on the second floor. Quickly I slip my newly pedicured feet in my shoes and start toward the door.

Xavier grabs my hand. "Where are you going?"

In his perfectly pressed khaki pants and light blue sport shirt, Xavier looks altogether delicious. And the salacious gleam in his eyes reveals what he's after.

"You're crazy. Guests are arriving." I'm not convincing in the slightest. If it weren't for the sake of propriety I would be tearing his clothes off right now. We haven't been alone all day, and it's beginning to show.

"I know." He juts his lower lip out, looking ever the petulant child.

I come in closer. I take his lower lip in my teeth and bite gently. Quickly I release him and walk away, my steps hasty. If I'm not fast enough he'll grab me. And we will be so very late to the party.

"Is that how it's going to be, Birthday Girl?" Xavier looks positively wicked as he smiles mischievously.

My gulp is audible. What have I gotten myself into?

Thankfully Xavier's attention has been taken up by Cade's father for most of the night. I was worried that there might be tension, given Xavier's previous bad boy ways and his influence on their oldest son. I watched as Xavier went straight to Mr. Blankenship and shook his hand, exchanging a few quiet words with the man.

Someone else has stolen all my attention tonight. She's perky, seemingly dim-witted, happy like a puppy, and captivated by my relationship with Xavier. Cade's sister means well, but her questions are annoying and intrusive.

At first Sunny was innocuous enough, gushing about Xavier's family home and how *incredible* it is. Of course I agree, the home is awe-inspiring, but does Sunny have to keep saying incredible like it's the only adjective she knows? She's about to graduate from college. Hasn't she learned more than one adjective by now?

Then Sunny decided that we're friends, so of course she should be asking me about my relationship with Xavier. Because that's what friends do, right? Right? *Wrong, Sunny.*

Jessica catches my eye and gives me a warning look. I glare at her, and she puts her hands together in front of her as if praying. *Please*, she mouths, pleading.

Fine, I mouth back, glowering. This is actually what friends do for each other. They endure an onslaught of questions, some inappropriate, for their beloved best friend.

Sunny starts by eyeing Xavier like he's for sale. "Wow," she says. "He's so hot."

"Umm-hmm." I agree. Her observation doesn't bother me, because he is hot. Anyone with working eyes can see that.

"You're so lucky, Lila." Her voice is wistful, and she's still looking at Xavier.

I'm not lucky, Sunny, I'm worthy. Why do I get the feeling she's picturing him as Prince Charming? Do I need to give her my lecture on how the princess doesn't actually need a prince to come rescue her?

"I suppose I am." My response is as contained as possible.

Sunny looks at me like I'm crazy. Am I supposed to be doing backflips over how lucky I am?

"Do you love him?"

It's her first overstep of the night. I don't like talking about my personal life with someone I hardly know, but I feel I have no choice. Or I could be totally rude and tell her to mind her own business. But I'm minding my manners tonight.

"Yes, I do."

Sunny smiles her bubbly, blinding smile. "Ohhh, you guys have already said *I love you*. That's so sweet."

Is it? Since I can't say what I think, I'll just form sarcastic responses in my head.

Sunny leans her blonde head in conspiratorially. "How's the sex?"

My mouth opens in surprise, and I stare at her. How could anybody think that's an appropriate question?

I love you, Jess, but I'm finished with your soon to be sister-in-law.

"You know what, Sunny? I think it's time for me to start playing photographer for this event. Excuse me."

I head upstairs for my camera. Hopefully Sunny will leave me alone if I'm hiding behind the lens.

And, thankfully, she does. Perhaps she has come down from the clouds for a moment and realized how nosy she was being.

I'm happy and busy taking pictures of the different groups of people chatting. April is the consummate hostess, going from group to group and spending a few minutes with everyone. Once I spot her standing alone at the back of the house, looking through the window toward the lake. Her expression is pensive. With her profile and then face reflected back in the window, it's a great shot. Mr. Townsend comes up behind her and lays his head on her shoulder, eyes closed. Snap, snap. What a sweet moment between them. I guess he isn't always so distant and cold.

Dinner is served buffet style. The caterers are standing behind the serving tables, slicing prime rib by request. I stand back and watch, taking more pictures of it all.

"Does the help want to eat?" Xavier is next to me with two plates of food.

The memory of my earlier lip-biting comes to mind. I lower the camera and look him head to toe. "I'm hungry."

Xavier looks at me and licks his lips. Is he remembering it too?

"Come," he orders.

I follow him into the kitchen, where he smiles politely at the caterers and sets our plates down.

He takes my hand and quickly leads me down a long hallway and into another bedroom. How many rooms does this place have? Through the bedroom is a bathroom. Xavier locks the door behind us. I take the camera off my neck and carefully set it on the toilet.

Xavier is all over me as soon as I'm free of my camera. He lifts me up by the waist and sets me back down on the edge of the vanity. It takes only seconds before we begin moving together.

CHAPTER TWENTY-TWO

Jessica and Cade's wedding day is here!

Last night was a success, with everyone from the two families getting along nicely. Jessica's parents have calmed down enough to at least be happy for her. And they seem to be making an effort to get along with each other this weekend, despite their ongoing divorce.

It seems Xavier and I got away with our tryst last night, mostly. We re-entered the party unnoticed, except for Jessica's eagle eye. She raised her eyebrows and shook her head. I grinned and lifted the camera up to my face. Back into hiding.

Languidly I stretch out on the enormous bed. Through the windows I can see the early morning light is just beginning to peek over the mountains. Xavier is still fast asleep, his mouth open slightly and his hair in disarray. He looks gorgeous. I resist the urge to wake him up for round two. He looks too peaceful.

Instead I pull on the soft robe hanging in the bathroom and make my way downstairs. I'm perfectly presentable in my pajama pants, tank top, and robe. In the kitchen I find a pot of coffee has already been brewed.

Hot coffee in hand, I head out to the deck. I want to sit and listen to the birds chirping in the trees.

April and Mr. Townsend are already sitting together at the table, coffee cups in hand.

Xavier certainly got his dark hair and eyebrows from his father. Mr. Townsend regards me with a friendlier look than he did yesterday, but not much. Affable he is not.

"May I join you?"

"Yes, of course, Lila. Please, sit down." Xavier's mother, on the other hand, is the epitome of genial. She gestures to the chair beside her. "Actually, I'm happy you're up early. I wanted to talk to you about something. Jessica came to me last night and asked if I could still get that photographer for today."

Jessica doesn't want me to be her photographer?

"Why?" I frown.

"She said she didn't think about how you being photographer would mean you would essentially miss her wedding. She wants to experience it with you, not have you stuck behind the camera taking pictures of everyone else."

Oh. I didn't think of it like that.

"Plus, you would have to walk down the aisle before her, grab your camera and go back up the aisle to start taking pictures of her walk. That doesn't sound very fun for the maid of honor. So I called my friend, and he's going to be able to make it work."

Actually, this is good. I'll be able to enjoy Jessica's wedding and be with Xavier. I'll still bring my camera with me, and now I can just use it when I think the shot is special.

"That's ok with me." I smile at April before taking a sip of my coffee.

"Wonderful! I would love to see some of your work. Xavier has bragged an awful lot about you."

Xavier has bragged about me? I hardly know why. He has seen very little of my work. Mostly my pictures are stored on my computer. I haven't done anything remarkable since Smiles by the Sea.

"Xavier is a bit biased."

"That he is. He also mentioned you won your scholarship to UNLV." April stares at me, her expression expectant. She's determined to make me boast about my work. I hate boasting.

"I photographed people from all walks of life enjoying the beach. It was fun. One of the photos was of a couple who had ridden in to the parking lot on motorcycles and wore all their leather down to the sand. The focus of the photos was that every person wore the same joyful expression, no matter their age, gender, lifestyle, what they were wearing, etc." I loved Smiles by the Sea, and I need to come up with something like that again soon. Four years at UNLV will culminate in one giant final project. I still haven't chosen a subject for the project.

April looks impressed. *Score one for me.*

"Lila, that sounds incredible. Can you send it to me? I would love to see it. Really."

I feel my blush.

"Sure. I'll send it as soon as I get home to my computer." A yawn sneaks up as I'm talking, and I try to stifle it.

April laughs. "Isn't it a bit early for you to be up? I slept in until very, very late when I was in college." April turns to her husband with an affectionate smile. "Remember?"

Finally, a hint of a smile moves Mr. Townsend's face muscles. "I do."

April turns back to me. "I was your age when I met Grant. You can call him Grant, by the way." April pointedly looks at at her husband. "You'll have to excuse his behavior. Grant is dealing with some stress that is completely separate from our activities this weekend."

Xavier did mention that his dad has big investments in various companies. Maybe something is going south and he stands to lose? But that doesn't explain the odd look of longing I saw yesterday. Mr. Townsend was looking at his wife like he missed her, when she was right in front of his face. I cannot figure this man out.

I respond in the most political way I can think of. "You and Mr. Townsend have been very generous, gracious hosts, and we appreciate your kindness."

"Planning this wedding has been so fun. Hopefully I'll get the chance to plan Xavier's wedding, whenever that is." April elbows me lightly, and her soft cashmere sweater brushes against my arm. It's quite warm, sitting in the full sunshine as we all are. Isn't April hot?

"Hmmm, I wonder when that will happen for Xavier?" It's far too early to be talking marriage, but I honestly can't imagine a life without him.

April laughs. "A mother can dream. I didn't get to see him get married the first time."

My face sours at the mention of Xavier's ex-wife.

"They were young, and it was a long time ago." April reminds me.

"Gigi has become a problem." I murmur. I'm not sure how much I should say, but I don't want to give April the impression that I'm jealous.

April rolls her eyes. "Oh Lord, what's that girl doing now?"

My eyebrows rise in surprise. "I take it you're familiar with her antics?"

April nods, her blonde hair shimmering in the sunlight. "We still lived in Vegas when they were married. Let's just say that I didn't think they were right for each other. But try telling that to a headstrong twenty year old with a penchant for trouble."

Mr. Townsend is shaking his head. He's probably imagining all of Xavier's teenage shenanigans. And their repercussions. April and Mr. Townsend share a knowing look.

April turns her gaze back to me. "Lila, you're so much better for him. I've never seen him so relaxed. Don't let whatever Gigi is pulling this time get between you. That girl has always been obsessed with him. And from what I know of her, she's probably deeply threatened by you."

Not that she's telling me anything I didn't already know, but I nod anyway. If only they didn't share ownership of Townsend. Then she would be out of our lives for good.

I smile brightly at Xavier's parents. *Fake it til you make it.*

"Everything will be just fine." Fervently I hope my words are true.

Time for a subject change. "April, please tell me how you keep your roses so healthy. Xavier planted a rosebush at my house, and it looks very unhappy."

April looks over to her row of colorful, beautiful blooms. "It's the desert, Lila. Roses won't flourish in the harsh desert clay."

That's what I was afraid she would say.

I've been in Jessica and Cade's room for most of the day. Xavier took Cade out of the house, presumably to let the bride get ready without the groom seeing her. I have no idea what they are up to.

Jessica and I are lounging on her bed, waiting for the hair stylist to arrive. In a few hours she will be Cade's wife, and she's already a tiny person's mother. I feel wistful as I curl up next to her. So much has happened in the last few months.

"You ok?"

"Yes." My voice is small. I hate being this emotional.

"Lila. Open up. It's just me and you."

I look up into Jessica's kind eyes. Tears trickle down my face. I'm not ready to let my best friend grow up and turn into a wife and mother.

"It's stupid, so stupid. I'm just sad that you're growing up."

Jessica runs her hand down the length of my hair. "Hey, don't worry. I'll always be your best friend. I'll make you nasty green juice any time."

I laugh, even though more tears are coming.

"What else?"

My stomach knots. "Gigi made a pass at Xavier."

I hear Jessica's sharp intake of breath. "What? When?" Her outrage is barely contained. Xavier's number one fan has just made Gigi public enemy number one.

I sit up so I'm facing Jessica. She looks beautiful, make-up understated and elegant. I can't believe this is her wedding day.

I take a deep breath, halting the tears. "It was a few nights ago. At Townsend. She did her cage dancing thing and then went into the office. She was crying because it was the anniversary of the day they lost their baby. I don't even know if that's true. Maybe she made it up. I wouldn't put it past her. Anyhow, she tried to kiss Xavier, and he told her that he loves me. Then she took off her top." I pause my re-telling to shudder. I'm thoroughly horrified that Xavier was recently exposed to Gigi's huge, perfect breasts.

Jessica wrinkles her nose. "Ew. Continue."

"So he tells her no again, that he doesn't love her. He loves me. Then she gets mad and storms out, telling him that he will fuck this up too."

"What a psycho."

"I know. But I have to think that she'll be done with all this crap now. I mean, who keeps coming back for more rejection?"

"A sane person would be done. But a woman like Gigi, who clearly believes Xavier is her possession? I'm not so sure."

239

I groan. "Ugh, why can't she just go away? She's beautiful, she has a great body, and her personality isn't totally terrible. Can't she find someone else?"

"How was Xavier when he told you all this?"

"Shaking like a leaf. I thought he was going to tell me that he cheated on me with her." Bile rises in my throat as I remember how I felt.

"Lila, why would you think that?" Jessica frowns at me. "Don't you trust him?"

"I trust him more now. Knowing that Gigi was all over him like that, and he shot her down. She makes me nervous, Jess. Xavier carries so much guilt over what happened with their baby. He thinks it's his fault. She uses that guilt to her advantage."

"She is so manipulative."

I nod. "I wish we could just be away from her."

"Maybe Xavier could buy her out?"

It's a good suggestion, but Jessica isn't the first person to think of it.

"He tried that six months ago. She refuses to sell."

"Good Lord." Jessica sighs the words.

"I know."

The knock on the door interrupts our heavy conversation. April peeks her head in, then opens the door all the way.

"Your hair stylist is here."

We climb off the bed as a tall, slim brunette walks in. I'm trying not to stare at her nose piercings or hair that has been dipped in purple dye, but it's hard. I settle for looking at the spot between her eyes.

"Have fun girls. Yell if you need anything." April closes the door behind her.

Jenna introduces herself, and we begin to plan out Jessica's hair. The pictures that Jessica has torn from wedding magazines help. I've taken the role of assistant, sitting on a stool next to Jenna and her handing bobby pins when she puts her hand out.

The house looks exquisite. The expansive stone terrace has been set up for use by the DJ and bartender. Beyond the stone patio are stairs that lead down to a lawn of deep green grass. White rose petals designate the aisle Jessica will walk down, and rows of wooden chairs flank it. The arch is covered with huge peonies in varying shades of purple. It reminds me of the bouquet Xavier sent to me following our first date. I love that April and Jessica chose purple. It looks magnificent against the green foliage surrounding us.

Jessica, Sunny, and I are standing on the side of the house, completely out of Cade's eyesight, waiting for the remaining guests to sit down. I glance up at the sky, where the sun is bright and shining. It's truly a perfect day.

Suddenly my arm is yanked, and I stumble in my heels against Xavier's chest. He lowers his lips to my ear and whispers very quietly. "You aren't supposed to look more beautiful than the bride." Sweet, but partial.

I'm no competition to Jessica today. She is radiant in her ivory lace gown with her hair curled and pulled back in an intricate bun.

I smile prettily up at Xavier. "Mr. Townsend, I do believe you're wearing rose colored glasses."

Xavier's hand falls over the curve of my backside and travels back up to my exposed neck. "I know I said

I like your red dress, but this purple one is very nice too."

I'm about to remind him that it has nearly twice the amount of fabric of my red dress, but decide against it. Why burst his bubble?

"How about later you peel me out of it?"

Xavier's groan reverberates through his chest. At just the wrong moment, April approaches.

"Sunny, Xavier, it's time. Cade's ready. All the guests are seated." April is all business. I like it.

Sunny and Xavier step forward. The way everything falls, Xavier will walk Sunny down the aisle. I'm the maid of honor, so my trip down the aisle will be solo. My walk back up the aisle after the ceremony will be with Cade's best man, his college roommate.

"Xavier, offer Sunny your arm. Sunny, take it. Walk like this." April demonstrates a slow, controlled gait. "Walk to where the rose petals start. Pause, so Greg can take your picture. Then continue down the aisle. Got it?"

I like this version of April. She's assertive and commanding. Two characteristics I appreciate.

Watching Xavier and Sunny's retreating backs makes me pout. I wish I were walking down the aisle with him.

Jessica grabs my hand. "I'm nervous." Her voice wavers.

I look up into frightened blue eyes. "What are you nervous about?"

Jessica looks panicky. "Is this too fast? Am I only marrying him because of this baby?" A manicured hand flies to her stomach, which hasn't developed a hint of baby bump yet.

I grab her shoulders and look her in the eyes. "Jess, am I your best friend?"

Her answering nod is slight. *She really is freaked out.*

"You know me, Jess. If I thought for one second that you were doing something stupid, I would tell you. I would raise that baby with you before I would let you do something truly asinine, like marry someone who isn't right for you." My voice is calm and certain.

"You mean it?" Jessica's eyes are wide and hopeful.

"Truer words have never been spoken." My voice rings with my sincerity.

April coughs delicately behind me.

"You're up, Lila."

I give Jessica a hug. "I'll see you out there," I whisper.

April grabs my hand and steers me around the side of the house and into the view of the guests.

"You will do just fine." I hear her say in a teary voice, then she releases me. *What?*

Of course I will do just fine walking down the aisle, but I get the feeling that isn't what April meant. I don't have time to ask, or even ponder it. The guests are watching as I approach the top of the aisle and pause, giving a wide smile to the photographer.

Showtime.

CHAPTER TWENTY-THREE

Jessica looks magnificent. From my place at the table, I have a great view of Jessica and Cade dancing. Camera ready, I snap a few pictures.

"Are those tears, stone-faced Mitchell?" Xavier teases me.

"No," I lie, flicking a tear off my cheek. "Just little balls of salted water."

Xavier's gaze turns from laughter to awe. "Lila, I love you. How did I get so lucky? I've done so many bad things. I feel like I need to claim you now, before you wise up and run away."

I laugh and shake my head. I know the truth. Xavier is the prize.

I lean over and plant a kiss on his cheek. "I think maybe your champagne is talking."

Xavier shakes his head adamantly. "Just me. And just me says, we should do something really crazy."

My stomach muscles clench, but my brain over-rides my desire, thankfully. "Oh, no no no. Last night in that bathroom was crazy enough. You can wait until we get back to our bedroom." I swear, this man is insatiable. *Not that I'm complaining.*

Xavier laughs. "I mean something even crazier. Let's get married. Now."

I burst out laughing. Who leaves Vegas and then has a quickie, spur of the moment wedding in Tahoe?

"I'm not joking, Lila." Xavier looks hurt.

Oops. Ok, I can see I need to tread lightly. Because there's no way I'm marrying Xavier tonight.

"My family isn't here. I can't get married without my family." It's the most reasonable excuse in my arsenal. The other reasons are more along the lines of, *We've only known each other for a couple months, We work opposite schedules, You have a psycho ex-wife who you work with, and she will probably gut me like a fish if I marry you.*

Xavier's jutted lower lip does not detract from his good looks in the least. In fact, it does quite the opposite.

"Besides, you married when you were twenty two and you said you were too young to know what a mistake you were making. I'm a year younger than you were." I remind him.

Xavier gives me a pained look. He doesn't like being reminded of his marriage to Gigi.

"That was different."

I rub his leg. "I know a way to cheer you up."

Excitement comes into his green eyes. "Now?"

I roll my eyes. "I meant a dance. But I'll let you feel me up as long as you can do it without other people noticing."

Xavier stands quickly, his chair scraping the floor. "Deal."

He grabs my hand and drags me, laughing behind him, to the dance floor.

It's well after midnight when everyone has finally left. There weren't very many people, but they could all agree on the music and flowing champagne. Cade's mom will be hungover tomorrow, no question.

Mrs. Blankenship was showing us all a thing or two on the dance floor. Cade looked ready to die of mortification when she busted out the *Sprinkler*.

The wedding showed no signs of having been planned with only two weeks notice. April must be a formidable presence. How else did she accomplish all this in a short timeframe?

Jessica is exhausted, leaning heavily against Cade. He bends down and literally sweeps her off her feet.

With a proud and happy glance to the four of us still standing in the kitchen, he nods courteously. "Goodnight everyone. I think my wife needs to sleep now." Cade walks out of the kitchen, Jessica nearly comatose in his arms.

I can't help my ear-splitting grin when Cade says the word 'wife'. He looked so content. I meant what I said to Jessica before the ceremony. I would've told her if I thought she was making a mistake. Cade is right for Jessica. I'm glad he found someone who can tolerate his serious and practical nature. It surely wouldn't be me. I much prefer Xavier and his playfulness, his arrogance, and his tenacity.

"Are you ready to hit the hay, Ms. Mitchell?" Xavier enunciates my name. He's still pouty because I didn't jump at his impromptu marriage proposal. Had I agreed, would he be calling me Mrs. Townsend right now? I can't deny the small thrill that runs through me as I think of becoming Xavier's wife.

"Ready, Mr. Townsend." My voice is sugary sweet.

Xavier hugs his mom and claps his dad on the back. I hug April and nod at Mr. Townsend.

"Thank you for this wedding. You've given my best friend the most special memories." Tears threaten for the umpteenth time tonight. *What is wrong with me? Get it together Mitchell.*

April beams. "It made me very happy to do it. Goodnight you two."

Xavier and I are almost to our room when I remember I left my camera downstairs. I run back down and into the kitchen, grabbing my camera off the counter. As I go back through the house, I see Xavier's parents standing on the terrace. They are holding each other, slow dancing under the white strings of lights. I raise my camera and take their picture.

I don't want to leave Tahoe. I love the quiet, the stillness. The unhurried pace, the lushness, the crisp air. The majestic mountains and shimmering lake put my heart at peace. Dare I say, it feels like home?

I've spent the morning at the waters edge with Xavier and my camera. The Townsend's have a dock on their property and a little stretch of beach. Xavier turned the camera on me once, but I don't particularly enjoy being the subject.

Now it's time to go back up to the house and say goodbye. The thought puts a lump in my throat. What is it about this place that keeps making me teary?

"Why do I feel like I'm marching toward the guillotine?" I ask Xavier as we wipe off our sandy feet and start up the path.

"That bad?"

I nod. This trip has made one thing very clear. Vegas is not my home. UNLV has been great, but come December, it will be time for me to leave. But where does that put me and Xavier? Could he sell Townsend? Go to another city and do something different? Is it even fair for me to ask that of him? All I know for sure is that I love Xavier so much, it makes my heart swell.

By the time our plane takes off, I'm more melancholy than I was at the lake this morning. I don't know what has come over me. I didn't feel like this when I left California to move to Nevada. Why is it so hard for me to say goodbye to a place I've only spent two days visiting? And to top off my mood, Xavier's in a mood of his own. He has been very quiet since we said goodbye to his parents. Is it because we have to go back to our real life, and Gigi?

Xavier will have to see his boundary-crossing ex-wife at work this week. And I'll have those stupid cameras on me when I return to The Pain Shoppe on Tuesday. Granite Alexa won't leave me alone now that he knows I'm dating Xavier Townsend. He's way too chatty with me, and the cameras are catching it all. Marco has done my hair four times since Xavier came to Alexa to take me to lunch. I know what that means. And here I thought my image would end up on the cutting room floor.

Xavier shifts in his seat, bumping into me. It's the third time in five minutes. He's not usually fidgety. Mr.

Smooth and In-Control boss man, fidgeting? Since when does Xavier display anything less than complete mastery of his movements?

"Are you ready to talk?" My curiosity has been raging since we left, and he went mute. I didn't want to ask on the drive to the airport with the new Mr. & Mrs. in the backseat, just in case what was bothering him was not for general consumption.

Fear and worry etch the plains of Xavier's face. He shakes his head, and I'm pretty sure I can see the gears in his head moving. A minute passes before he sighs.

"My mom is so thin. She kept wearing those loose sweaters, but when I hugged her, I could feel how skinny she was. She had breast cancer a long time ago, and she beat it. What if it's back?" Xavier's voice chokes on the last word.

I pull him toward me, holding him as much as our restrictive space allows.

"Don't you think your parents would tell you if something like that were going on? They would want you to know."

"You'd think so. They should tell me. But my mom, she's a martyr. It would be just like her to chose not to tell me so I don't feel sad or scared."

"What about your dad?"

"Dad will do whatever my mom wants. He never could tell her no." Xavier pulls back from me and looks away while he speaks. "My dad was weird this weekend too."

"Is he always that reserved?" It's the nicest word I can think of to describe Mr. Townsend.

"He has never been emotionally demonstrative towards me, if that's what you mean." Xavier gives me a sideways glance.

I nod. *Yes, that's exactly what I mean.*

"How was he different this weekend?"

Xavier shakes his head. "It's hard to describe. I just got the feeling he was on edge. Like, waiting for something."

"Well, maybe he was just waiting for all of this weekend's events to happen." My suggestion sounds lame. It was clear that April was the planner and executor of our whole weekend.

Xavier shrugs. "Maybe."

He leans forward to grab a magazine that was left in the seat back pocket by a previous passenger. I take the hint and shut up.

I don't know what to say to this man, my boyfriend who I know so well in some ways and barely know in others. I'm at a loss for how to make Xavier feel better. It must be like this in every new relationship, and lets face it, we're still new. We might be in love, and I'm closer to him than anybody besides Jessica, but it will take time for me to learn how to handle him. The learning curve is frustrating. I sigh and resume the e-book I downloaded before we left.

We've returned to the intense desert heat and parted way with the newlyweds. They're headed to a posh hotel for the night. It's the only honeymoon they'll get because Cade didn't want to ask for time off after working at SFA for only two months.

Xavier pulls up in front of my house after a silent drive. In a matter of weeks the sale will be final, and this will be Cade and Jessica's house.

"Are you staying tonight?" I ask Xavier hopefully. I don't want to be apart from him, even after being together all weekend. I haven't had my fill of him yet.

Xavier shakes his head. "I need to get back to my place."

Your place is a freaking hotel. It's not like anything could have gone wrong while you were gone.

I'm starting to feel angry. Xavier's silence has followed us all the way home. I understand he's scared and worried, but why is he shutting me out?

Xavier kisses my cheek in a subdued way and gets back into his car. "I'll call you tomorrow."

I watch, astonished, as Xavier drives away. He has never acted so aloof before.

Gigi's warnings come floating unbidden into my head. *Xavier is trouble. He will only hurt you. He hurts every person he gets involved with.*

No. I won't think like that. Xavier is upset because he's afraid his mother is sick again. That's it. End of story.

I turn away from the street and meander into the dark house, my suitcase bumping along behind me.

CHAPTER TWENTY-FOUR

I'm so sick of Granite Alexa pretending we're friends. He was snottier than a two-year-old with a cold until he found out Xavier is my boyfriend. Now its "Hey, girl" when I walk into The Pain Shoppe. I can barely contain my disdain. Besides, it's not really me Granite wants to know. In Granite's warped, reality show-focused mind, Xavier will increase his star status. Which is really stupid, because it's not like the general population knows who Xavier Townsend is. Nobody stops him on the street. It's just the upper echelons of the Vegas crowd who know him.

It's not really the cross-dresser extraordinaire that has me in such an atrocious mood today. I haven't heard from Xavier in two days. *Two days!*

I called him yesterday morning and left a message. And I haven't heard back. I refuse to be the girlfriend who feels entitled to blow up his phone just because he's my boyfriend. Xavier will call when he's over this weird mood.

Yesterday totally sucked though. Jessica and Cade went to her first doctors appointment and came home bearing a little black and white picture. A tiny white arrow pointed to a spot in the picture and proclaimed

BABY! It's now proudly displayed on the fridge. Baby's first portrait.

Jessica and Cade left for work soon after their appointment, and I was at home, mulling over how this weekend ended on such a low point. My house is spotless, thanks to my need for distraction. And then I ordered a book about growing plants in the desert. I refuse to let the roses go down without a fight.

I thought work would be a welcome distraction from my silent phone, but I was wrong. I've only been here a few hours, and I want to punch Granite. He was all over me the second I walked in, gushing about my trip to Tahoe like an overeager puppy.

Jeri and Marco are just as bad. They want to hear all about the shotgun wedding and how gorgeous everything was. Jeri already knew Xavier's parents were loaded, a little fact I had no idea about. She asked about their house as soon as she spotted me.

"Is it, like, right on the water?" Today her lipstick is a watermelon shade. Very summer.

I nod. I have to pretend like nothing is bothering me. As much as Jeri gossips at work, I'm sure she's gossip queen outside of work, and she knows way more people than I ever want to. Channeling Sunny's bright smile and energy, I launch into the description of the cabin-mansion and the floor-to-ceiling windows. The house is truly drool-worthy, so I don't have to fake my excitement when recalling the details.

"The wedding was beautiful, and we had a great time. Xavier's parents were wonderful hosts." And this concludes my story. *Now run along so I can be in a bad mood again.*

The rest of my day trips along, and before I know it, I'm back home, sitting in the kitchen with the newlyweds while Cade cooks dinner.

"Is Xavier coming over before work tonight?" Jessica has noticed his absence but hasn't asked me about it yet.

"Probably not." My phone vibrates on the table next to my water glass. It's a message from Xavier.

I'm sorry. I just freaked out about my mom. I needed to think through some stuff. Can I come over tonight? I'll let someone else close the club.

Relief fills me. Everything is fine. I get it. I need space sometimes too. I respond, telling him I will see him tonight, whenever he gets in.

"I guess Xavier will come over at some point tonight. I'll leave the key under the mat for him. I'm sure we'll be asleep by the time he can break away from Townsend."

Cade sets a casserole dish on a mat in the center of the table. The enchiladas smell mouth-watering. This man can cook. I'm certainly going to enjoy the home-cooked meals while it lasts.

I dig in, suddenly ravenous. I didn't realize my appetite went on a hiatus with Xavier's communications. It's back now, with a vengeance.

At five a.m. I wake up to an empty bed. Where is Xavier? My head is groggy and my eyes are still partially closed from sleep, but I climb from bed and traipse clumsily to the bathroom. Once I'm done, I go downstairs and out to the front door, checking under the mat. The key is still there. I grab the metal, warm from the never-ending Vegas heat, and close the door.

After a stop in the kitchen for a glass of water, I head back up to my room. Worry is gnawing at me. What if Xavier was hurt? Was he in a car accident? So many drunk drivers are out at the time when Xavier would have been driving. I'm taking the stairs double time now, water sloshing over the sides of the glass.

I rush to my phone on my nightstand. There's one message, sent at one a.m., but it's not from my boyfriend.

Gigi's text consists of three words:

I told you.

I scroll down to the picture she has included. My stomach lurches as I absorb the image.

"Oh God," I moan in pain. The water glass drops from my hand and hits my nightstand, shattering.

"No, no, no. No, no, no." If I say it over and over, it won't be true. The image of Xavier and a blond women, lips locked against one another, won't be real.

Jessica's in my room now, bending over me where I sit on the floor. I can see Cade's feet at the door, but I don't have the will to lift my head.

"Lila, what's wrong?" Jessica asks.

"Xavier," I choke out.

"Is he hurt?"

I shake my head. No, Xavier isn't hurt. He's the one doling out the pain.

"My phone." It's all I can say. The picture is ricocheting around my brain, making it impossible to say much. Xavier was kissing someone else. Gigi took a picture of it. Xavier was literally caught in the act. Gigi said this would happen. I'm beyond stupid.

Jessica lets out a cry of indignation."No." But the picture cannot lie.

Jessica's arms are around me, holding me. I can't get ahold of my emotions. There are so many swirling around inside me. Which one is dominant? Anger. I'm really fucking pissed.

Cade, the voice of reason, sits on the floor in front of the ball of limbs that is me and Jessica.

"Lets just approach this calmly." His deep voice rumbles quietly, directing the scene before him. "We don't know the context of this picture. There's probably a lot more to this story."

"How is any of this explainable?" hisses Jessica.

Cade lifts his hands. "I don't know. But shouldn't we give Xavier a chance?"

An idea occurs to me. Disentangling myself from Jessica's embrace, I stand on legs that are shaky but getting stronger by the second. Jessica and Cade watch me cautiously from their seats on the floor.

"Oh, Xavier is going to get his chance. Right now."

Cade stares at me like I'm a mystical creature.

"Maybe you should calm down before you go to see Xavier." Cade's suggestion is just so…Cade.

"You know firsthand I'm not a person who waits until extreme emotions have passed before facing a situation."

Jessica looks from me to Cade, not understanding. I don't have time to explain. Cade can fill her in if he wants to.

I head into my closet and shut the door, then exchange my pajamas for jeans and a tank top. My audience is still seated on the floor, talking softly. I can't hear what they're saying.

In the bathroom, I make myself presentable as quickly as possible. When I come back out, the twosome are waiting expectantly.

"What?"

Cade looks to Jessica. Apparently she has been nominated as speaker.

She steps forward, holding out my phone. The screen is mercifully dark. I don't think I could handle seeing that offensive picture again.

"We want to drive you to The Martin. Just in case, umm..." Jessica looks uncomfortable.

I wait as patiently as possible under the circumstances.

Jessica sighs and finishes her statement. "In case things don't go well."

"Fine." I mutter. I shove my feet in my sandals and turn to Jessica and Cade. "Meet me in the kitchen in five minutes. If you take longer than that, I'll go by myself." With a warning look at Jess and Cade I head out my bedroom door.

Cade looked completely terrified at my words, but Jessica knows better. This is what I'm doing to protect myself. This toughness, my resolve, my determination, is to keep me from falling apart. I will see this through, I will make Xavier answer for his actions. And I won't think about the outcome, not yet. One step at a time.

We're silent on the drive. I stare out the window from my spot in the backseat of Cade's sensible, kid-friendly mid-size SUV.

I haven't looked at the picture again, and I don't want to. It's seared in my brain, an image of my boyfriend and a blonde locked at the lips. Cade, ever helpful and pragmatic, mentioned context. *We don't know the context of the picture.*

Of all people, I understand context. To interpret the content of a photograph, you look at the four w's: who, what, when, and where. But to think critically about a photograph, you consider a fifth w: why. Why did Gigi choose to take that picture?

"You guys!" I blurt out, making Jessica jump. These are the first words spoken on our drive, and we're nearly to The Martin.

Jessica looks back with wide eyes. She looks nervous. *For* me or *because* of me?

"Listen, I was just thinking about photography and a class I took. The context of the picture of Xavier and that...girl. Well, I know the who, what, when, and where of the picture, but I don't know the why. Why did Gigi take the picture? Why from that angle? Why did she emphasize the sides of their faces but not one face more than the other? Why did she choose that exact moment and not another one? Why did she send me only one picture?" I'm sounding off my questions like rapid-fire.

"Well," Cade starts, "I don't know why. Maybe she—"

"Cade, you don't know the answers. I can only guess, but Gigi knows."

I shake my head, clearing out my annoyance at Cade. It's a good thing he works in the financial industry. He belongs with numbers.

"My point is, Gigi wanted me to see this image and react. Gigi has made it clear she wants to be with Xavier. This is another attempt to blow up my relationship. Whatever happened last night at Townsend, Gigi has something to do with it. I'm not saying Xavier is innocent." The image comes to my mind again and I shudder. "What I'm saying is that this situation has Gigi's handiwork all over it." Finally I stop talking and sit back against the seat, proud of the way I figured it out.

Jessica turns to face me.

"Lila, didn't Gigi say something really weird to you after you were leaving coffee with her? You needed luck?"

I can still hear her words. *Good luck. You're going to need it.*

"Holy crap, Jessica!" My brain is firing off, alarm bells ringing. "This is what she meant. First she made that ridiculous and naked pass at Xavier, and I know she had something to do with this."

Jessica shakes her head. "This girl is demented. Can you ever imagine wanting someone so bad that you would act like this?"

"No." I shake my head. "But I don't have any screws loose."

Cade opens his mouth to make a joke.

"Don't," I warn, pointing my finger at him.

We laugh, a weird feeling that releases some of the tension in the car. My stomach is still in knots, but I feel better now that I understand Gigi is playing a role in this. Somehow, someway, Gigi had her hand in it.

The early morning drive down the strip looks absolutely depressing. Gone are the energizing bright lights, the magic. The sun, a dose of reality, shines down on the tall towers. Some people are out, many of them dressed in last night's party clothes. Two girls carry their stilettos and are walking in bare feet. I hope they sanitize more than just their feet when they get home.

The Martin is positively blinding in the sun's light. My heart hammers. What's going to happen? Will I still have a boyfriend when I get back in this car? Or will I be exchanging Xavier for a broken heart?

The thought is so unpleasant that I shake my head, trying to clear it out.

Cade stops and rolls down his window. The valet walks over.

"We're just dropping her off and waiting down there." Cade points to where they will park. The valet nods and goes back to his booth. There's nobody else in the driveway, so it wouldn't matter if Cade stayed right where he is.

"We'll be right here when you need us, ok?" Cade's voice is sincere.

I nod and take a deep breath.

Soon I'm through the turnstile at The Martin. Past the lobby, toward the elevator, waiting for the doors to open, taking me up,up,up to Xavier's floor. And in that two minutes, I prep myself.

You are Lila Mitchell. You don't do bullshit. Xavier played some role in this, and he will answer for that. Gigi is not one hundred percent to blame.

My words are strong in my head, but still my legs are shaking beneath me. The elevator doors open, and I step off. The closer I get to Xavier's room, the more I want to throw up. How could Xavier put me in this position? Falling into whatever trap Gigi designed for him and causing this angst. It's so brainless on his part. I won't forget to tell him so.

I raise my hand and knock on Xavier's door, two hard, angry knocks.

Through the door I hear Xavier's voice. "That was quick. Thank God, because you need to eat something."

What the fuck?

The door opens and there he is, my boyfriend, in shorts and a T-shirt. Behind him stands a blonde women, wearing nothing but one of Xavier's shirts. She looks confused.

The blood drains from my face as I take in the scene. This is so much more than a picture on a phone. This is so much worse than I thought.

Xavier looks back at the blonde and then to me, horror on his face. He opens his mouth but nothing comes out.

Well, I'm not speechless. I look him right in his lying, cheating face.

"Fuck. You." Each word is separate, clearly pronounced.

"Lila, I know this looks bad, but I can explain."

"Save it." I snap. I'm trying so hard to keep the tears at bay. *Don't let him see you cry.* But there's no stopping the raw pain in my heart. The tears pour onto my face. With all the strength I have left, I manage one last sentence before I know I'll be unable to speak. "Gigi was right."

Xavier stands frozen. His lips are trembling, and he looks devastated.

I turn and walk back down the hall, toward the elevator. Behind me I hear the soft click of Xavier's door closing, and then he roars a profanity.

I sob the whole way down the elevator and out to the waiting car. People are looking, but I don't care. Jessica jumps out before I make it to the car, rushing to me. Cade has the back door open, and we climb in. I curl into a ball on the seat, the tears flowing. Jessica sits next to me and rubs my back while Cade drives us home.

CHAPTER TWENTY-FIVE

A summer romance. Just a fling. That's all it was. Except it wasn't.

No matter how I spin it, it was real. I loved Xavier. And I know he loved me too. So how did he manage to do just what Gigi claimed he would do?

I still can't figure it out. My mind goes over it all, detail by tiny detail, trying so hard to see the fissures in our relationship. Should I, could I, have seen this coming? Aside from the warnings from his lunatic ex-wife, Xavier never gave me any indication that he would hurt me. And then, in the blink of an eye, it was over. I was first-hand witness to his infidelity.

Xavier has left me message after message after message. *Lila, please, you don't understand. Lila, just answer my calls. Lila, stop being so fucking stubborn.* He won't get a response from me. I won't be going back for a second serving of heartbreak. Fool me twice, shame on me.

I allowed myself two weeks to wallow. Two weeks to eat whatever I wanted and lay around. Two weeks to cry shamelessly and read sappy romance novels and cry some more.

And now the timer has gone off on my two week pity-fest. Whatever I feel, I'll have to lock it up. I'll move on, I'll stay strong. Eventually my heart will be whole again. In the meantime, while I'm waiting for the holes in my heart to mend, I have shit to do.

My final semester begins next week, and I have a major project to start. I have one class, and my only grade for the entire semester rides on creating a meaningful project. Next week I will receive the parameters of the project, and the rest is up to me. This class will consist only of need-based meetings that I request. Aside from my regular check-ins to update the professor on my progress, this is a totally independent study. This is where I show I have what it takes to be a photographer. Do I create meaning with my photographs, or do I just take pretty pictures?

This is why I gave myself a two week allowance to give in to my broken heart. Crying into my pillow stifles all the focus and creativity I need to come up with a project. Would I really let my feelings ruin almost four years of hard work and a lifetime's passion?

Absolutely not.

Today is the first day after my two week broken-hearted sob fest. And I'm a woman with a plan. First, I'll exercise. I like the toned version of me, and I want to keep it up. Lord knows all the ice cream I've consumed in the last fourteen days needs to be melted off. Unfortunately, the only exercise I've ever enjoyed is hot yoga. I could find another studio, but I'm a creature of habit. I know the class times, the layout, and most of the instructors. It's a Thursday morning, so I won't see Xavier there. He works Wednesday nights at Townsend and sleeps until noon on Thursdays.

It annoys me that I can recall Xavier's schedule with such ease, but what am I supposed to do? Unlearn it? It will take time to forget it, to forget his smile, his emerald eyes, the feel of his soft brown hair, the way his brows furrowed when he was concentrating, the lift of his chin when he was being arrogant. And there it is, the too familiar tugging in my heart. My stupid, stupid, heart.

Jessica's surprised when she finds me out of bed before her this morning. She blinks when she walks into the kitchen. In her tight pajama camisole, she has the tiniest hint of a baby bump, probably not noticeable by someone who doesn't know she's expecting.

"Hey, girl. Everything ok?" Jessica looks wary. I can't blame her for proceeding with caution. For the past two weeks I *may* have acted like a grumpy bear woken early from hibernation. Either that or sobbing.

"No, everything isn't ok. But it will have to be, because my time is up."

Jessica is bewildered. "You gave the process of getting over Xavier an expiration date?"

Of course this would baffle the girl who could nurse a broken heart until her next boyfriend came along. But for me, it works.

"Yes."

"And now you're over him?" Jessica pauses to snap her fingers. "Just like that?" Her look is dubious.

I sigh."Not at all. I still love him. But I'm over crying about him. I can't wallow in self-pity. I have a life to continue."

Jessica shakes her head, and I'm not sure whether she's in awe or thinks I'm crazy. Perhaps a little of both.

She grabs the greek yogurt from the fridge. I watch as she puts a scoop in a bowl and piles fresh fruit and granola on top. She comes to the table and sits with me, happily digging in.

"Lila, you never cease to amaze me. How do you plan to continue this life of yours?"

"Well, for starters, I'm going to keep up with yoga. I've finally found a form of exercise that doesn't feel like torture."

Jessica pauses mid-bite, raising an eyebrow. "At a new studio?"

When I shake my head, she continues. "Are you sure that's a good idea?"

"I won't see Xavier today. And I want to go. After two weeks of binge-eating and laying around, I'm ready to exercise. I don't want to wait. Speaking of." I stand, pointing at the clock on the microwave. "Gotta run. Well, not really. I hate running. Gotta yoga."

Jessica laughs, and I bend to kiss the top of her head. She has been an incredible friend.

I walk out the door in all my moisture-wicking-yoga-clothed glory. My yoga mat is slung over my shoulder, and my hair is piled on top of my head. I feel a semblance of peace just knowing where I'm headed. I know what I'm doing is the right decision for me. *My heartbreak will not keep me down.*

The yoga studio is a serene place. Every yogi who walks in is calm, smiling. They exchange quiet, pleasant conversation before heading into the room where they practice. I recognize a handful of people and say hello.

In this setting I'm confident and friendly. In the UNLV cafeteria I want to hurl my tray down and tell them all how senseless they behave. Finally I have discovered some places where I feel comfortable. I like to be in Tahoe, and I like to practice yoga. That's two.

Tahoe makes me think of Xavier though, and that hurts. Xavier and his green eyes, his witty comebacks, his confidence, his willingness to challenge my smart mouth. Ouch, ouch, ouch. For all my bravado and strength of mind, I still can't turn off my heart. My heart wants the man who cheated on me. My eyes sting as I think of him.

No! This isn't going to happen here. I'm here to feel centered, to be at peace, to try and soothe the storm raging inside me. There is no room for Xavier in my yoga practice.

I'm already on my mat in child's pose when the instructor walks in. I smirk when I see it's Brandon, the instructor who rubbed my lower back and got Xavier in a tizzy. How ironic, Xavier gets worked up about another man touching me in a setting as innocent as this when he can kiss and presumably bed the blonde woman. *Which event crossed the line, Xavier?*

Brandon closes the door and starts his music. "Good morning everyone. I want you all to think about setting an intention for your practice today."

Immediately I know what my intention will be. It may be fruitless, but my intent is to forget about Xavier, if only for an hour.

The door to the studio opens for a latecomer, distracting me. It's generally considered poor yoga etiquette to come to class late. I look into the mirror to see who has joined us.

Xavier.

No no no no no!

My heart pounds. My focus is gone. Everything inside me is in turmoil. How am I going to get through this? I can't leave now, it would get everyone's attention, including his.

Thankfully the class is full, and we're far apart. With any luck he won't see me. I'll just hang out here after the class finishes and wait for him to leave.

What the hell is he doing here on a Thursday morning? Did he change his schedule? Why? Is it because of the blonde?

Dammit, I can't focus, not now. I have to use the mirrors to see what people around me are doing because I can't pay attention to Brandon's instructions. I steal a look across the room at Xavier. I can't help it.

Xavier is standing upright, staring at me with his mouth open. He takes a step toward me, but I give him my nastiest look and turn my gaze away. For the rest of the hour, I make it a goal to keep my eyes forward. And when a pose makes it so that I have to face Xavier's way, I close my eyes. I will not, cannot give in to him. Xavier is too charming, and I won't listen to his excuses for the blonde.

Finally the stretching begins, and we're almost done. Brandon comes up behind me, just as he did the last time, and rubs my lower back. It feels quite good and makes me think I should book a massage. And then Brandon's hands move a little lower and off to the side. *That's definitely not my lower back anymore.* Just as before, his hand travels up the length of my spine. He gets to my neck and squeezes it lightly, then moves away from me. *Ok. That guy definitely just touched my ass.*

I glance at Xavier to see if he noticed. He's sitting, not stretching, and he looks pissed. *Yep, he saw it.* But he doesn't have a right to be pissed about it, not anymore.

After our final poses and savasana, the class is over. I turn my back to Xavier and roll up my mat. I know I won't get out of here without talking to Xavier. He won't let me.

"Did you enjoy your ass rub?" Xavier's voice is acid behind me.

I don't turn around. Hearing his voice, even in a nasty tone, makes me want to cry. I miss him. I gather my strength and stand, turning to face him. It's my first close up of his face, and I'm pleased to see he doesn't look well. His eyes look tired and sad. *Well, good.*

Xavier's face softens when our eyes meet. He takes a step toward me, but I put my hand out, palm facing him.

"I have no interest in doing this with you. I didn't come here to see you. I thought you wouldn't be here today." My voice is strong, but quiet. Even so, the people around us notice.

"Lila, quit being so fucking stubborn and talk to me."

"Why would I talk to you?" I hiss. "There are no excuses for what I saw."

"Yes, there are, and if you would just listen—"

"I don't want to hear more lies from your mouth. You did what you said you would never do to me, and that's the end of it. Just let me move on. Quit making it worse." I stare at him, strong and full of conviction.

Just then Brandon, yoga instructor and opportunistic boundary crosser, inserts himself into our heated conversation.

"Is this guy bothering you?" Brandon glances from me to Xavier and back to me again, his face concerned.

Oh, Brandon, you shouldn't have. Really.

Xavier answers for me. "No, I'm not fucking bothering her. *I* am her boyfriend. Does your kumbaya brain compute? You need to stop rubbing her ass, or I'm going to squash you."

Oh, my God!

Xavier's eyes flash. He looks like he's about to do just that.

I have to get out of here.

Without looking at either man, I hurry toward the exit. I have no idea how Brandon has reacted to Xavier's lashing. I need to get my purse and shoes from my cubby, and fast, before Xavier can follow me out here. Hearing his voice, seeing his face, makes me want to fall into his arms and forget everything. And that is unacceptable.

I'm almost to my car when Xavier calls to me.

"Lila, wait." His voice sounds far away, and I'm so grateful for that. I look behind me, and now he's jogging to catch up.

I toss my mat in my car with a flourish worthy of Granite Alexa and spin around to face Xavier. So much for a quiet morning of peaceful yoga practice.

I lift my hand in the universal stop signal, and he does.

My voice is icy. "Let me be perfectly clear about something. You're not my boyfriend."

Xavier glares at me. "That guy was interested in you."

"So what?" I explode, my arms flying up. "It's not your problem anymore. Oh, and speaking of problems, please tell your ex-wife to stop calling me. Ignoring calls from two different people is becoming a full time job."

Xavier rolls his eyes. "Why the hell is she calling you?"

"I know why she's calling. To gloat. To say her big fat 'I told you so.'"

"Fuck her, Lila. Just quit being stubborn for three minutes, and you'll see that this is one big misunderstanding." Xavier's green eyes are pleading, but there isn't an ounce of softening in my heart.

I stand with my arms crossed, staring Xavier down. "I didn't come here to talk to you. I have no interest in your lies. You cheated on me. And really, weren't you always going to?" My tone conveys my disgust and contempt as I unearth this hideous realization. Xavier never stood a chance against his impulse to cheat. He likes the nightlife and the energy he finds in the pulsing beats of the music pounding through Townsend. The attention and glory he gets from owning the hottest nightclub in Vegas are inextricably tied to his psyche. Of course I wasn't enough.

His eyes are wide in shock and disappointment, his mouth settling into an angry line. This only incites my own rage. What does he have to be mad about? Xavier should be groveling on the floor, begging for forgiveness. Not that he would get it.

"You always thought I would cheat, didn't you? You were never going to trust me." Xavier shakes his head. The anger, so evident on his face just moments before, is gone. Now he just looks crestfallen.

I don't know why he looks so upset, and I'm not staying around to delve any deeper. My well-rubbed ass is out of here.

"Move out of the way of my car or I will back over you."

In happier days Xavier would have laughed at a statement like that and sang "Lila, Lila, full of fire." But now, on this awful morning of ugly truths, he gives me one last mournful look and walks away.

Once I'm safely inside my car, the floodgates open. If I hadn't seen Xavier today, my resolve to stop crying would have stayed strong. But this morning has proved too much for me. As I drive past the yoga studio I spot Brandon inside near the window. Was he watching me and Xavier? It doesn't matter. I'll never show my face in his class again.

CHAPTER TWENTY-SIX

College. Thank God for it. I've always liked going to class, learning and challenging myself. But right now I love it more than ever.

Honestly, I would love anything that would take up my time. After my run-in with Xavier last week, I've been struggling to maintain balance. I find myself wondering where he is, what he's doing, and, mostly, *who* he's doing it with. I know nothing of the blonde woman. Was it once? Are they dating now? If they're dating, why did he look so affected by me last week at our awful yoga encounter? I know all these questions could be answered simply by returning one of his calls.

The idea of calling Xavier, of even giving him an inch to put some of my questions to rest, is abhorrent to me. Xavier broke my trust, though according to him, I never really trusted him. He violated the code of conduct of our relationship. Most of all, most heartbreakingly of all, he slept with the blonde. He put his hands on her in places where he has touched me. That vile thought makes me so sick to my stomach, so fist-clenchingly angry, that I'll never reach out to him.

Back in school, I'll finally have a goal that doesn't have to do with Xavier. No more daily goals of thinking about him less, crying less, forgetting about him more. School and this project are for me only. The goal of finding a project and making meaning with it will be created by me and for me. Xavier isn't allowed in this space. And that's why I have some semblance of a smile on my face as I drive to my first meeting with my professor.

I pull into a parking spot at UNLV and head into the building. Because this is a student-led course, my meeting will be one-on-one with Professor Stein. Per his email, he expects me to bring some recent samples of my work and an idea sheet. My idea sheet is blank, but I'm not concerned. Inspiration can strike at any moment.

Prof. Stein probably doesn't remember me, but two years ago I took his class on Digital Photography. Because of his class, I talked my parents into buying me a killer digital camera, and its been my weapon of choice ever since.

I arrive at his office door and knock.

"Come in," his voice booms. Oh yeah. I forgot how loud he is.

I push through and step inside. The hole he calls an office is littered with visual entertainment. The walls are covered in photographs, and papers are stacked on every surface. In the center of the chaos sits Professor Stein, brown haired and bearded, reminiscent of Paul Bunyan.

"Miss Mitchell, hello." Professor Stein rises to shake my hand. He is tall like Bunyan too, and his height is comical inside this tiny office.

I take his hand. His grip is strong.

"Thank you for spending some time with me today. And please, call me Lila." I smile at him. Miss Mitchell is what my sister's students call her.

"Well then," the lumberjack behind the desk says cheerfully, "you can call me Paul."

My stomach contracts with my effort not to laugh. It's my first laugh in weeks, and I have to swallow it.

The corners of my mouth tip up in a smile. "All right, Paul."

"Lila, have you given any thought to what your final project will be?"

"A lot of thought, no inspiration yet."

Paul strokes his beard and leans back. His chair squeaks in protest. *So much weight for such a small chair.*

He holds a large, flat palm out in front of him. "Did you bring some work?"

I pass my folio over to him. In it are pictures of Fulton Gardens, some of Tahoe, other random shots. One of Xavier's parents dancing under the lights on the patio after Cade and Jessica's wedding. Paul holds up a picture of a wilted rose with a spider on it, eyes questioning me.

"I was feeling maudlin that day," I explain. The day after I found Xavier with the blonde I'd gone outside to hack down the rose bush. But then I spotted the spider on the one and only red bloom and ran for my camera. A symbol of evil perched on a dying rose. How fitting.

Paul nods and keeps going through my photos. He arrives at the one of April and Grant.

"What's the backstory here?"

I sigh silently. Of course he would choose to ask me about that one. I included it because it was a display of emotion. Different than the landscapes of Tahoe and flora of Fulton Gardens.

"That was taken very late at night, after the couple in the photo hosted a wedding."

"Why is he in pain?"

It's the same question I've had ever since I first loaded the picture onto my computer. I didn't see it when I took the picture, but after, when I zoomed in on the dancing couple, it was easy to see. Mr. Townsend's eyebrows are furrowed, and his nose is scrunched, like he's crying.

"I don't know. When I took the photo, I couldn't see his emotion. It was just a sweet moment between two people who have been married for thirty years. When I got it home and studied it, I saw the tears."

"This is interesting. Is there any more opportunity here?" Paul holds up the picture. "That isn't Las Vegas."

"It's Lake Tahoe. I was there a few weeks ago." Even as I say the name, I miss being there.

"Gotcha. Well," Paul flips through a few more, landing on the one I hoped he would. "Who is this woman?"

I smile and sit up straighter, happy to be off the subject of the Townsend's. "That is Ms. Barbara Fulton. She and her family own Fulton Gardens."

"You know her well?"

"I've had tea with her. And explored the grounds of the garden twice." I swallow, images of being there with Xavier flowing freely through my head. My heart aches. For Xavier, for the time, for the innocence of our first date.

"Why did you choose to take this picture?" Paul cocks his head to the side, studying the image and then me. He's learning my style, my motivations. I could tell him exactly what he wants to know if he would just ask, but fine, if the lumberjack prefers to learn this way.

"I'm interested in capturing beauty and emotion in real time. To me, beauty is more than a highly stylized model or a dressed up bride. There is beauty in Mrs. Fulton's eyes. Look at her wrinkles. There's wisdom and life experience there. To me, getting to be that age and having those experiences to make you as peaceful and relaxed as she is in that picture, *that* is beautiful."

Paul looks stunned. "I have to say Lila, I've never heard a student as young as yourself refer to an old woman's wrinkles as beautiful."

I shrug. "It's how I feel."

Paul runs his hand along his beard again. "I see. How did you get her to make a face like this? She appears to be thinking, but not too hard."

"I asked her what advice she would give to me on my wedding day. When she paused to consider it, I took the picture. I wanted to get the emotion on her face as her thought process was working."

"Brilliant, Lila. Brilliant."

I smile and duck my head.

"You can change your mind, but I think you might know which direction your project is going." Paul holds up the photo of Mrs. Fulton.

I was hoping he would say that.

Paul flips back to the picture of the Townsend's. "I still think there's something more to this picture."

"Perhaps." Not that I'll ever find out what.

Paul's interest in the photo makes me think he likes to read mystery novels. There are probably scenes of a gumshoe detective and various plot lines going through his head right now.

With a disappointed sigh, the lumberjack replaces the photo in my folio and hands it back to me. *So sorry the crying man will remain a mystery to you, Mr. Bunyan.*

"Well, Lila, I look forward to your work on Mrs. Fulton. It will be very interesting to see what you come up with."

"Thank you. I'll be in touch."

I begin my trek back to my car, head filled with thoughts about my project. How can I take Fulton Gardens and apply my style to it? And how, oh how, am I ever going to be able to get through it without thinking of Xavier and the magic that once was?

"Whoa, whoa whoa. You're going to do your project about Fulton Gardens? Don't you remember what happened when you went back to the yoga studio?" Jessica has paused her tea making to place her hands firmly on her slowly expanding hips. The look on her face tells me she thinks I'm the village idiot.

I smile anyway. Despite the borderline insulting look on her face, she exudes radiance. Pregnancy agrees with her. Her strawberry blonde hair is silky and thick, her skin luminous.

The delicate, pregnant flower in front of me rolls her eyes. "Why are you smiling?"

I shrug. "Because you look cute, even if you're suggesting that I'm a moron."

Jessica shakes her head, her hair shimmering under our kitchen light. She resumes filling the tea kettle. "You know, it's funny. For the last three years I've been trying to lose twenty pounds, and now that I have I'm supposed to gain it all back."

I make a show of rubbing my belly. "If Cade doesn't stop cooking all those down home meals, I'm going to gain sympathy weight. Are you sure he isn't from the South?"

Jessica's blue eyes narrow. "Stop trying to change the subject."

I feign innocence. "Where were we?"

"Fulton Gardens." Jessica sets the bright blue tea kettle on the hot stove.

I rub my temples and sigh. I really don't want to talk about this.

"What do you want me to say, Jess?"

"Do you think this is a good idea?"

"Yes. No. Maybe. I really don't know. My chances of running into Xavier there are the same as running into him anywhere. I already found a new yoga studio, obviously I won't be stepping foot in Townsend, I have no plans to go gambling in The Martin. If I want to avoid him completely I'll have to move."

Actually, moving away from Vegas isn't totally out of the question. After December there will be no reason for me to stay. And it's not as if I've ever felt at home in this damn desert.

Jessica shakes her head. "No way. I can't handle talking about you moving away. And I'm not talking about running into Xavier at Fulton Gardens. I'm talking about running into memories and emotions."

"Very poetic."

Jessica pinches my arm. I'm too slow to dodge her and end up rubbing the injured piece of flesh.

"I'm serious. Is choosing Fulton Gardens for your project really a good idea?"

Have the pregnancy hormones turned her into a badger?

I shrug, my nonchalance as fake as Granite Alexa's name. "It's no big deal. We only went once."

Jessica scrutinizes me. The tea kettle whistles from the stovetop.

Jessica turns off the stove. "Do you want a cup?"

"No thanks."

"Would you prefer some green juice?"

I wrinkle my nose. "No thanks."

Jessica laughs. "So just me and Cade then."

I watch mindlessly as she prepares tea for two, my thoughts moving to my future. Where will I be in January? I just have to get through these next four months and graduate. I have to focus on my project. No more Xavier to distract me.

Fulton Gardens is bursting with color. The heady scent of flowers is heavy in the hot, dry air. And my heart is heavy in my chest. Jessica was right. But it's too late now. The Fultons are expecting me.

I spend the morning following Mrs. Fulton around, getting a feel for what she does. Basically, she sits at a desk and greets people and makes everyone fall in love with her. Who doesn't love a sweet and charming old woman?

From what I can tell, Mrs. Fulton's son, Eric, and daughter, Samantha, are responsible for the operation. Her son does all the accounting and invoices, her daughter is the horticulturist. And they both fret over their mother.

So far I've gotten a good picture of them all together, but it was too posed. I've wandered through the lovely gardens and observed Samantha working with some of the other gardeners. Those pictures are good too, but they don't convey anything aside from teamwork. I don't mention Grant Townsend to Samantha. What am I supposed to say? "Hey, I know your high school sweetheart..." No thanks. By the end of my day at Fulton Gardens, I'm confident there isn't much to make a project from.

I leave with a thank you to the Fultons and tell them I'll see them soon. That's probably not true, unless I come back for a visit. I need to find a new project ASAP. And I need to find a way to tell Mrs. Fulton that my creativity went in a different direction, or something along those lines.

My drive home is quiet as I consider my options. There aren't many. I'm dusty and grimy from a day spent walking through the gardens and sweating under the hot Vegas sun. I'm ready for a shower and dinner.

My phone rings from its spot in my cup holder. Without taking my eyes off the road I grab it and answer. It's either Jessica or my mom. Xavier and Gigi have both stopped calling.

"Hello?"

"Lila, thank God."

Xavier. My stomach flips and turns, doing cart-wheels inside me. Even his frantic voice affects me so.

"Yes?"

"It's my mom." Xavier's voice is pained. Immediately I want to hold him, soothe him. I push the thought away.

"I knew it," he says. "I knew she was sick. She was just too thin. Dammit!" He explodes. I can picture him banging his fist on any nearby hard surface.

Oh shit. April. All her sweaters, her extreme happiness at seeing all of us and having a weekend together. Mr. Townsend's pained expressions, his longing for his wife. And the words April spoke before I stepped onto the aisle for my maid of honor duties. *You will do just fine.* Now I understand what she meant.

"Xavier." My voice is a whisper. I don't know what to say.

"Please come to Tahoe. Please. I can't do this without you." Xavier's plea claws at my heart.

But you hurt me. You cheated on me.

I shake my head, clearing out my initial reaction. I can do this for April. Not for Xavier.

"Ok."

I hear his intake of breath. *Well, I'm surprised I agreed, too.*

"I'll book you on a flight for tomorrow. I'm almost to the airport now. Lila, thank you."

"I'll see you tomorrow Xavier. Have a safe flight."

I turn off my phone and toss it onto the seat, the tears falling down my face.

CHAPTER TWENTY-SEVEN

Jessica notices my distress the second I walk in the door. With those eagle eyes of hers, she'll make a great mom.

"What's wrong? Are you having a relapse?" Jessica keeps waiting for me to fall back into the pit, needing more ice cream and bad TV in order to properly mourn my relationship with Xavier. It's not going to happen. If anything this experience has reminded me just how much I hate wallowing.

I shake my head. "You better sit down. Is Cade here?"

"Kitchen." Her eyes are wide, scared.

"Cade." She calls. He comes immediately.

Jessica explains. "Lila wants to tell us something, and she wants me to sit."

I gesture to the couch. Both Jessica and Cade lower themselves onto it.

"Xavier called me on my way home from work and—"

"Did you answer?" Jessica demands.

"Yes, now listen. April is sick. Xavier didn't go into any details, but he's on his way to Tahoe now. She had cancer about seven years ago, and he was really worried that she was sick again. He just had a feeling after being in Tahoe. That's why he was so quiet on the way home."

Cade puts his arm around Jessica, who's already crying.

"Now what? Do we wait to hear from Xavier?" Cade looks unshaken, always dependable in situations like this.

"I'm going to Tahoe tomorrow."

Jessica blinks up at me through wet lashes. "Are you sure that's a good idea?"

I sigh, sinking down into the chair across from her. "No. But what was I supposed to say? He sounded so sad. And I want to see April. I'm almost positive she knew she was sick while we were there. So many things are making sense now." The puzzle falls together perfectly in my head.

Jessica nods as I tell her about everything I noticed and April's words before I walked down the aisle.

"At the time I just assumed she was referring to me walking ahead of you and doing it the right way. But now I'm pretty sure that's not what she meant."

Jessica just shakes her head. "I wish we could go. The house closes this week, and we have all of that to handle."

"It's best if you stay here."

She nods, still crying.

"Come eat dinner, honey. Feed our baby, ok?" Cade smiles softly at Jessica. He practically worships the ground she walks on. I used to think it was irritating, but now I think it's cute. At least he won't cheat on her with some blonde.

Cade stands and pulls Jessica up with him.

"Coming, Lila?" Cade asks.

I shake my head. "I'm going to shower and get packed. I don't know which flight Xavier will put me on, and I want to be ready."

I watch Jessica and Cade's retreating forms. Cade reaches over to gently rub Jessica's back. I'm so happy for my best friend.

While I pack, I call my mom and tell her what's happening. She knows Xavier and I have broken up, but she doesn't know why. I just couldn't bear to smudge his name, even though he deserves it. Like Jessica, my mom wants to know if it's a good idea to go to Tahoe. I give her the same answer I gave Jessica.

Before I go to bed, I load the newest photographs onto my computer. The pictures are good, but they don't tell a story. As I'm studying the photos an idea hits me. I type a quick email out to all three Fulton's and attach my pictures from today. I've given them my photos with full copyright consent. They may use them how ever they wish.

An email comes through while I'm writing to the Fulton's. I hit send and open up the flight confirmation email. I'm headed to Tahoe tomorrow on the ten a.m. flight. The same one I took with Xavier over a month ago. Same flight, very different trip.

I've landed in Reno and picked up my rental car.

Now I have this forty-five minute drive to think, to consider what I'm doing here, to wonder how this will all play out. I have no idea how sick April really is, but

Xavier sounded distraught. Wouldn't he have been calmer if the prognosis was good? Probably.

I have to prepare myself. Xavier's charm is too potent to ignore. His nearness will be a challenge. I'm definitely not staying with the Townsend's. I need to book a hotel.

Nerves are welling up in my stomach. I thought I had mentally prepared myself on the drive here, but now with the Townsends' massive residence staring up at me, I'm not so sure.

Before I can step inside that house, I need to gather my wits. Ten deep breaths, the yoga kind. Chirping birds accompany my even breathing. Ok, I'm ready.

My start is interrupted by the sound of footsteps and a loudly muttered expletive. My head swivels toward the noise.

There he is. Oh, my heart. My battered, beaten heart. Xavier has just come around the corner of the house, arms full of logs. In his gray cashmere sweater he looks better than anyone has a right to. My knees weaken at just the mere sight of him.

My chin lifts in defiance, and I watch him until he sees me. He startles.

"Lila, you appeared out of nowhere." He looks immensely relieved.

"I'm fairly sure you know how I got here." I'm too quick to respond with a rude comment. Sighing, I rein it in.

Xavier empties his armful of wood onto the deck as I walk toward him. My intention is to give him a supportive, friendly hug. As soon as I'm within reach,

Xavier grabs me and pulls me forward. His arm wraps around my waist and his hand cradles the back of my head. His face is buried in my hair.

"Lila," his whisper is pained. "I need you so badly."

I'm stunned into submission. The electricity from our first handshake at Townsend is still there, an undercurrent running all over our bodies. My skin feels so alive right now. Why does my heart need and want this man so much?

"I'm here," I croon softly, holding the large man with the broken heart.

Xavier keeps his face in my hair. I feel his chest rising and falling with his soft sobs.

When Xavier is done crying, he lets me go and takes my hand, pulling me to the steps and gesturing for me to sit down.

We sit facing each other, but I make it a point to put some space between us. I need some physical distance to clear my head.

"How bad is it?" I dread the answer to the question.

"Bad. She knew when we were here that her breast cancer was back. It's spread to her bones. She didn't want to upset everyone, so she asked my dad to wait to tell me." Xavier's red eyes begin tearing up again. His next sentence is choked. "She has three months, tops."

I gasp. There must be a way to fight this. Chemo, an experimental drug, something. I want to argue with him, but I'm sure they've looked into every option.

"I'm so sorry. What can I do to help?"

Xavier looks at me with apprehension.

"What is it? Anything. Well, almost anything." With Xavier you never know.

"There's one area I could really use your help in." Xavier sighs and runs a hand through his hair.

Uh oh. I'm not going to like this.

"Go on."

Xavier makes a face. "I haven't told my parents about us. They still think we're together."

My eyes bulge. "What? Are you kidding?" Each word is enunciated. "Let me guess, I have to pretend we're still together for April's sake."

Xavier nods. "She loves you, Lila. She thinks you're the perfect woman for me. And you are."

I give Xavier a warning glance. "Don't get me started."

"I would love to get you started. Then maybe you would actually listen."

"Stop. I'm here to see April and be a friend to you. I didn't sign on for an acting job."

"Lila, please. Knowing that we broke up would be so upsetting for her. I can't bear to upset her, not now."

"Why didn't you tell them before you knew about your mothers condition?"

"I was hoping we would get back together."

I snort. "That won't be happening."

Xavier stares at me. He looks annoyed.

"What?" I demand.

"You drive me crazy."

"You don't drive me anywhere." I say stubbornly. That's such a lie. Xavier drives me all sorts of places that I no longer should go.

"Please do this Lila. Please."

I sigh. "Ok, I'll pretend like we haven't broken up. For your mom. But don't take advantage of the situation."

"Who, me?" Xavier stands and pulls me up. "Don't you have luggage?"

"In the car." I point over to the rental car. "No need to bring it in. I'm staying in a hotel tonight."

Xavier's mouth sets in a hard line. "We can discuss that later. Right now my mom is waiting to see you. My dad went to the grocery store." He stoops to pick up the wood he went outside for in the first place.

I nod, taking a deep breath and squaring my shoulders. I'm not sure what I'll see when I walk through that front door.

April is sitting in the big, overstuffed armchair in the living room. A large sweater makes it hard to see her diminishing frame, but I can see in her face that she has lost weight. Her cheek bones stick out noticeably.

A huge grin spreads over April's face when we walk in. I smile back, but inside my heart is wrenching.

"Lila." April says my name like I'm someone very special to her.

"Hey." I hurry to her and bend down, gently folding her into a hug. I try not to be affected by how frail she is. What will she be like in another month's time?

"How are you doing, dear?" April looks at me with waiting eyes.

"Well, I..." My voice halts. I look to Xavier. He's standing at the glass window, staring despondently out at the lake. "I was doing well, until Xavier told me you're sick." My answer is totally honest.

April nods. "A bit of a shock, huh?"

"Yes." I sink down on the floor in front of April. I just want to be near her.

April, with her legs folded up beside her in the large chair, bends forward and runs her hand through my hair.

"Such pretty hair. I always wanted to be a brunette."

With eyes closed I relax into her fingers as she strokes my hair. I can't help the tears that are falling down my cheeks. I want to know this woman better, and I won't get to.

When I open my eyes I meet Xavier's gaze in the reflection from the window. He's crying too.

"Lila, how long are you staying? You can stay as long as you like."

It's a struggle not to let my tears show through in my voice. "I'm not sure. A few days, probably."

"I'll be sure to tell the cook. We hired someone to make meals for the time being. Grant is a lousy cook and, well, I'm not really up to the task."

I smile. "I can help in any way you need. But you might not want me to cook. My talents lie outside the kitchen."

April laughs lightly. "I'll keep that in mind."

"Do you need anything right now?" I ask, ready to be put to work.

"Just sit here with me and tell me all about your inspiration for those photos you sent me. They were just wonderful."

April is referring to Smiles by the Sea. As promised, I sent the photos to her when I arrived home after my last trip here. Right before her son invited the blonde into his bed.

I launch into the story of how I got inspired, detailing my life growing up in an ocean side town and seeing vacationers experience the beach, some for the first time. Xavier comes and sits beside me, listening intently. He hasn't heard this before.

When I finish Xavier reaches for my hand and squeezes it. "I've always wanted to hear you talk more about your photography."

Surreptitiously I take my hand back and use it to gesture. Xavier looks hurt but recovers quickly.

"What are you working on now?" April asks.

"Well, I'm supposed to be creating a final project for my last class. It's a very independent class, and this project is my one and only task for the entire semester. I spent yesterday at Fulton Gardens trying to cultivate some idea of using the owners and the garden in my project, but I don't think it will work out."

Xavier stares at me. My return visit to Fulton Gardens is, of course, news to him.

"You spent yesterday at Fulton Gardens?" His voice is soft.

"Yes." My voice is even.

Your mom is watching, fool. Act right.

"Did you think of our first date?" Xavier looks so affected. April's going to pick up on the vibe if he keeps it up.

I smile and touch Xavier's cheek. His skin warms under my touch. "Of course I thought of our first date.

And how you're still just as wonderful as you were that evening."

My words snap Xavier out of his surprise. He remembers and rejoins the charade.

"Maybe we can go back again sometime."

I nod and smile at him. *This is so fake.*

April looks overjoyed watching us talk. And that's why I'm doing this.

"What do you kids have planned while Lila is here?" April sits back in her chair and pulls a throw blanket across her lap.

Xavier stands. "Well, first I'm going to build that fire you asked for a while ago."

I watch as Xavier arranges logs and stuffs balls of newspaper under the them. He strikes a long match against the stone fireplace and sets the wood aflame.

This man can build a fire, run a nightclub in Vegas, and do hot yoga classes like they don't even faze him, but he can't manage to stay monogamous. It's truly baffling.

CHAPTER TWENTY-EIGHT

April has fallen asleep in the armchair. She looks so peaceful, sleeping next to the fire in this exquisite home.

Quickly and quietly I rise from my spot on the floor next to her. I want to take her picture.

Xavier looks at me with narrowed eyes, but I dismiss him with a wave. April is asleep, and I don't have to pretend right now. The charade is exhausting.

I'm back quickly with my camera. Thank goodness I decided to pack it at the last minute.

Xavier sees what I'm doing and tries to move out of my shot, but I get a couple in before he can. Then I set it up and snap a few of April.

Xavier has his hand out for my camera. "May I?"

I bring up the last few shots and hand it over.

"Look at her." Xavier exhales slowly as he looks at my photos. "She looks so peaceful."

I take the camera back. "These are for when she isn't here anymore. Right now she's here. Look at her, not the picture." My voice is gently chiding.

"You're right." Xavier chokes up again. "Thank you for coming."

"Of course," I say simply. I wouldn't miss saying goodbye to April. "Actually, I guess I'm the one who should say thank you."

Xavier looks bewildered. "Why?"

"For giving me the opportunity to see her again."

Xavier sighs. "I called you without even thinking, Lila. I hung up the phone with my dad, called the airline while I threw clothes into a bag, then called you. I needed you. I still need you."

"We're broken up." I want to ask about the blonde, but I don't. We can't have that fight right now.

"I'm painfully aware of that." His tone is bitter.

From behind us Mr. Townsend clears his throat. Together we turn to look at him. I glance at Xavier and wonder if I look as guilty as he does. Did his dad hear us? We were speaking in hushed tones, but who knows?

"Are there more groceries to bring in?" Xavier asks.

Mr. Townsend nods, taking in the sight of his wife cuddled under a blanket and asleep next to the fire. Xavier heads outside, leaving me to navigate this land mine by myself.

"Hello, Lila." Mr. Townsend gives me a small smile and walks toward the kitchen with two bags in each hand. Dutifully I follow.

"How are you, Mr. Townsend?"

"Been better. Call me Grant."

"Um, ok." I'm not at ease enough with this person to call him by his first name, but I'll have to get over it.

"Did I just overhear you and Xavier say you're broken up?" Grant sets the groceries on the counter and turns to me, eyebrows raised expectantly.

Oh shit.

"Yes." I bite my lip nervously.

Grant nods. "That's what I thought. Do me a favor, and don't tell my wife. She thinks of you as her replacement. And I don't want her getting upset."

Her replacement? *You will do just fine.* Aprils words from just before the wedding ceremony. But...no. Xavier and I aren't together anymore. I won't be replacing April, not that I ever could anyway. I can't believe how important this is to April. Now I'm more committed than ever to giving the performance of a lifetime.

"You don't need to worry." I assure Xavier's father. "Xavier and I already agreed to pretend for her sake."

"Good."

I watch as Grant puts away groceries. Xavier walks in, two bags in each hand.

"That's the rest of them." He announces, setting them down on the counter. I join in the unloading. Anything to be busy right now.

If Xavier notices the tension, he doesn't say anything. We work in silence, me unloading while Xavier and his father put away.

When the job is finished, Mr. Townsend looks at us. The stress in his eyes is evident. "The cook will be here soon to start dinner. I'm going for a walk. Call me the second your mother wakes up." He turns and walks away.

After the door closes behind him, I turn to Xavier, who's staring at the place where his father disappeared. "I can sit with her if there's something you need to do."

"I just want to be near her."

Together we go back out to the living room and sit down on the rug in front of the fire. I open my camera and start looking through the pictures. Xavier stares out the window. The setting is so romantic, but the reality is not.

When April wakes, Xavier types out a quick message to his father. Mr. Townsend is back quickly, entering the room with eyes only for his wife. Xavier and I leave the room to give them some space.

"I think I'll go get a room," I announce quietly, veering toward the front door.

"Can't you just stay?"

"I can't sleep in a bed with you."

"So stay in a different room." I can hear the exasperation in his voice. "This will be a hell of a lot harder to pull off if you aren't here in the morning."

"I need some distance. This is overwhelming."

Xavier runs a hand through his hair, eyes closed. "Fine," he says through clenched teeth. "I'll book a room for you. But don't go until my mother is asleep for the night. And please be back before eight a.m."

"Yes sir," I retort, my own teeth clenched. I force myself to stop before I say something I'll regret.

Xavier is angrily pressing buttons on his phone. He finishes his furious dialing and looks at me. "You can be really difficult, you know that?"

I raise my eyebrows, but he turns away, walking farther away from the living room to make the secret reservation for me.

I'm just standing my ground. That doesn't make me difficult.

Dinner was probably delicious, but I was hardly able to appreciate the coq au vin. April ate very little, while Grant begged her to eat as though she were a baby. It was almost too much to watch. I can't understand Xavier's dad. He's distant and even cold with everyone but his wife. Is it his way of experiencing grief? I can't see how it's helping April.

Right now it doesn't matter because I'm safely in my hotel room, far away from Xavier and all the confusing feelings that come along with being in such close proximity to him. I'm emotionally shot, thanks to the tension between us and knowing that every moment with April is quantifiable. I've taken a long, hot shower, and now all I want is a bed.

When I hear the knock on my hotel room door, I glare at it. That had better be a maid.

Slowly I rise up from my seat at the window and walk toward the door. The person knocks again. I sigh. I know only one person who's that impatient.

I check the peephole. It's Xavier.

I thought I put on a fine performance today. Does he want to rehearse lines for tomorrow?

"Can I help you?" I ask with irritation as the door swings open.

Xavier barges in without being invited.

"Come on in. It's fine. I wasn't about to go to sleep."

"Good." Xavier matches my tone. "Glad to hear it. Thanks for the invite."

For some reason I feel the childish urge to stick my tongue out at him.

"What are you doing here?" My arms are crossed. I'm wearing only my tank top and boxer shorts. The wet hair on my back is cold and making two things, ahem, *pointier* than usual.

"We need to talk. And this time you can't run away from me, you can't send me to voicemail, and we don't have the presence of my parents to stop us."

"Ohhhh, no no no no. I didn't come to Tahoe to hear you out. You don't deserve it."

"Too fucking bad. You need to know the truth. It's killing me."

"Truth?" I screech, letting go. "The truth is that I received a picture of you kissing a blonde girl, and then I chose to give you the benefit of the doubt, considering who sent the picture. I went to your place to ask you about it, and I find the same blonde half naked and wearing one of your shirts. The writing was on the wall, Xavier. Don't even bother lying to me." My voice is an octave below screaming. Who the hell does Xavier think he is? Does he think he can cheat on me and be forgiven? Does he think I need him so badly that I'll prostrate myself for him and swallow his lies? I love myself too much for all that.

"Dammit. Would you just open your mind for a second?" Now Xavier is yelling. "It was all a set up. Gigi wanted me to cheat on you."

Unbelievable. This guy is unbelievable. "If that's true, then you, for all your business brains, fell for it. Hook, line and sinker. How stupid do you feel?" I don't doubt Gigi's involvement in whatever happened that night, but that doesn't explain the half naked woman in his room. Gigi doesn't have that much power.

Xavier's retort is scathing. "About as stupid as you should feel. Nothing happened between me and Chloe."

"Oh, she has a name. Great, I can finally give the home-wrecking blonde a name. I was starting to feel rude for referring to her as *whore*." Not that I've been calling her that, but I'm spitting mad and the words are already out of my mouth.

Xavier smirks at me. "Lila, Lila, full of fire."

"Don't you say that to me." I point my trembling finger at him, my voice sliding through clenched teeth.

Xavier takes a step toward me. The look on his face is familiar, both admiring and sensual. "Lila, you have never been more fiery." Another step closer. "It tells me how much you care."

"Stop where you are. If you have nothing else to say, we're done here, and you can leave." I feel shaky inside. I have to assume Xavier is lying. The scene of him in his hotel room and that girl, Chloe, in his shirt, looked just too 'morning after'.

"I will talk until you believe me."

We face each other, my stubbornness mirrored by Xavier's. I break first.

"Fine. If it means you'll leave sooner, then the floor is yours."

Xavier wastes no time launching into what he has been dying to tell me for a month. His story is rushed, as though I've set a timer, and he's racing against the clock.

"Chloe grabbed me and kissed me, and Gigi took a picture. I was so angry that I left, and I was going to go to your house. Then I got a call from the club that there was some girl who met the criteria for having been given a roofie, so I came back. It was Chloe. She seriously couldn't talk or walk. I didn't know what to do with her, so I took her back to my room to let her sleep it off. When she woke up in the morning, she started coming on to me. I pushed her away, she told me everything about Gigi's plan to get me to cheat, and then you showed up."

My brain is working through all of Xavier's words. Could this be true? My heart is singing, joyful beams of hope shooting out. My brain, unlike my heart, is skeptical.

"Who's Chloe?"

Xavier's face is triumphant. "Somebody I dated a long time ago, after Gigi."

"Why would she go along with Gigi?"

Xavier has the grace to look embarrassed. "Probably because I cheated on her, and she's still angry about it."

My response is acerbic. "Well, well, Xavier, you really have some fans in the female population."

Xavier holds up his hands. "I know, I know, I know. I haven't been the greatest guy. But I was to you."

I stare at him. If this is all true, there's only one thing left that's bothering me.

"Why would you take Chloe back to your room?" The thought of it makes me angry. Really angry. I feel the heat coming back into my body. Xavier would go crazy if I had a guy, an ex no less, stay in my house. The yoga instructor barely touched me and Xavier lost his top.

"She needed help."

"And it had to be from you? There was no one else who could help her?"

Xavier looks stunned.

"Don't look at me with such surprise, like this thought has never occurred to you. You didn't have to take her back to your room. I mean, come on." I'm yelling again. "Did you think I was going to do a happy dance when I found out you'd been caring for your ex? Even if I hadn't shown up and found you the way I did. First I have to deal with Gigi literally taking off her top and sitting in your lap, and then Chloe kisses you and manages to spend the night in your room and wear only your shirt. And you proclaim your innocence all the while. Xavier, a yoga instructor rubbed my lower back two times during the class *he was teaching* and you tried to fight him. How is any of this fair?" I'm almost in tears.

"Hey, baby, it's ok." Xavier's voice is suddenly soft, caring. He walks closer.

My eyes flash. I've heard his words, his excuses, but I don't know what to believe. What if he's lying? I can't stand the thought of being the naive girl who swallowed his lies.

Xavier grabs me, pulling me into his chest. Oh my, the smell of him, so familiar. I've missed it so much. I want to fold, to throw my cards in and take the easy route. I stand frozen against Xavier's chest, considering his words.

I can't. I knew he would do this, charm his way back to me. Gigi, for all her manipulating, told me the truth the first night I met her. Xavier leaves a trail of broken hearts. I knew from the moment he took me on our first date to Fulton Gardens that he was too good at all this, too practiced. All the flowers, the sweet sentiments, the well-placed compliments. I feel the heat starting up in my limbs again. I'm still in his arms, and he's stroking my hair as though he has been forgiven.

I'm so mad I want to bite him. Without thinking, my mouth opens and my jaws clamp down on his chest. I taste the cotton of his shirt.

"What the fuck?"

I let go and look back at him, my eyes gleaming with my anger. It feels good to release the pent up fire I feel inside.

"Did you bite me?" He looks horrified and also...turned on?

I'm about to respond when his mouth suddenly comes down on mine, and our tongues dance. We are ill-timed and angry. None of it's sensual, all of it carnal. I have a deep need to lash out, to release my anger. And Xavier is willing.

With one swift move Xavier sits down on the bed and lifts me onto his lap. *I'm home.* My lovesick heart breathes with relief. Thank God my brain knows better.

"You asshole," I hiss, delivering a swift blow to his back with my fist.

Oh, that felt good. I do it again. And again. Xavier is silent, absorbing my blows to his back, focusing his attention on removing my clothes.

It's erotic and contagious, but I can't let this go. I have to know, before I'm swept away.

His hair is in my hands, and I'm pulling, watching his face register pain.

"The garden, the rose bush, telling me you loved me, the weekend here with your parents. Was it all a fucking lie? Was it a part of your game?" I tug harder, enjoying this more than I ever knew I would.

Somewhere in my brain I know this is balancing on BDSM.

"No." Xavier's response is a groan. If I didn't know better, I would guess he might be enjoying this. At least a little.

I drag his head back up with my hands.

"Tell me," I whisper, my lips against his ear.

His voice is strained. "None of it was a lie. I've never done that for anybody. The rosebush... It was meant for us. I thought we could grow as it grew. I've wanted you and only you since the second I saw you. Something about you made me see that I could have a new path, I didn't have to act like I used to. Nothing happened between me and Chloe." His face is in my hair, and his breath melts against my ear.

I groan. "Don't say her name."

"Please Lila. Please. Be mine again."

His whisper is a plea, and it's all I need to hear. My anger has evaporated. I believe him.

My mouth is on his again, and I speak against his lips.

"I'm yours, Xavier. I always was." There's no use in denying what I've known since the second I broke up with him. My heart totally and completely belongs to Xavier. As does my body.

Xavier's mouth finds mine again, and I'm lost in the sweetness of our reunion.

CHAPTER TWENTY-NINE

I wake up to a bright, shining Lake Tahoe morning. My heart warms immediately when I sit up and see the shining lake above the tree tops. My happy place. For a brief moment I feel pure joy. Then I remember Xavier's mom is dying. And soon. Too soon.

Next to me, Xavier is still sleeping. Even in sleep, worry furrows his eyebrows.

Shit... What have I done? I promised myself I wouldn't go back to him. What if last night was a bunch of lies? I bite my lip as I ponder his words. *None of it was a lie... Please. Be mine again... I've wanted you and only you since the second I saw you...* Shit. I hate feeling this way. I glance at his face again and feel even more conflicted. How can I hate and love him at the same time?

I need to clear my head. Quietly I sneak out of bed and go to my suitcase. Toiletry bag in hand I walk to the bathroom, making it a point not to glance at the man in my bed.

The hot shower doesn't accomplish anything. My shoulders are as tense as they were before, but at least I feel clean. The fresh clothes help too. Fresh clothes, fresh start. Clear mind. I still haven't looked Xavier's way. I can't bear to.

I'm putting my toiletry bag back into my suitcase when I see it. The long, white envelope Jessica handed to me before I left Vegas yesterday. Until now I'd completely forgotten about the hand addressed letter that had Jessica so curious. I'd been in a hurry to get to the airport and thrown it in my bag just before I dumped everything else on top and ran for my car.

I turn the envelope over, studying it. With big loops and wide arcs, the handwriting obviously belongs to a female. I take the letter to the chair next to the window and open it very quietly.

I skip to the bottom of the letter to see the signature. Gigi. My stomach drops. *What now?* She has done and said enough. Finally I brave a glance at Xavier. His eyebrows are still furrowed. *Poor guy.* I can't imagine what it must feel like to face loss the way he has to.

I look back down at the letter. I hate that I'm wondering what she has to say. I hate that I don't trust Xavier.

I take a deep, quiet yoga breath and start to read.

Lila,

Snail mail isn't really my thing. I'm writing because you won't answer my calls. And I don't know your email address, and this is too much for a text. So an old-fashioned letter it is. First, you should know that I've been seeing a therapist for the last month. I realized that I had some unresolved issues. These issues were making me behave in ways that weren't healthy.

When I first met you, I really was trying to keep you away from Xavier for your own good. His track record isn't great, and he has hurt enough people. His tendency to use and toss has earned him some enemies. And then you came along, seeming so innocent and wide-eyed. I knew he would pounce. And, to be honest, I wasn't sure your preference, and I liked you too. But soon it was clear you like men, and I really was trying to be a friend.

In typical Xavier fashion, he caught you in his net, and it was a done deal. I started to feel a lot of bad feelings, mostly toward Xavier. How could he turn into this nice guy for you after cheating on me? And then I was thinking, what if Xavier and I could work again, now that he's figured out how to be faithful? What if he could be the husband he should have been for me? We could have another baby, and my heart would finally begin to heal. According to my therapist, a lot of my actions in the last few months were brought on by grief. This letter is a step toward getting better, so I can move forward.

I came on to Xavier one night. I don't know if he told you. He rejected me, said it was you he loved. You can't imagine how angry that made me. I was his wife! So then I did something really awful, one final thing. I set Xavier up to cheat on you. I was just so sure that once he had the opportunity with someone other than me, he would do it. Because he used to be that guy. I invited Chloe, a girl Xavier dated, to Townsend.

She was in on it. As I said, Xavier has a few female enemies. She was supposed to flirt, do whatever, and kiss him. And I was going to take a picture of the kiss and send it to you. As you know, that part appeared to work out. What I didn't capture was the moment after Chloe kissed him. Xavier was so surprised and angry. He pushed her away and walked out. She was supposed to make him want to kiss her, but she just grabbed him. I knew my picture idea wasn't going to work, because he was going to tell you what happened. I had to do something more to get him to cheat, so I gave her something that would make her beyond crazy and need help. Then I told a bouncer who had just started his shift to watch Chloe and call Xavier, because she was a friend of his. Within minutes she was totally out of it, and Xavier came back into the club. I saw him talking to her, and then he left with her. He was carrying her, because she couldn't walk. I knew that I had set Xavier up with the perfect opportunity to cheat. Xavier would nurse Chloe through this and, once Chloe came to, he would have all the opportunity in the world. Like me, Chloe didn't understand how Xavier turned into a nice guy for you.

Chloe told me how you showed up at Xavier's very early the next morning. When she saw you in person and how hurt you were, she felt awful. She was upset that she took part in something that hurt another person.

Xavier didn't cheat on you. He slept on the couch that night, and Chloe passed out in his bed. She was in his shirt because she woke up feeling better, showered, and wanted something clean to wear. She tried to seduce him, and he flat out rejected her. She told him the whole plan, and he wasn't even angry. He just shook his head and told her he had ordered breakfast, and she could leave after she ate. And then you showed up.

I don't know how you turned him into a fine, upstanding gentleman, but congratulations. You did it. You can go back to him, if you haven't already. But given what I now know of you, you have a lot more fire inside you than what I originally thought.

I won't bother you or Xavier anymore. I'm getting help and working through my grief and other things. Good luck. And this time I actually mean it.

Gigi

Relief fills me. Xavier was telling the truth. I want to cry tears of joy. Since I'm not much of a crier, I settle for a gigantic smile.

"I see last night still has you smiling."

I look up to see Xavier propped up on one elbow, watching me.

I giggle. I can't help but feel elated. I take the letter and bound over to the bed, then jump in.

"I've missed your laugh." Xavier reaches out and plays with a lock of my hair.

"I missed a lot more than your laugh. Look." I dangle the open letter between us.

A dark look comes onto Xavier's face.

"I found it in my suitcase this morning. Jessica gave it to me yesterday when I was rushing to get to the airport and I forgot about it. I didn't read it until a few minutes ago. It's just like you said."

Xavier takes the letter. I sit quietly while he reads it, watching his face register all her words. He looks disgusted.

Xavier finishes, balls up the paper, and throws it in a perfect arc to the wastebasket near the desk.

He takes my hand and traces patterns on the top. "I'm happy you believed me first, before you saw this letter."

"Me too. But I did have a minor freak out when I woke up this morning."

"You made it really hard to let me tell you the truth."

"The situation appeared to have the truth written all over it."

"Can we forget all this ever happened? We've been apart for a month, and there are some things we need to catch up on." Xavier's eyebrows wiggle suggestively. He looks so sexy with his hair all messed up.

"Like current events?" I tease.

"Something like that," he murmurs, reaching for me.

Xavier pulls me under the covers, and I'm laughing again at the absurdity of it all.

In the midst of pain and heartbreak over Xavier's mother, we have found our way back to one another.

Something tells me that if Xavier and I didn't have to get out of bed, we would've been there all day. We have more important places to be, though.

April is awake now after a morning nap, according to the text Grant sent Xavier. We have to hustle. April will only be up for a while before she will tire and be ready to rest again. Xavier needs every minute he can get with his mother.

We check out of the hotel and drive the few miles to the Townsend's house. Xavier is on edge. He all but yelled at the bellboy who dropped my bag when he was loading it into the Land Rover.

Xavier drives through the large iron gates and pulls up to the house. Before he can climb out I grab his hand and squeeze.

"I know this is awful, but just treat her like normal. Give her a gentle hug and love her. Think about what you would want if you were in her place."

He stares at me with unfathomable eyes, his voice hushed. "I'm terrified."

I nod. "I know." I wipe at the tears on my face.

"Lila." My name is a sorrowful moan on his lips. His eyes begin to water.

I shake my head. "Lock it up. Don't let it overtake you. Your mom wants to see us happy. We need to give that to her. We can cry on our own time." My words are strong, but inside I feel weak.

I hand Xavier a tissue from the large stash in my purse, and we both blow our noses.

"Let's go," Xavier says.

He grabs my hand as we head up the stairs to the front door, then pauses to kiss me before we walk in.

"This time we don't have to fake it."

My heart sings at his words. Would I have gotten over Xavier eventually? Yes, I would have. But I would much rather be here, right next to him, his partner.

April seemed more energetic this morning. She was beyond happy to see me and Xavier, and adamant that she felt well enough to eat lunch on the terrace. We were all happy to see her appetite. Grant was the friendliest I've ever seen him, regaling us with a story from their honeymoon about the glass-bottom boat tour from hell. We were in stitches as he described the green faces of everyone on the boat. For a second, I forgot the reason we were there. But only for a second.

"Dare I say the cook's chicken salad is better than my own?" April asks, delicately wiping the sides of her mouth with a napkin.

"Never," Xavier declares from his spot beside me. His arm is around me, and I'm leaning into him. It's heaven.

"Aww, thanks." April smiles sweetly at her son. Her hands gesture wide toward the sky. "Boys, the day is beautiful. What do you think about having yourselves an afternoon on the golf course? You could get in nine holes before it gets too dark."

Xavier and his father share a look.

"Why do I get the feeling you're trying to get rid of us?" Grant smiles good-naturedly.

"Because I am." April announces cheerfully.

Grant stands, and Xavier follows suit. Reluctantly I let him go. Now that we are back together, I don't want to spend a second without him.

"All right, all right, if you insist." Grant feigns a martyr's expression. "I guess we'll have to spend the afternoon golfing. Let's go, son."

Xavier gives me a quick goodbye kiss.

"I have to change, and then we can leave." Xavier breaks away from me and glances at his dad. Mr. Townsend has looked both confused and surprised more than once since we showed up today, and he has the same look on his face right now. I'm sure Xavier will fill him in on our reconnection over Bloody Mary's on the golf course.

"Goodbye, dear," April pats the hand Mr. Townsend placed on her shoulder when he bent to kiss her cheek. "Have fun."

I watch, forlorn, as Xavier and his father retreat into the house. It sounds stupid, but I already miss him. I sigh and turn my attention back to April.

She's watching me with suppressed mirth.

"Did I miss the joke?" I ask with a smile.

"It's only for the afternoon, Lila. Your love will be home before you know it."

I blush. Am I that obvious?

April waves her hand. "Don't worry. I know what that feels like. The magic in the beginning of the relationship is very special."

I nod. It feels even more special now that Xavier and I have found our way back to one another.

"Are you excited to have more time with Xavier soon?"

I stare at April's serene face, confused.

"Why would I have more time with Xavier? Because I'm here, you mean?"

April shakes her head. "No. I mean when Xavier sells Townsend."

What the hell? Xavier's selling Townsend?

"You didn't know?" April looks taken aback.

I shake my head slowly, trying to come to grips with it.

April's hand flies to her mouth. "Oh no. Maybe it was supposed to be a surprise?"

I should explain. What would Xavier feel about me telling his mother the truth? But one look at her face and the worry etched there, and I know I have to.

"I didn't know because Xavier and I have been apart for the last month. It was the Gigi situation. We worked everything out last night."

April's eyes widen. "But you came here yesterday."

I nod. "As soon as Xavier called."

She narrows her eyes. "Were you hoping to get back together with him?"

I turn to take in the beautiful vista, not sure how to explain. "I thought…it doesn't matter what I thought, but I was wrong. I had no intention of going back to him, but I still cared about him." I turn back to April. "About you."

"Lila, you really are something."

"Your son says I'm full of fire."

Aprils laughs. "Yes, I think you might be. Full of a fire that burns with tenacity and love and compassion."

I blush. Am I full of those things?

April shakes her head. "I can't believe you didn't know about Townsend. Xavier has a buyer. They're just working on the logistics with the lawyers."

Selling Townsend. No more big shot club owner, no more half-naked girls dancing in cages, no more odd work hours. I'm relieved. But why did Xavier decide to sell the club he poured his heart into creating?

Worry furrows April's brow. "I hope Xavier won't be upset that I told you."

I place my hand on her forearm and feel a stab of sadness at how small her arm has become. "He won't be, April. Promise."

April smiles. "I can see how happy you and Xavier are together. Whatever that problem is with Gigi, I hope it has resolved itself."

I nod slowly, recalling Gigi's letter. "I believe it has."

April nods. "Good. Lila, while we're still alone, there's something I need to discuss with you."

I gulp. Here it is, the reason why she kicked Grant and Xavier out for the afternoon.

"I'm all ears."

April's response is no-nonsense. "Grant already knows my final wishes. I'll be cremated. Unfortunately I can't donate my organs, thanks to the cancer. I've asked Grant to spread my ashes in the places we visited together. He's going to take a year and travel. He'll need that year." April's voice grows small, and she cries silently.

I swipe at my own tears. *Oh, April, what will we all do without you?*

"These damn tears," April says with annoyance. "They come so frequently these days."

I laugh despite my despair. I feel the same way. "I've cried more in the last month than I have in my whole life."

April laughs with me. "I see so much of myself in you. Maybe that's one of the reasons Xavier loves you so. They say boys marry their mothers."

"Boys marry their mothers..." I echo her words. April is strong, poised, and kind. I can only hope to be like her someday.

"Lila, I have an idea. I ran it past Grant last night, and he's ok with it. But you can say no if it's something you don't think you can do."

"Whatever you need."

April holds up her palm. "Just hear my idea first. You may not want to."

I'll do whatever I can for Xavier's mother.

"What do you think of using your talents to take pictures of my remaining months? You mentioned you're in need of a final project."

It's not at all what I thought she was going to ask. I expected a request to help Xavier and Grant, or my assistance tying up loose ends. But this? Does she really want photos of herself as she grows sicker and weaker?

However, this could be a really great project. What if I can capture the grief cycle as it plays out? Grant and Xavier are in the unique position of knowing they will lose their loved one, so they'll be able to spend quality time with her before she passes. That will make for some really special moments. And then emotions will change as the time draws closer. This could work. But, I have to know if this is something April really wants.

"From the standpoint of the photographer, I think it's a great idea. But, April, are you sure?"

"I listened to you yesterday explaining your aesthetic nature. You said it yourself, you like capturing emotion. And this way Grant and Xavier can look back on the pictures and remember our time together. They will see the love and happiness in your photos and know that I went with their love surrounding me."

I'm astounded. April is putting a lot of faith in my abilities.

My mind is already working on the logistics. "It would mean I'd have to stay here, in Tahoe."

"Of course you would live with us. I would want you here, even if you didn't have any talent with a camera."

How can I do this? How can I watch from behind a lens as April deteriorates? And what about Xavier? He might not like this idea. I can't say no, but I can't say yes.

"Let me think about it, ok?" My palms are sweating just from considering it.

"Of course, Lila. I understand what I'm asking of you." April draws her feet up into her chair and tips her head back, letting the sun shine down on her face.

"What is it like?" I ask without thinking. Did I just say that? Where is my filter? "I shouldn't have asked that. I'm so sorry April."

April doesn't even open her eyes. She keeps her head up to the sky and responds.

"You can ask me anything Lila. And it's very frightening. Not the dying part. The part where I leave Grant and Xavier."

I watch her, admiring April's grace and beauty as she drinks in the sun. I have an idea.

"April, would you mind if I took your picture? You look very peaceful and beautiful right now."

April smiles but still doesn't open her eyes. "After seeing what you can do with a camera, you can take my picture any time you want."

My chair sounds against the wood deck as I stand. I hurry inside for my camera. I snatch it off the table in the living room and rush back before anything can change the shot. I love the way the sunshine filters through the leaves in the trees.

April hasn't moved. I bend a little at the waist so I'm the same height as her chair, then snap a few photos.

"Did you get what you need?" April opens one eye and looks at me.

"Yes, thank you."

"Good. Would you mind walking me to my room? I think I'll take a nap while the guys are still out."

"Of course." I gently take her arm.

She doesn't need much help, but I think she wants me there in case she does. We walk through the house toward her bedroom. I watch as she climbs into her massive bed and settles in. She's dwarfed by the billowy covers.

"Thank you. For everything. For the pictures, for loving my son. For loving me."

She drifts off almost immediately.

CHAPTER THIRTY

I find my luggage in Xavier's room. I hadn't even thought about where I was sleeping, but obviously Xavier has. I have to keep from hugging myself with glee. I'm so happy we're back together.

I set about unpacking my bag and hanging up my clothes in Xavier's closet. If I decide to stay I'm going to need more clothes. Winter things. The nights are already chilly, and it's only September.

Once I'm settled in the first thing I do is call Jessica. She's at work but takes my call anyway.

"Finally." Jessica snaps into the phone. I picture her face, eyebrows pinched together.

"Hello to you too."

"I've been waiting for you to call. How's April?" Jessica's worry pierces through her irritation.

I take a deep breath. "April's breast cancer is stage four and has spread to her bones. The doctors expect her to live three more months."

I sense Jessica's panic in her silence. After a moment I can make out the sounds of crying.

"Jess, maybe you can come for a visit. April would love that. Just a short weekend trip. Probably before things start to get really bad."

Jessica sniffles. "That's a good idea. Maybe I can go back with you, if you're going out there again. When are you coming home?"

"I'm not sure." I explain April's request.

"LL, how will you do that? It'll be so hard. Won't it be awkward with Xavier? Or is he coming back to Vegas?"

"Um, about tha—"

"Lila... " Jessica says my name like a warning.

"Don't freak, Jess, but —"

"Are you kidding me?" Jessica breaks in. She still isn't as shrill as Granite.

"Jess, it's so crazy. It was all a set up that Xavier very stupidly fell for. Gigi planned the whole thing, and that blonde went along with it."

I wander over to the glass wall and stare out at the lake while I recount Gigi's letter and how it corroborated what Xavier had already told me.

"That's insane. I hope she stays far away from you guys from now on."

"She might, actually. Xavier is selling his part of Townsend."

"What?" Another screech. Still not as bad as Granite. "Lila, you're like one headline after another."

"I know. Let's move on from me. How's the little monkey?"

Jessica sighs in exasperation. "Lila, you know Cade doesn't like it when you call our baby a monkey."

"Cade can kiss my ass." I say cheerfully.

I picture Jessica giving me a dirty look through the phone.

No need to upset a pregnant lady. "Ok, fine. How is Baby Blankenship doing?"

I listen as Jessica fills me in on her most recent doctor's appointment and the anomalies of having another person growing inside her.

Xavier walks in just as Jessica is informing me that pregnant woman, do, in fact, have cravings, and they are intense. I wink at him and signal one minute.

"Hey, Jess, I have to go, but really quick, tell me about the closing. Are you and Cade homeowners now?"

"Yep." Jessica says with pride.

"Congratulations!" I'm happy for my best friend and her husband, but of course this means I'm officially homeless. "You can move my stuff into the spare bedroom if you want to make my room the baby's room."

"That would be perfect. Thanks Lila. Give my love to everyone, and maybe we can make it out there in a couple weeks. See if that works and get back to me."

"Will do. Oh, and before I forget, can you please take care of the rosebush for me?"

Jessica snorts. "Hate to break it to you LL, but that thing is a goner. Guess you have quite the black thumb."

I glance out the enormous windows of our bedroom down to the row of exquisite rose bushes on the edge of the property. It wasn't my black thumb that killed the rosebush. Nothing so delicate can survive in the hostile desert.

"I'll be in touch soon to plan your trip out here."

We hang up, and I walk over to Xavier. I want answers about the sale of Townsend. But first, I want a kiss.

"Aren't you a sight for sore eyes." Xavier looks me over appreciatively.

In jeans, a T-shirt, and messy hair I'm hardly enticing.

"Well, it's not exactly my little red dress."

"Come here, you."

I practically float to Xavier's open arms. I inhale the scent of his skin. Wait, shouldn't he smell like sweat and sunscreen? My dad always does after a day on the golf course.

I lean back to look at him. "Why do you still smell so good?"

"Quit asking questions." Xavier brings his mouth down on mine.

I kiss him back, but I'm too curious about Townsend to let the embrace develop into more. I let him go and sit on the bed, watching an obviously disappointed Xavier change out of his khaki pants and collared sport shirt. It's very golf. I don't like it. I prefer his usual jeans and soft v-necks.

"So, dear boyfriend of mine, when were you going to tell me about Townsend?"

Xavier looks at me, pausing the process of pulling on his shirt. He frowns.

"That was supposed to be a surprise."

On goes the shirt. Too bad. Xavier's bare chest is quite a sight.

"I don't think your mom knew that."

Xavier shakes his head. "Probably not. What do you want to know?"

I tick the questions off on my fingers. "Why? When? What will you do now? Where will you go? Will you stay in Vegas?"

Xavier sits next to me on the bed.

"I decided to sell Townsend after that awful night at the club. I'd been thinking about it ever since I met you. It just didn't seem like the right job for me anymore. It fit the lifestyle of the person I used to be. Roughly three weeks ago, I got an offer. The buyer thinks I'm crazy to sell." Xavier shrugs. "He can have the place. For the right price, anyway. We've been hammering out the details ever since. What were your other questions?"

"What's next for you? Will you get a different job?"

"I'm not sure of what's next. With my mom sick, I'm going to stay here and spend all the time I can with her. And I'm hoping you'll stay with me. I know you have a life in Vegas, but yesterday you made it sound like this final course is independent. And Alexa is a job you were probably going to quit after graduation anyhow. What do you think?"

"I think your mother already beat you to the punch." I explain April's request.

"Would it be your final project?"

"Yes. The aim of the project would be to capture the stages of grief. You and your dad are in a situation where you know her death is coming soon, and you've already begun the grieving process. It doesn't always work that way. Sometimes people are taken from us quickly, and the grief process is started in a totally different way. You have the opportunity to celebrate your mom right now and spend quality time with her."

"And you're sure my mom wants this?"

"It was her idea. She said your dad is on board already."

Xavier puts his arms around my waist. "Well, I am too. Hearing you talk yesterday about Smiles by the Sea and what you look for when taking pictures, well, you sounded so happy. Why don't you talk about it more?"

"It's very personal. I don't know if you've noticed, but I'm not super comfortable with showing my emotions. With photography, the emotions are silent but evident. It's like speaking without hearing anyone talk."

"Dare I say, Birthday Girl, that you're actually quite emotional? I think you would have to be, to have the kind of passion you have."

"That's what I'm scared of." My voice drops to a whisper.

"What?" Xavier's eyes squint with concern.

"How can I possibly take pictures of your mom while she slowly loses her battle? I don't think I can be detached enough to do this project justice. And what about you? How can I see a poignant moment and capture it with a camera instead of experiencing it with you?" My voice breaks. "I don't want to disappoint your mom, but I don't know if I have it in me." I'm crying softly now, knowing I will agree to April's request, but at what personal cost?

"Lila, sweet Lila, please don't cry. You can say no. My mom will understand."

I wipe the last of my tears and gaze up at Xavier. How is it that he's consoling me, when he's the one whose mom is dying? My resolve strengthens. I can do this. I can give April what she wants and still be there for Xavier.

"I'll do it."

"Lila, don't. You don't have to put yourself through this."

"Yes, I do. Compared to what April is doing for you and your dad, this is nothing. I want to do this, Xavier." A few more tears run down my cheeks.

Xavier brushes the last of my tears away. "Lila, Lila, full of fire. Look at those tears. And here I thought you weren't much of a crier."

I grin and poke Xavier in the ribs. "I certainly have cried my fair share in the last four weeks."

Xavier shakes his head regretfully. "I wish your tears weren't about me. I'm sorry all that shit happened. I should've known what Gigi and Chloe were up to. I'm not naive. I think meeting you has turned me soft."

I gasp in mock horror. "Xavier Townsend, a softie? First you fall in love with a California girl, then you sell your hot Vegas nightclub? Have you lost your edge?"

Xavier growls playfully, knocking me into the bed. He climbs on top of me, his full weight pressing me into the mattress. Gently he nips at my ear.

"Not even close. I happen to know a fiery woman who needs a man with edge to challenge her."

I'm giggling. "Ok, ok, I get it. You still have your manly prowess."

Xavier makes his voice extra deep. "That's right." He props up one elbow and leans on his hand, gazing down at me.

My fingers come up to trace patterns on his shoulder and down his bicep. My mind is already moving forward, making plans for my stay.

"I need to call Granite and quit. Without two weeks notice. He won't be very happy with me." Quitting like this means I won't get to fulfill my fantasy of calling Granite by his real name right to his haughty face. *I quit Sheldon, you overbearing, rude, narcissistic jackass.* "He'll probably just be annoyed that he can't get any more footage of you for his stupid reality show."

Xavier waves his hand flippantly. "Don't worry about Granite Alexa. I'll take care of it for you."

I roll my eyes. "I can fight my own battles."

"But the guy is way nicer to me than he is to you. And I still own Townsend. That will give Granite and his friends six more days to be VIPs. I'll call him tonight."

And just like that, my problem, and my job, have vanished. But I still need to go shopping.

"Are there some clothing stores around here? I need winter things. Real winter things, not just sweaters."

"You probably need a lot of stuff, and so do I." Xavier frowns as he says this. It's hard not to think about the reason why we will be in Lake Tahoe.

"We can shop online tonight and buy what we need. The lawyers are wrapping up the sale of Townsend tomorrow, and I'm about to come into a large sum of money." Xavier winks at me.

"What about all your stuff in your hotel room? Don't you need anything from there?"

Xavier shakes his head. "I packed for a long trip. I'm sure the hotel manager will send me whatever I missed. What about you? Do you need things from home?"

Mentally I glance around my room back in Vegas. There isn't much I need. It really isn't my home anymore, if it ever was.

"Jess will send me something if I need it. She'll be going through my room soon anyway and moving everything to the extra bedroom. Time to make room for baby."

Xavier shakes his head. "Everything has happened so fast."

"No kidding."

Xavier reaches into his pocket with his free hand and holds up a small, sparkling object.

"Is this too fast?"

My stomach drops. *Holy shit.*

"What is that?" My voice is breathy.

"The reason I don't smell like an afternoon on the golf course."

"Is that what I think it is?"

"Birthday Girl, I just spent the last month without you. That was enough to know I never want to be without you again."

"Xavier, I —"

"Lila, I don't want to hear it unless your answer is yes."

"Then you're in luck."

Xavier's eyes light up. "Really?"

326

"Put the ring on my finger already!"

Xavier beams. He sits up and takes my hand.

"Lila Mitchell, will you marry me?"

I giggle, my utter joy bubbling over. "Yes."

Xavier slips on the ring and I curl and flex my fingers, feeling the sensation of the cool metal.

My grin is wide as I look up at Xavier. *My fiancé!*

"I think this is where you kiss me."

Xavier laughs and lies down, covering me with his weight once more. Our kisses have always been passionate, but this one is different. This kiss has jubilation and promise in it.

As much as I would like for our celebration to continue, we have to stay rooted in reality at least until the day is over.

I break away first and plant a sweet kiss on Xavier's cheek.

"I'll take a raincheck. And it expires tonight."

I giggle again as Xavier rolls off me and stands. He holds out his hand, and I take it, reluctantly standing.

"Let's go downstairs and see if my mom is awake yet. You ready?"

I grab my camera and hang it around my neck. "You won't see me without this for a while."

"It looks good on you."

"You look good on me."

"Why, yes, I do."

I smirk. "Always so humble."

Xavier runs a thumb down the length of my cheek, green eyes shining with love. "Always so beautiful, so loving, so challenging, so full of fire."

"Why, thank you."

"Lila, I mean it. I love you." Xavier's voice is clear, full of meaning.

"I love you too." *And I will love you forever, Xavier.*

My camera bumps up against Xavier's chest as I lean in to kiss him.

We laugh together when he reaches down to pull the camera aside.

"Maybe it doesn't have to be there all the time." Xavier's voice is husky as he leans in to plant a sweet, light kiss on my lips.

"Agreed." I grab Xavier's hand and pull him through the door. "Come on. Let's go see if your mom's awake. I think we have some news to share with her."

Epilogue

ONE YEAR LATER

The sound of her breath is everything.

Life.

Vitality.

Proof that a higher being exists.

Five tiny fingers, already imprinted, curl around one of mine.

Her rosy lips part, and I brace myself for her wail, but instead she stays asleep.

Six pounds of utter perfection feels like air in my arms, and yet the weight of my love for her could bring me to my knees.

Suddenly the world's problems are my problems too. All because this little girl was born. I want to cure diseases, feed the hungry, fight global warming, plant trees, buy an electric car, do anything to make this world better for her.

Right now I'll just settle for sitting here in the rocking chair with my daughter curled on my chest, her cheek resting on top of my heart.

With tired, new mother eyes, I survey the nursery. The canvas photo of Xavier kissing my swollen belly is on the wall across from me. We had so much fun at that photo session, safe from the knowledge that just four days later we would become parents, one month earlier than we expected.

Xavier was my rock through the emergency c-section. His voice hid the fear his eyes revealed.

"We're going to be a happy family a little earlier than we expected. That's all." He smiled at me and brushed the hair from my face, tucking it back into the surgical cap.

"I can't feel half my body," I whispered with tears in my eyes. It was not how I was supposed to deliver. I wanted to push our daughter out myself.

"I know, baby," he whispered back, eyes on mine.

"Can you see her yet?"

He glanced over the sheet at the team of doctors and nurses at the bottom half of my body.

"Not yet."

"What's happening?" I yelled, terrified. I'd been in a state of panic since I woke up that morning and saw the blood.

"Almost there, Lila." Came Dr. Monroe's voice from beyond the sheet. "You'll have your baby girl in less than a minute."

No pain, but I felt a tugging sensation. *She's leaving me.*

And then a hollowness. An absence of something.

"Where is she?" I cried.

I turned my head, searching, finding her tiny figure in a nurses arms, being laid in a plastic bin that sat under something that looked like a heater. My heartbeats faltered. *Not this April, too.* Two doctors stood over her, touching her, looking at her, but what were they looking for?

"Why isn't she crying?" I asked Xavier.

"I don't know," he said, tears pouring.

And then she wailed. Angels sang, bells rang, my heart soared. Her cry was the most beautiful sound I'd ever heard.

They brought her to me, placed her on my chest, and my heart left my body. It went right into her, where it embedded itself into her tiny chest. Every breath she took made my heart explode with happiness.

"She looks great." Dr. Monroe stood off to one side of the hospital bed. "Four weeks early, and she's as perfect as can be. She's strong. Her apgar was great."

I couldn't tear my eyes away from my daughter long enough to look him in the eye while I thanked him.

"Does she have a name? Sometimes when babies come early they go a couple days without a name."

"April," Xavier and I answered in unison.

Like there was ever an option.

The memory fades, and my gaze finds the picture of my daughter's namesake. Xavier's mother, before she was sick. Before I knew her. Smiling for the camera, her arms thrown around her husband. I look back down to the bundle in my arms.

"One day we will tell you all about your grandma. How she was brave and kind, how she faced her diagnosis with poise and grace." I whisper the promise into the air around my sleeping baby. My eyes close, and I drift off, the motion of the rocker lulling me asleep.

I'm awakened by the lovestruck voice of my husband. "How are my girls doing?"

Xavier strides into the nursery, dropping a kiss on my cheek. With a featherlight touch he caresses the side of April's head.

"I can't believe she's here with us." He says, awed.

"Technically she should still be in my stomach for another week."

"She wasn't going to let that stop her. Fiery little thing." He kisses me again, this time on the mouth. "I know someone a lot like her."

"Me too." I laugh quietly. "How's the restaurant?"

Xavier smiles when he hears the word *restaurant*. It was his mother's idea. A few days after Xavier and I became Tahoe residents April mentioned the sale of a space overlooking the lake. We could all see Xavier's restless energy building, and we'd only been there a short time. It's the perfect job for the man who loves seeing people have a good time. And the planning and development gave Xavier a place to direct his grief when it overwhelmed him. April probably knew that it would. *She was so good at knowing those things.*

"Good. Matt handled everything while I was out." He backs up until he's leaning against the crib. "Everyone loves your photos. Especially the one of that guy making a face while his wife laughs at him. The food looks great in that one."

"They're just saying that because they were taken by the boss's wife."

"No way. The concept was genius."

"I wouldn't go that far." It was easy to get people into the restaurant for a soft opening and take their pictures while they enjoyed the place.

"Can you please just take a compliment?"

April's tiny head moves around on my chest. Xavier rushes forward, gingerly lifting the baby from me and snuggling her into his arms.

"I've missed you all day, sweet girl." He puts his nose to her head and inhales. "How am I supposed to go to work everyday when I have you two ladies here? I don't want to work ever again."

"It's not like you have to." The sale of Townsend left him wealthy, and that's not even considering his family's fortune. Our wedding certainly didn't put a dent in his bank account. It was low-key and rushed. We were racing his mother's clock, and we made it with six weeks to spare. *I'll never forget the smile on her face after it was official. Or the joy when we told her we were expecting.* She was incredibly sick, skin stretched across her face, but her eyes danced.

Xavier shakes his head. "I want to. I need to. Working does something good for my soul." He grins at me over her soft little tufts of brown hair, his smile full of love and contentment. It is the look of a man who has finally reached the point where he has longed to be.

"This moment is one I've dreamed of since we learned you were pregnant." His eyes are tender, shiny. "I couldn't wait to stare at my beautiful wife while I held a piece of her in my arms."

Oh my heart, be still. This man's words have the power to undo me.

I watch him bring his nose to our daughter's head again, hear his inhale as he takes in her sweet baby scent.

There's no part of me that understands how I got this lucky. One year ago I was trying to decide if I should give Xavier a chance, and now here we are. Our journey wasn't smooth, but each bump revealed what was weak about us. To be together we needed strength, tenacity, two willing hearts, and a fire that burned so bright it incinerated his ghosts and my fears.

I don't fear Xavier's past anymore. When I look at him, I only see my husband.

Our future is determined by us, and only us.

Coming November 10th…
A second chance romance novel
that explores the devastation of loss,
the beauty in losing yourself,
and the transcendent power of grief.

The Day He Went Away

Chapter One - Kate

His hands are on my hips. He squeezes, fingers digging into my skin, and I like it. I try to open my eyes but they won't obey. I don't know who's making me feel this way, but I know I'm not scared. His five o'clock shadow gently scrapes my cheek as his face drags across mine. Just before his lips touch mine, his scent fills my nose.

I know who it is.
The scent of his skin is seared into my soul.
My best friend.
My Ethan.

The creak of metal brings me back to reality, and I shake off the images.

I swivel my chair and cross my ankles, pretending to listen to Belinda as she introduces her new client and the concepts she's working on.

The conference room at work is not the place to relive that dream. The earth-shattering, mind-bending, rule breaking dream. *My Ethan dream.*

His hands. On me. Touching me in a whole new way.

"Kate, where are you with your new client?"

I look into the expectant eyes of my boss, Lynn, and the bright red lipstick that never seems to leave her lips.

I clear my throat, buying myself a few seconds. *Rookie move.*

"Kate and I are still in the planning phase of the Rodgers account." Sarah, seated on my right, speaks up.

Ethan's fingers digging into my skin.

Focus.

Lynn looks at Sarah and regards her with cool eyes. She flicks her eyes back to me. "But you're taking the lead on Rodgers, right, Kate?"

I nod. "For the remainder of the morning I'll focus on getting all the information as complete as possible and the releases perfected. I'm taking a half day today, and I'll be out until the twenty-seventh. Sarah will run with everything I've created. And I'll be available for any questions or to help in any way, of course."

Lynn sighs. Just a tiny, barely perceptible sigh, and I hope Sarah didn't pick up on it. Sarah is capable of completing tasks without me. Besides, I'm going to make it foolproof. Everything will be so perfect that Sarah will have to *work* to make a mistake.

Lynn sets her sights on someone on the other side of the long, dark wood table, and I relax. My mind wanders back to Ethan's lips…hands…

A totally different hand taps my knee.

Sarah's giving me her irritated look.

"Thanks for saving me," I mouth.

She scribbles on her notepad and slides it to me. *Are you okay? That wasn't like you.*

I give her a thumbs up and turn my attention to Lynn. I can't be caught daydreaming again. Totally unacceptable.

But that dream... For weeks I haven't been able to get it out of my head. But I have to. Ethan will be here this afternoon.

There's work to be done before I can head to the airport. Everything needs to be handled before I can take time off from Simone PR.

Ten days. With Ethan Shepherd.

My best friend.

And also the person who has been on my mind while I'm asleep.

How many times am I going to relive the dream when I'm awake?

I'm trying to pay attention to what Lynn's saying, I really am, but... *His scratchy face on my skin...* I'm a goner. Might as well give in and let myself enjoy the daydream.

"Kate, seriously?"

Sarah stares down at me, hands on her hips. I look around. The room is empty. My cheeks warm.

"I'm sorry, my mind is elsewhere today."

"That's clear. Want to tell me where?"

I bite my lip. I've hardly dared to tell myself where my mind has been. There's no way I'm telling anybody else.

I rise from my seat and lead the way out of the now empty conference room. Sarah is on my heels.

"We have some work to do. Let's get to it." I throw the directive behind me.

I'm Kate Masters, and I'm back in control.

It's funny how, when I think I'm in control, something happens to remind me how wrong I am. Not haha funny, but funny like *of course you have no control over Ethan's flight home.* If I'd checked my phone before I ran out of work, I would've known his plane is late. But I was busy, pushing it to the final second before jumping from my seat and thundering to the elevator. *There had been so much to accomplish before I left.*

At work Sarah kept reminding me of the time. And asking why I'd been a space cadet in the morning meeting.

I know something's up. Does it have to do with Ethan?

No, why would anything be up with Ethan?

Because you're taking a lot of time off work to spend with him, and you've been weird for weeks. And extra weird today.

I took time off to spend with him last summer when he was home.

But you weren't absent minded and forgetful and—

Weird?

Yes.

Everything is cool. Promise. I just need to get through all this work before I can leave.

Now I'm sitting in front of terminal four security at the airport with forty-five minutes to spare.

Forty-five minutes to think.

About Ethan.

About how Ethan and I have been best friends since we were five. *Two decades.*

And about my dream. And what it means.

I've never dreamed of Ethan before. Not like that, anyway.

Ethan has always been… Well, Ethan.

But now he's not.

Now he's *Ethan.*

And that terrifies me. It shakes the foundation of my life. I've spent a lot of time building the solid, stable floor I stand on. Having feelings for Ethan is like taking a sledgehammer to one of the wooden planks. I need Ethan the way I need air and water to live. Ethan's unyielding, loyal friendship is my safe haven. He's the only person I don't try to be perfect for. Everyone else… They expect it. Perfection. And I don't do disappointment.

But these feelings… They've consumed me. Infiltrated my heart and swallowed me whole.

And they're already affecting my behavior. Last night he called from the airport in Germany, and I turned into a thirteen-year-old with a crush, stammering and sweating. When he asked what was wrong, I assured him I was great, just preoccupied with work. He believed me. *I think.*

What if I told him everything?

I know what would happen.

I sigh and glance at the time on my phone. Twenty more minutes until he arrives. I look up, survey the weaving security line, watch the TSA employees with their stiff shoulders, and look again at the stream of people exiting the concourses, fresh from their flights arrival. My fingers tap my knees. I need a change of scenery. These gray walls are driving me crazy. *Or maybe it's me and all this overthinking.*

I rise from the seat I've been planted in too long. The blood rushes into my left foot, and it tingles. I wobble, but make it to the restroom without an embarrassing scene.

Instead of walking toward a stall, I go to the mirror. Ethan has seen me thousands of times—at my absolute best and complete worst. Still, I fuss with my hair and check my makeup. *Brown hair still brown, lower lip still bigger than upper lip, one ear still a millimeter higher than the other. Makeup in place.* I look down at my red shirt, happy I remembered clothes to change into. I didn't want to greet Ethan in my sensible blouse and gray slacks. *It's possible I chose this color for a reason...*

After all our years together, physical appearance falls low on the yardstick by which we measure one another. We'd made mud pies together, scraped our knees on the harsh asphalt of the street we grew up on, and spent days cooped up together while we battled chicken pox. Our pain, happiness, heartbreaks, and successes are wrapped up within each other, intertwined in a way only time can accomplish.

My fingers curl around the edge of the sink, knuckles growing whiter. *If I let these feelings take control, things might not end well.*

Our friendship is strong, but feelings like this make us fragile.

The strength of our relationship has been the one thing I could always count on. While I was busy achieving, accomplishing, *mastering*, Ethan was by my side. He's the only person who didn't need me to achieve, accomplish, or master in order to love me.

Something implicit exists between us, an unspoken declaration, and it states that nothing will ever divide us. I felt it the day I watched a moving truck pull up to the empty house across the street. A little boy bounded out and somersaulted his way across the front yard, and my five-year-old self *knew*. Twenty years together hasn't changed it.

I look into the mirror and watch the emotions ripple over my face. Excitement, fear, apprehension. Fear dominates.

But there isn't anything concrete to be scared of. I can't reach out and take hold of what has my heart racing.

My fear is a shadow, pursuing me soundlessly. *If you tell him you have feelings for him, you'll lose. Would you really risk Ethan? He's your biggest fan, your other half, your... soulmate.* I shake my head. I can't think like that.

"Get it together, Masters." Saying my last name out loud makes me feel better. Like I'm in control. *Kate will Master it... Master of Everything.* I loved those nicknames at first, but now they're a reminder of the impossibly high expectations people had for me. Or maybe I just had them for myself. With a last name like Masters, what else could I become but an over-achieving perfectionist? Of course, the last name didn't rub off on my little brother. I picture him tucking his wild, shoulder length hair behind his ears, and shake my head. *Running an organic beet farm... The opposite of everything my dad wanted for him.* I've given Noah the grief my dad would have, if he were alive. Honestly, it's probably time to let my little brother own his career choice, as exasperating as it is.

Running off to Noah's modest farm in Oregon doesn't sound too bad right now. I'd love to escape my mind for a while.

Stop being unrealistic. I need to deal with these feelings. I need to be practical, pragmatic, level-headed, and logical.

Telling Ethan about my dream would be foolish. Telling him about how I can't stop thinking of him would be irrational. What I need to do is forget about it.

Because I know how he would respond if I came clean.

My dependable, loyal, compassionate Ethan. He's been in love with me for ten years. And he's never been shy about telling me.

Once a year, on our shared birthday, he asks if I've changed my mind yet.

His caramel eyes radiate with hope after the question leaves his lips. *And I always tell him no.*

But now… My God, what am I doing?

I can't.

Absolutely, unequivocally, without a doubt.

I need to do less dreaming and more forgetting.

The fear in my seizing stomach tells me I'm making the right choice. If I give in to my feelings and Ethan and I fail at a relationship, I'll lose him forever.

I cannot tolerate a life without Ethan. So my mouth will stay shut.

His visit home will be like all the others. We'll have order, structure, and solid plans. I like those things, I *need* those things. And Ethan understands that about me. He's always been that for me. Nobody knows me like Ethan.

I just want *us,* the Kate and Ethan I'm used to. Ease embodies our time together, like an old, comfy sweatshirt, worn from time and use, but continuing to serve its purpose. *We're sweatshirts.*

If I tell him…well, we won't be sweatshirts anymore. We'll be crisp and stiff, new clothes from a new store.

And I can't have that. I need my best friend.

The bright lights of the airport blind me when I walk out of the women's room. I blink a few times. It's louder now. Lots of people, enthusiastic greetings. I stand on the periphery and scan the area.

There he is, walking down the long, wide hallway, away from the concourse. *Ethan!* My insides go topsy-turvy, my heart hammers like it wants to leap out of me and run to him. *Calm down. He's still the same person you've known since before you could ride a bike.*

Ethan strides past security and slows, peering around and above the people who are in the midst of their own reunions.

His jet black hair shines in the light overhead. For a brief moment, I'm struck by how different he looks. It's not the classic military hair cut or the tan fatigues he's wearing that make him look so different. It's his face, his shoulders, his chest, even his neck, that have changed. He looks so *big*, so strong.

Something even more alarming than Ethan's changed appearance is snaking its way through me. The warmth spreads, starting in my heart and running out to the tips of my fingers and all the way down to my toes. My skin feels alive.

Desire. That's what this feeling is. My brain tells my body to stop, but my body isn't listening.

Ethan hasn't seen me yet. *Petite girl problems.* His warm brown eyes continue to scan the throng of people. I'm halfway to him when his eyes meet mine. His face lights up.

My feet accelerate. Deftly I dodge elbows and purses as I make my way toward him. I smile, but he just stares at me, transfixed, like my face isn't the same face he's known for most of his life. Finally, he smiles back, but his eyes continue to stare at me, absorbing me in a way that puts a blush on my cheeks.

Ethan finally comes to life, dropping the bag from his shoulder and taking a few steps forward.

I don't even stop to think about what I'm doing. The talk I had with myself in the bathroom flies out the window. This is *Ethan*, my best friend, and I've missed him so much, it's become a physical ache.

As soon as we're close enough I launch myself at him. My legs wrap around his waist and he catches me, arms encircling my back, holding me up. I let my face fall into his neck, feeling comforted by what I find there. I inhale deeply, breathe him in, and his familiar scent tattoos my heart.

I'm in love with him.

I can lie to myself as much as I want when I'm alone. But right now, with my nose pressed to his skin, my heart knows my truth.

His hand falls down my back, rises, falls again. My shoulders shudder and bow. My insides twist and arc, a convolution of confused excitement.

I break first, jumping down and backing away from the circle of Ethan's arms. Heat fills my cheeks as I peek up at him.

His eyes bore into mine. He squints, like he's trying to wrap his mind around what just happened. I should apologize for leaping into his arms like a gazelle. My lack of control is mortifying.

Ethan grins his beautiful, happy smile and lifts his left hand up to my face, his thumb tracing its way along my jawbone. *He's never touched me like this.*

I lean into it, forgetting myself again. I can't help it. *This must be how he felt all these years.* Why did it take me so long?

His hand is touching me. *Ethan.* And now my stomach is starting to feel funny, and it's *Ethan* making me feel this way.

I want to grab him and kiss him right there, in the middle of this mass of people, but I don't.

I take a step back, forcing his hand to drop. His eyebrows draw together as though he's trying to solve a difficult math problem. *Well, haven't you been a difficult problem for years? And now you're acting like this.*

I'm not ready to tell him. I want to say the words, but they aren't there. Adrenaline courses through me, and I hate how it makes me feel. I want my control back.

Ethan's staring at me, waiting for me to explain my behavior.

"Are you hungry?" It's a lame question. I wish I could do better.

His eyes narrow like he's evaluating. Whatever he's thinking of, he makes a choice. "I'll grab my bag, and we can go." He turns, walking to his backpack lying on the ground a few feet away.

Oh, thank God. He's letting it go.

He hefts it to his shoulder. "I know it's the middle of the afternoon, but I'm hungry. Starving, actually. Airplane food." He wrinkles his nose. "I ate in Philly on my layover, but that was almost six hours ago. I had a Philly cheese steak. It sucked. Don't you think it should have been better, considering where I was? Maybe ordering one at an airport wasn't the best idea. And the snacks they handed out on the flight were crap."

Yes, this is definitely my best friend. Live, in the flesh, and acting like himself. His chatter is infectious. I find myself smiling as I picture him working his way through the bad cheese steak while he waited for his next flight.

"Okay, so no cheese steaks, peanuts, or pretzels. Where would you like to go?"

"You won't believe this, but I want a burger. A good old drive-thru burger."

It's my turn to wrinkle my nose. "That's gross, but I won't deny you. Your wish is my command. After all, you do spend your days protecting me."

As usual, one word of the war, and Ethan withdraws instantly. I shouldn't have said anything. I know better. But I'm so grateful to him for giving up his civilian life for me…for everybody.

I let his withdrawal pass without comment.

In baggage claim, he grabs his green duffel like it weighs nothing, then nods to the door. "Take me anywhere. Surprise me."

We reach my car, and there's that familiar stab of disappointment when I see it. *Dad wasn't even alive when I bought this car, and still I chose something that would've made him happy. Even if it didn't make me happy.* I can still hear him expounding the virtues of Hondas. *Reliable, safe, trustworthy.*

Ethan grins. "Good old Helen the Honda. Gotta love her."

I give him a side-eye and he laughs.

"Can I drive?" His eyebrows raise with hope.

"No way."

He gives me a dirty look and tosses his bag in the back seat. *My God, those muscles. Since when?* I climb into my car and blink a few times, trying to clear my head. This is Ethan. I'm looking at *Ethan* like he's a piece of meat. Or a treat. Yes, a treat. A gorgeous, raven-haired, caramel-eyed delectable man. *One who can dig his fingers into my skin and run his stubble across my face and—*

"Kate, what's with you?"

I feel the flush in my cheeks. There's no way Ethan will miss it.

"Nothing. Why?"

Ethan's eyes narrow. "I asked you where we're going. Twice. And you're blushing."

I don't answer. I just point the car towards downtown Phoenix and drive.

Dear Reader,

Thank you so much for spending your precious time reading my debut novel, **Full of Fire**. I truly hope you enjoyed following Lila and Xavier's journey. The main characters story may have come to a close, but I found myself wondering about Gigi's side of the story. The more I thought about her, the more I thought she had a side of the story that deserved telling. You can find Gigi's story, titled **Full of Fury: A Full of Fire Novella,** for free on jennifermillikinwrites.com.

Next up for me is a project that is very personal. Unlike Full of Fire, which was conceived by a crazy dream I had one night, The Day He Went Away has its roots in reality. You can visit my blog to find out more about the true story behind that book. The Day He Went Away will be available for pre-order November 1st, and releases November 10th.

I would love to connect with you. Feel free to write me at jennifermillikinwrites@gmail.com and visit me on facebook.com/JenniferMillikinwrites. I'm also on Instagram and Twitter at jenmillwrites.

Thank you again for reading **Full of Fire** and spending your time with me.

In gratitude,

Jennifer Millikin

Acknowledgements

First and foremost, my husband. Thank you, thank you, thank you for not being afraid of a strong woman with a dream. You've never tried to hold me down.

A big, hearty thank you goes to my best friends, Rachel and Kristan. Your support for me is never-ending.

To my editor, Robin Patchen. You made the editing process as painless as it possibly can be. Thank you for the positive and rewarding experience.

My sweet daughter. You may only be three, but your larger than life personality, sassy attitude, and strength inspired the character of Lila Mitchell.

About the Author

Jennifer Millikin is a romance and women's fiction author who enjoys writing about strong female protagonists. She is the author of Full of Fire and Full of Fury: A Full of Fire novella. Upcoming projects include the November 10th release of her newest novel, The Day He Went Away. Jennifer graduated from Arizona State University with a degree in Communication Studies and lives with her husband and two young children in Scottsdale, Arizona. When she isn't chasing after her little ones she can be found gulping coffee in her office, typing furiously at her keyboard and reenacting scenes. Visit Jennifer at jennifermillikin-writes.com and request your free copy of Full of Fury: A Full of Fire Novella. Find Jennifer on Facebook, Twitter and Instagram.

Made in the USA
Middletown, DE
14 June 2021